HOUND
OF THE
BISCUIT BARREL

HOUND OF THE BISCUIT BARREL
Neil S. Reddy

ISBN 978-0-9954753-8-0

Cover Illustration by Tim Youster
Author photo by D Edwards.
Dank House Manor Publications 2022

ACKNOWLEDGMENTS
Previously published in 2017 by Weasel Press USA as
Taxi Sam in Pink Noir.
Significantly rewritten and revised 2021 for this UK
edition and used with permission.

For D. Edwards

PROLOGUE

This is a simple story, of a simple man. I am that simple man. I'm not doing myself down, that was also the official opinion of my old headmaster and two social workers. I'm a chump who found himself on the wrong side of a corrupt secret society, a fool who went on to kill four, might be five, complete strangers. A bungling oddball, who fought a beast born of the bowels of hell, blew up his best friend and killed a police officer... and got away with the lot.

Not exactly the story of everyday life in the Lincolnshire Fens, but a simple story none the less. I'm telling this tale, so that those that didn't survive will be remembered - that and to make a few quid. Some of the fallen I will remember fondly, others I hope are being buggered in hell by a steam driven sandpaper covered cock of alarming girth... although now that I've put that to paper, I can think of one amongst their number who might have wished such a fate on himself, but more of that later... welcome to sunny Broston.

Chapter 1
MONTY'S FALSE ONE

It was Tuesday morning, and I was busy in my workshop, with no idea of the mire of degradation and violence the future had in store for me. But I do recall experiencing an unsettling internal conflict, distracting me from my day's work. Perhaps I should have been more wary, more alert to the omens, but as my old Dad would have said; 'Omens are just so much bollocks. Better to get stuck in and have a broom handy just in case you need it,' - smart fella my Dad. So, let's start with the aforementioned conflict; in my head it sounded something like this; 'shall I finish cutting off this breast or eat a custard cream biscuit?'

Now I'm sure you'll agree, the call of the custard cream biscuit, is not to be taken lightly. It is a deep and soulful yearning. Eating a custard cream is one of the very few pleasures in life that truly delivers on its promises. I have yet to come across the custard cream biscuit that failed to deliver, but equally, is there anything in the world as satisfying as palpitating a soon to be severed breast? The dichotomy of the breast, pert and firm and yet soft and malleable. If there's anything in the world, more satisfying than palpitating a soon to be severed breast, you can be sure it's been taxed, banned or hidden in a big box with the words, 'The Devil's Own,' written in gold and fire all over it. There I was, caught between two yearnings, scalpel poised, steel to flesh when the phone rang.

I answered, 'Sam&SonTaxidermists,' my words sliding into a slurred mess. Familiarity breeds cacology – I am Sam, as was my dad. He'd passed away three years before all this happened, and none of this would have happened if he'd still been around. But there I was, all alone, Sam, Son of Sam, Taxidermist.

'Good afternoon, Major Monty Turney here, Broston Grove.' The tone of voice was meant to impress, but I knew the name and had seen the Major's face in the local suck-up rag many times. They referred to him as one of the town's 'Leading Lights,' and 'Our Leading Local Historian.' His voice was loaded with all the self-importance that such guff encourages. I'd bought one of his books, read one page and put it in my oven to rot.

'And what can I do for you Major?'

'I was wondering do you undertake restoration work?'

'I'm not proud. I'd work for the Queen, if she was willing to pay cash.'

The Major cleared his throat, 'do you think you could pop over this afternoon, and give me your opinion on an item?'

I gave my answer with a low growl, 'that depends?'

'I beg your pardon?'

'I said it depends on why you can't bring it here? I'm a very busy man Major, cats to skin, voles to hollow-out, that kind of thing.' I regard the goading of self-important men as my civil obligation.

'I think it would be best if you could view it here.' I could hear his teeth grinding, he wasn't used to backchat from tradesmen. 'It's a rather delicate item.'

Delicate means money; which meant it was time to cut the crap and play nice, 'in that case, no problem, I'm sure I can fit you in.'

'You know where the Grove is I expect?'

'It's by the 'For Sale' sign isn't it?' That was another dig at the Major's vanity, but I'll explain that later.

The Major cleared his throat, 'yes, that's right. Can you see me this morning? ASAP and all that, you know, carpe diem.'

I looked at the defrosted barn owl on the workbench. It would keep for another day in the fridge; 'I can be there in fifteen minutes Major?'

'Very good.' He hung up, and I had the distinct feeling I was under starters orders.

I threw the owl in the fridge, tossed two custard creams down my throat, and jumped on my dad's old bike. Taxidermy is not a growth industry. So although I can drive, I can't afford a car, and why waste a perfectly good bike? They built them to last in my dad's day, its frame could support an elephant. I've seen thinner scaffolding holding up our local church; but by god does the bastard squeak.

It's an easy ride to the Grove. You go around the back of the park, then alongside the river which mustn't be confused with the town's larger tidal inlet, because that route would take you in completely the wrong direction, then... hold on a minute... I just realised I'm describing a journey you'll never need to make, so why bother? The point is you end up on Karma Roundabout; not its official name of course, but the three blind bends that converge on the penny-sized roundabout, seem to bring out the fatalist in everyone that uses it. Fuck indicators, shut your eyes and go for it. Death may be coming in the other direction but if it happens, it happens. I put my head down and peddled hard, narrowly missing a white van, whose fuckwit driver, was connected to his mobile phone and a pasty. If you survive the Karma Roundabout, you can easily drive past Burton Grove, without even seeing it. This is partly due to the stout, six-foot high, box hedging that surrounds it, and partly due to the 'For Sale' sign that obscures the front entrance. To the left of the sign are a fine set of wrought iron gates, eight feet high, covered with wrought iron monkeys, climbing wrought iron vines that bloom into burnished wrought iron irises - nothing fancy, the very epitome of understatement. Also, a real bugger to get the bike through.

The Grove itself is all grey stone walls, twisted brick chimneys, and narrow lead lined sash windows. Best not to mention the dubious pointing that you could push a sandwich into. The Grove has been 'For Sale,' longer than I can remember, and I fear it will be 'For Sale,' until the day it falls down. As tumbling Tudor buildings go, it's a fine pile of waterlogged bricks.

'Afternoon, Sam isn't it. Pleased to meet you.' The Major strode across the gravel drive and gripped my hand with a good firmly; just like his nanny must have taught him to do; 'Very prompt, very good. Come on through, it's a bit warmer inside.'

The Major walked with a slight stoop, but it didn't slow him down any, the old sod fairly galloped along. Off he went with his faded military baring; shoulders back, chest forward, black swagger stick a wobbling. I wasn't impressed. As far as I'm concerned that much show could only mean one thing, a pent-up pen pusher in deep denial, but I kept my mouth shut and my opinions to myself; after all, the customer is always trite.

The Major marched me along a narrow wood-panelled corridor, that smelt of mice and toadstools; a servant's corridor, from which generations of resentment seeped. A butler or two had envisaged beating in their master's head behind those walls; I'm telling you that for nothing. We emerged into a large room at the back of the house, where the walls were stained darker than good gravy. The furniture was a disappointment, mostly because there wasn't any.

'Are you moving out Major?'

'Eventually, most of the rooms are like this now,' he declared to the floor, 'just a few things left to sort out.'

'What will the local rag do for stories when you go? And all your local history fans; they will be disappointed.'

The Major coughed, slapped his stick into his palm and straightened his back; well, as much as he could. The verbal foreplay was clearly over; he wanted to get down to business. He made a great show of looking me over. I suspected he didn't like what he saw. Most people don't. I always felt I pulled off a convincing version of Oliver Reed's Bill Sykes; minus the dog - if you don't count the stuffed ones I had back at the shop. But everybody else just seems to see a walking, misshapen, hairy turnip.

'Are you a man to be trusted?' the Major asked, pointing his swagger stick at my chest.

'Does it prove much if I say yes?'

'Indeed, self-recommendation is no recommendation at all. But I can look a man in the eye and know him, know him to his very core. And besides, you've been recommended to me. But I'd be obliged if you'd answer my question sir, are you a man to be trusted?'

The pompous old twat was clearly paranoid. And I don't like looking people in the eye, it makes me feel brittle. I didn't want to play the Major's army games; 'So you don't trust personal recommendations, but you're willing to take my word, is that it?'

'The eye sir, the eye holds it all. I trust my own judgement.'

I wasn't in the mood to affirm someone else's superior social standing; no matter how justified it was. 'Major, I'm the only taxidermist within sixty odd miles. There's only three of us in the county. The other two are both good men, but no better than me. I'm the one that's here now, so why not chance your arm?' It was then I realised, I was looking the Major in the eye. I'd been had. The wily old bastard held my gaze. I began to wonder, what was he playing at? Why all the phoney cloak and dagger theatrics? The 3-watt bulb at the back of my brain flickered into life, illuminating the single blank domino, that totters there from time to time. The Major was running an insurance scam. The wanker had already claimed for the piece, and now wanted it repaired on the quiet. Whoever had recommended me to Turney, must have told the Major I'd take on dodgy work, and keep my mouth shut; so it had to be somebody who knew me well.

'Forgive me young man,' the Major flustered, 'I can see you are a man I can trust. I'm afraid my doubts were initiated by your guarantor, Fast Luke; not the most salubrious of gents.'

I nearly dislocated my eyebrows in shock, 'you know Fast Luke?'

'What concerns me sir, is that you know him. Are you of the same tribe?'

'Am I what?'

'The same tribe sir. Of the same inclination?'

What was the old duffer talking about? My mind domino tottered, casting a shadow over Fast Luke; I saw the purple fingernails, the lipstick and the attitude that could stop buses. And then I understood, 'do you mean, am I gay? What the hell is that to you?'

'No please, don't misunderstand me. It's just that he's a… colourful character and this is rather a discreet assignment.'

Assignment?! the old duffer really did take himself way too seriously. But to be fair, 'colourful' was a rather placid way of describing Fast Luke; a day-glow rainbow in loon pants riding a fiery unicorn into the sun; would have been more accurate.

'Why don't we just get down to business Major?'

'Indeed, indeed…' the Major's face relaxed and some of the starch seemed to drop from his shoulders, 'very well then…would you wait here for a moment please?'

He left the room, and I began to wonder how Luke and the Major ever crossed paths; whirling visions of the two of them indulging in some twisted sadomasochistic role-play; probably involving that black cane; formed in my head; thankfully I didn't have a chance to take this too far as the Major returned quickly. He was carrying a dark wooden box, that immediately caught my attention. It was almost three feet long, just over a foot high and about six inches wide - I give it to you in imperial because it was built in the age of Empire, and there was nothing metric about that dark old box. The thing was held together with brass screws, and a puzzling combination of mortise and dovetail joints. Placing the box on the floor between us with great care, the Major stepped back; 'There you go, please give me your opinion.'

I began my appraisal. It was most definitely a wooden box. There were no hinges, but I could see two small brass hooks held a sliding top panel in place. I flicked them open and slid the panel aside.

'Bugger.'

'Is that your professional opinion?' the Major chortled.

'Too right it is, I've never seen one outside of a museum.'

He nodded sagely, 'how old would you say it is?'

I knew I was being tested, and I really didn't mind, as the box held a treasure. 'Hard to tell but this sort of thing was popular in the nineteenth century, it could be later but not by much.'

The box held what is known as a curiosity, and this one was a very curious curiosity, and of exceptional quality. 'In fact, it could be a lot earlier. May I? Is it fixed to the box?'

'Four small spikes through the feet. It lifts out.'

I took a pair of rubber gloves from my pocket and snapped them on; sweaty hands do cruel things to

15

curiosities; and carefully dislodged the creature from the box. It was heavier than I'd expected, 'it's got some heft,' I commented.

'Is that significant?'

'It's unusual. Most pieces of this size are formed with sawdust or woodwool. Feels too heavy to be plaster. Could be led shot I guess, which might help us to date it. But what we need is a name.' I searched the piece, and the box for a tag or a brass plaque, but there was none. 'Have you ever seen a tag Major? We taxidermists do love our tags, and this beast deserves one.'

'I'm afraid not. I discovered it in the attic when I first moved in here, nearly thirty years ago.'

'That's a shame. Well, it's a Sphinx of some kind. Maybe a Chimera; have you had it valued before?'

The Major shook his head, 'no it's never been out of this house. What do you think its components are?'

I carried the beast to the window to see it better. 'The head's simian. The ears are fox. Those yellow eyes are handmade; could be amber. Let's hope so for the valuation. The body's a terrier, probably a Jack Russell, judging by the colour and girth. The front legs are feline; some poor street tabby no doubt. Not sure about the rear legs…' They were grey with large padded opposable paws but looked too delicate to be simian. 'The rarer the animal parts, the more expensive the piece was to make. I think these could be from a lemur. It would have cost a bit to make. The tail is a cobra of course. The wings…' A pair of black wings were set into the upper back; slightly in front of and above, a pair of grey wings that were folded flat against the creature's solid flank. 'Raven and a gull, a black-headed gull I think.' It was monstrously beautiful, and in prime condition, it certainly didn't require any attention from me.

'You're the historian Major, wasn't this place owned by the Massingbred family?' The Massingbred's were once local bigwigs, part of the original Fellowship of Upstanding Gentlemen - or the Lodge as we now called them - until their son Alfie crossed the Lodge and had to flee the country. It's a story every schoolkid in Broston knows and delights in. There's no love lost on the Lodge in this town, but I'll tell you about that later. 'Is there no mention of this thing in the family history.'

'None. As I said, I found it quite by accident in the loft.'

I didn't want to piss down the old guy's pipe, but provenance is everything. A tag containing the taxidermist's zoological name for the beast was best. It was the stamp of the creator. The taxidermist playing God and Adam, by making and naming the beast. Without the tag; the curiosity's value was greatly reduced. Unless we could locate the maker's mark. Just like quality silverware, each quality curiosity would have its maker's mark. My Dad used a scratched farthing to identify his handywork. I use a folded custard cream wrapper. But as these marks are hidden inside the pieces, finding one, would mean dismantling the beast. And I really didn't want to do that, it would have been a disrespectful act of vandalism.

'If we can determine who made it. If it's a known name, and not just some lucky amateur,' I ventured, 'we could have a real find here. A real auction house highlight.'

'Does it look amateur?' the Major pressed.

'Not on your nellie Major. This is quality, real quality, anyone can see that, but unless you can prove some provenance, the price will drop.'

'A pity indeed, but as you say; I'm a historian not some antique tout. I'm more interested in its origins than its value.'

Lying bastard. I didn't believe a word of it. I looked around the empty room. It occurred to me that the Major had been selling off his belongings to keep up the payments on the house, and this strange creature was his last throw of the dice. I'd just blown his paper boat out of the water, and he was too proud to show it. I actually felt sorry for the old git.

I carefully placed the creature back into its box, and wagged my gloved finger in the Major's face, 'to be honest Major, I wouldn't fuck around. I'd get this straight down to London. Go to a museum or a major auction house, get their experts to trawl through their books. Something like this has got to be listed somewhere.'
'Indeed, indeed, thank you.' The colour had drained from the old man's face. 'Do you have any contacts? Someone you could recommend? Someone you could approach on my behalf? I rather like the idea of it going into a museum.'

'Sure, I can dig out a name or two.' In truth the only contacts I had were vets and some dodgy gamekeepers, but a possible finder's fee was worth the effort.

The Major rubbed his hands together, and then looked me straight in the eye – why do people do that? 'I'm sorry about earlier Sam. It's just that…well in my day people like Luke were considered a security risk you know. Frowned on, definitely frowned on.'

I don't know who the Major thought he was kidding. I really wasn't buying his old soldier act. I felt sorry for the old man. Fancy having so much starch in your draws, you had to keep up a sham of being something you weren't, even that late in life.

'Like I said Major, your business is your business and none of mine.'

'Yes, yes and it is appreciated. Still, old habits you know, hard to break, hush hush and all that. Did you serve?' he asked raising an imperious eyebrow.

'In the forces? No, not me Major. I got thrown out of the Boy Scouts for bringing my dog Fluffy to camp.'

'Really, sounds a bit O.T.T to me, boy and his dog and all that.'

'Yeah, I thought so too, but I had just mounted him; it was my first big job, not my best obviously; gave some of the lads nightmares; parents complained, you know how it goes.'

'Indeed…I see…' the Major faltered, '… you know what Dr Johnson says, 'Every man thinks less of himself for not being a soldier.'

'Never thought much of myself to begin with Major, never felt the need.'

The Major huffed, picked up the box and marched out of the room. Two minutes later he walked back in, swinging his silly stick, and pulling a brown leather wallet from his trousers, 'so how much do I owe you?'

I bit my lip and gave him the biggest smile I could gather, 'Nothing at all Major. It was a pleasure. I wouldn't have missed it for the world.'

The old man rocked on his heels, 'Really, are you sure? I'm prepared to pay… surely, for time taken if nothing else.'

I thought about the council tax and the electric bill and said, 'all right slip us a fiver for some custard creams and we'll call it square.'

I got back to the shop just in time to miss a delivery of chemicals I'd been waiting on for three weeks, which meant I had to spend an hour on the phone negotiating a fresh delivery window with an automated service, that clearly hated dealing with me as much as I hated dealing with it. I wrote the new date and time on the wall, and noticed it was my dad's birthday. I felt a rush of emotion I knew I needed to smother before it overwhelmed me. I set the sign on the door to; 'Come in and shout – I'm round back,' and set about carving up the barn owl. There's nothing like scraping away muscle and sinew, to ease the body and concentrate the mind. Dad used to say; 'The man who can lose himself in his work is a happy man.' My Dad was a very happy man. And I guess I am too, unless I'm having to deal with man-hating delivery algorithms that are intent on bringing down humanity.

By midnight the owl was just about done. All I needed to do was fix it to a perch, and the job was jobbed; but it's never a good idea to rush these things. I crunched up a custard cream biscuit and set about locking up for the night; the bird wasn't going anywhere. That's when I heard the unmistakable clatter, of someone falling over my dad's bike. I stepped back into the workshop and turned off the lights. I could hear three muffled male voices beyond the door. The door handle creaked as it turned. A torch beam hit me square in the face. Someone shouted, 'Get him.'

I wasn't worried. They were clearly amateurs; they'd only brought one torch and they didn't know the ground. They immediately collided with my dissecting bench and had to take the torch beam off me to figure out their route. It was all I needed. I took hold of my favourite scarf - I call it Monkey Scarf, but I'll explain that later. I gave Monkey Scarf a quick whirl and flicked it forward into the torch beam; the four-inch lead pipe in the business end of the scarf did the rest.

'My nose!' – one down and lights out.

'There he is…' a panicked voice shouted; I flicked Monkey Scarf into the darkness and again it connected, 'Argh! He's broken my nose!' Two out of three, not bad.

'Let's go, let's go!' a third voice pleaded.

I went for them like a thundering god of war, a raging Viking berserker defending his homeland; only to be felled by an unseen punch to the chin.

I woke up cold, stiff and tied to my chair, with the sound of the morning church bells rumbling through my floorboards. My workroom had been trashed. The barn owl was stomped to pieces at my feet, along with a full packet of custard cream biscuits.

'Bugger.'

The rope wasn't hard to dislodge. All I had to do was break my favourite chair. Once I was free, I did a quick inventory. Although plenty was smashed, nothing was missing. I lifted half a custard cream from the floor and did some thinking. The voices I'd heard had been male but not young. Not young but they'd still been inexperienced amateurs; the damage I'd been able to inflict proved that; their lucky knockout shot, proved nothing. Druggies would have taken something to sell, or purloined some solvent to enjoy at their leisure, but my considerable stock of solvents was untouched. So why break in? It was odd, and when things get odd, there's only one person in town to turn to; I got onto the blower.

A Western Cowboy drawl picked up at the other end, 'Hi there, Chez Luke, how can I help you?'

'Is he there?'

'I'm afraid not, can I take a message?'

'Is he still at work? What time is it?' I hadn't counted the church bells, but it felt early.

'Do what?' the American accent broke into a lazy Fens drawl, 'I'm not the fucking speaking clock mate, who is this?'

I hate being called mate, it makes me think of wildlife programs, and all the animals I've yet to have in my workshop. 'Listen here pal. Just tell him Sam called, and I need a word.' I slapped the receiver down, picked Monkey Scarf from the floor, and laid him over my shoulders, the weight was very reassuring. I looked over my wrecked workshop; somebody had to answer for it.

Dad's bike was lying on its side in the alley. It looked like someone had stomped on the front wheel; but you'd need a tank to really damage that brute. I dragged it up and set off back to the Grove. If Fast Luke wasn't available, I was sure the Major had something to tell me.

In nearly forty years of business, our shop had never been broken into, but one visit to the Grove, and I was fighting off raiders, the whole thing tasted like rotten rabbit.

I dropped the bike onto the gravel drive, and rang the doorbell, followed by a couple of good thumps on the old oak door, but there was no answer. I stepped back; I could see all the curtains upstairs were open. The old codger had to be hiding inside. Spitting verbs and venom, I stomped around to the back of the house, and nearly fell over a splintered door laying across the path. Somebody had made a decent job of turning it into kindling. It had been kicked in, kicked over and kicked out. I ran into the house, and found myself in a kitchen that had been given much the same treatment as my workshop.

'Major!' I shouted, running into a dark panelled corridor. A set of stairs went up into the darkness on my left, but intuition drove me forward to the end of the corridor. I barged through another heavy oak door, and found myself in the furniture free room, I'd seen the previous day. The Major lay spread-eagled in the middle of the floor, wearing nothing but striped pyjama bottoms and a waistcoat of bruises. I dropped to my knees and checked for a pulse. He was cold, but still there. His face was swelling, and he had a nasty cut above his right eye. Panic flared within me; I didn't know what to do; my head was all over the place. One moment I was looking at the Major, and then I was looking down at my dad, after he'd fallen down our stairs. A flashback I guess you could call it. I froze. I was totally useless when Dad went too. I went to pieces and stayed that way for weeks. As I looked at the Major, I felt the urge to run away welling up within me, but before I knew I'd done it, I'd taken off my jacket and covered him up. Doing something seemed to quell the rush, and I was able to push Dad's face into the background and focus on the job at hand.

'Can you hear me Major?' The response was no more than a whine. I swallowed hard and took two deep breaths. I told myself to think, 'he needs help, more help than you can give him. I need to get help.' I fled the room, charged through the front door, across the gravel drive, and barged through the gates. Straight into the path of a speeding black something, with screeching wheels. Luckily for me the driver was a bit handy and managed to skim around me. I watched the car go, raising my hands in helpless protest, as it disappeared from view. I still had my hands above my head, when I turned to see a delivery truck the size of Denmark, bearing down on me. I shut my eyes as the airbrakes hissed.

'What the fuck do you think you're playing at?!' the driver railed as he jumped down from his cab, all fists and spit.

'There's an old man in there. He's been beaten up. Call an ambulance.'

He did better than that. He called an ambulance, put out emergency triangles and directed traffic through, until the ambulance turned up. It's good to know there are still some decent folks out there; difficult to believe they're lorry drivers but there it is.

PC Dobbs, who didn't look old enough to buy his own beer, arrived just as the ambulance crew were rushing the Major away. The baby copper asked all the obvious questions twice, and then told me to hang around, until the grown-up coppers arrived, no doubt so they could ask the same questions all over again.

'Do I really need to?' I asked, 'you do have my address.'

'I think its best sir. This is the third time I've been called out to this address in six months. Must be the eighth incident this year. I told the old fella to move out, or get a dog, but he wouldn't have it. That's how he lost all his furniture you know, bastards broke in and took it while he was asleep.

'He wasn't so lucky this time.'

'Exactly, they did a good job on him. Any help you could give us in apprehending them would be appreciated. Best to stick around, I'm sure the detective won't be long.' Dobbs' radio squawked. He gave me a nod, and then walked briskly out through the kitchen. Leaving me staring at the space on the floor where the Major had been. I noted thin smears of dried blood encircling the space. I tried to count the footprints. I couldn't be sure, they'd been too much through traffic, but it occurred to me that the Major and I may have shared the same unwelcome guests.

'What the fuck are you doing here Sam?'

I turned to see Bull standing in the doorway. How to describe Detective Benjamin Bull? His name says it all really – imagine a bull in a cheap suit, chewing on a bag of wasps – a big mean bastard; that about covers it.

'Detective Bull. I thought you'd been promoted to the big city.'

'Of course you did...'

Bull and I had history. He'd led the Simple Shirley investigation; and made a right hash of it. A much beloved local girl had been found dead in the town's park, killed by taxine poisoning as it turned out. The Bull concluded that Shirley was to blame. The misadventure of a mentally disabled girl, accidentally chewing Yew tree seeds – a ridiculously lazy conclusion. Shirley's family asked Fast Luke and I to look into it, and in less than two weeks we'd identified a culprit and gained a confession; admittedly with the use of a stuffed rat and a jar of Vaseline, but we got the job done. One Ceril Aldwick, local Newsagent, had been buying Shirley's sexual favours with sweets for years. Shirley's threat to make his foul attentions known, had proved too much for him, so he put ground Yew tree seeds into her sherbet dip to shut her up. The thought of Ceril braving the prison showers, still gives me a warm glow.

'… so, when did taxidermists start doing house calls?' Bull sneered, 'what was it, between you and the old boy, business or pleasure?'

Bull liked to think he was intimidating, but I don't scare so easy. If there's one thing taxidermy teaches you it's this – they've all got necks. 'Have you lost weight Bull? Or just hot air?'

'Business or pleasure?'

'Our business and none of yours, and the pleasures all mine.'

Bull's face formed a grin that could have cut a throat, 'so, for some, as yet unspecified reason, you were visiting the Major this morning. You tried the front door but got no answer, so you came in the back and found him…?'

'There, right there, half dead, after receiving a damn good kicking. I did wonder if some of your boys hadn't paid him a visit, but then I thought; an old man like the Major, probably too much for the local boobies to handle.'

'Very funny. I'm going to ask you one more time Sam; why the visit? Was the Major putting some work your way, if so, why not just say so, and save us all some time?'

Yeah, why not? I don't know, I can't say, maybe I just didn't like the tone of his voice or maybe it's because Bull was Bull; 'Fair enough, if it helps your investigation here it is. The Major and I go way back, what that old man doesn't know about the erotic application of egg whisks isn't worth knowing.'

Bull intensified his glare by two notches, boiling the blood behind his eyes, 'cut the crap Sam. How do you know him? Are you working for him?'

'Oh alright then, have it your way; we belong to the same table turning group.'

'Table turning group?'

'Yeah, we turn tables together but we take turns, it's the latest thing from America. All the celebs are at it. It's a lot more complex than it sounds. Some people turn left, some people like to turn right. It's all about accepting who you are. You should look into it. Unload some of that latent homosexual tension.'

Bull's fist clenched as he took a step towards me, 'is there some reason you're being an arsehole Sam?'

'Sure there is.' I waited for the silence to thicken, 'I don't want you to feel lonely.'

'Why...are...you...here?' his voice had dropped to a low rumble I could feel in my chest.

I stepped into his gravity field, 'what's...it...to...you?'

Bull smiled and somewhere in the universe a fairy vomited itself to death, 'okay Sam. I take it you can verify your whereabouts last night?'

'I was tied to a chair entertaining three gentlemen.'

'And I have no problem believing it. In that case, I'd like to thank you for your cooperation in this matter.'

'Fine, go-ahead.'

'But I won't.'

I headed back to the shop. I needed a shower, or at least a wipe down with an oily rag. My morning exertions had bolstered my, 'Odour de Bill Sykes,' and it was getting a bit too much even for my stomach. Back at the workshop, I wedged the bike between the workbench and the backdoor; getting at the crown jewels would be easier than getting past that bastard's bulk.

I'd grown up in the flat above the shop. It's not much...and there's not a lot to add to that. Two bedrooms, a bathroom and something called a kitchen, which apparently has something to do with preparing food.

As soon as I reached the top of the suitcase sized landing, I knew something was wrong. There was nothing obviously out of place, but I was certain someone had been up there. I checked the door to Dad's old room. I'd put a padlock on the door after he passed. I never went in there. I couldn't face going in there. The screws holding the latch had taken some punishment, when someone had tried to force their way in. I stood there, head against the door, struggling to settle my breathing. Even if they had forced the lock, they wouldn't have got past the six-inch nails, I'd driven through door and frame; not without taking half the fucking wall out. So why hadn't they? They'd had plenty of time to kick it in last night when I was out cold. Unless it hadn't happened last night; what if this was fresh work? I turned my back on Dad's room and faced my own. I hardly ever go in there, it's easier to sleep downstairs in the workshop, but I keep the door closed because of mice and now it was open. Not fully, but just enough for someone to be standing behind it, someone whose search I'd disturbed. I lifted Monkey Scarf from around my neck, twisted it around my fist, and made ready to ruin my intruder's day.

I'm sure you've realised by now, that Monkey Scarf, is more monkey than scarf. It is in fact two thirds of a Siamang Gibbon, A zoo reared beast, that died a natural death, after a long and happy life. Which makes Monkey Scarf a totally legal and above-board item: well almost, the stuffed exhibit I returned to the zoo, is actually two thirds dyed human hair from 'Cuts R Us,' and a well-crafted coconut husk; but they'll never know. One arm of the scarf is stuffed with very flexible, squishy silicon, the middle section is stuffed with washed wool - very comfy - and the other arm is lined with a sleeve of leather around three articulated lead truncheons; and it's all my own design. Fine workmanship, even if I do say so myself. I had murder in my heart at that moment. There are two things I believe in, a man's home is his castle, and don't fuck with the Monkey Scarf.

I kicked the door hard and followed it through, Monkey Scarf raised, teeth set to kill. There was no-one there, but the room had been searched, and whoever did it didn't mind me knowing. There was an empty ketchup bottle on my bed, and a note written in foot high red letters across my wall.

GIVE IT UP

The phone downstairs rang. I trudged back down and picked up the receiver.

'Get the message?' it was a male voice. I could feel his stupid toothy grin on the other end of the line.

'You're lucky, I took a degree in condiments.'

'Funny guy. We want it back.'

'Denial is good for the soul. Much like a swift kick to the happy-sacks. Come over and I'll show you.'

'We want it returned to us tonight, or you'll be meeting up with the Major sooner than you think.' Bloody amateur; he was telling me more than he knew.

'Okay, but there's a price.'

I heard the phone being clamped to his chest. He hadn't expected that. He was checking in with someone. His voice had a more agreeable tone when he came back on the line, 'how much?'

'I'm not a greedy man. Five hundred quid.'

'Deal.'

I've heard slower mousetraps. A real amateur; he didn't even pretend to haggle. This meant, whatever they wanted, it was worth more than five hundred to them.

'Great, we exchange merchandise tonight. Midnight on the Sluice Bridge. You come alone and so do I. Any nonsense and you'll be fishing for it, agreed.'

'Agreed. Midnight.'

'And one more thing. If one of you wankers, steps foot inside my place again, I'll carve you into fucking dog food, understand.'

The line toned out.

I ran myself a shower, and made liberal with the Fairy Washing-Up Liquid, whilst I thought about what I'd learnt. They didn't have what they wanted and were willing to pay. They thought I had it, which meant they didn't know where it was, which was something we had in common, but at least I had a better idea where it wasn't. But then again, I had no idea what, 'it' was; but what else could it be but that bloody curiosity. I do believe I sang in the shower; probably 'Get it On' by T-Rex. You can't go wrong with a bit of T-Rex – I love the Rex. And when your days go wrong, remember, get it on, bang a gong, and you're sure to feel better – that's bloody philosophy that is.

It was already past noon when I set out for the hospital. The Major had been admitted to a ward on the second floor, but they weren't keen on him having visitors. So I told the story of my part in the Major's rescue, and was soon ushered through like an honoured guest. The old guy looked worse than when I'd found him. The bruises were flowering over his face, and where he wasn't a bouquet of colour, he was as pale as the sheet that was tucked under his chin. I pulled the blue plastic chair to the bed and put my mouth close to his ear.

'Major, it's Sam.' His eyes opened. 'I need to know where you hid it.' His head barely moved. 'Listen Major, they've done you over and had a go at me, and I don't intend to let them get away with it.' His eyes met mine. 'Major, you need to trust me. I don't mean for them to have it. I think I can get one over on them, but they're going to keep at it, and there's no one protecting your place now. They could be tearing down the walls as we speak. Do you really think it's that well-hidden?'

He blinked slowly; I could see the effort cost him. His eyes shut and his lips parted as a dry whisper of a voice left his aching body; 'Fast Luke.'

I was round at Chez Luke in less than half an hour. It's just an ex-council house, mid-terrace, nothing special. Although the inflatable, six-foot high, white rabbit in the front garden does set it apart from its neighbours. It also has a really irritating doorbell, an off-key version of 'Somewhere over the rainbow.' Luke's ability to embrace a cliché that risks setting the gay community back twenty years was truly astounding; but I don't buy into it, the nail polish doesn't fool me, the man's a shark, and anybody who forgets that is buggered for sure. The door was opened by a tall youth in a tight white t-shirt and jeans; which could have been used as an andrological tool had they been any tighter.

'Yeah, what is it man,' it was that fake American accent again. He was giving me his best James Dean leer, 'what do you want?'

I tried playing it friendly, 'I spoke to you this morning. Is he in?'

'Maybe he is, maybe he isn't...'

I didn't have time for his act. I grabbed – I'll call him Buff Guy 32 for now - by the throat, stepped through the door and shoved him up against the wall. 'Luke! Are you in here or not? If you are you'd better come quick before I throttle the life out of your latest toy-boy.'

A gasp of outrage came from somewhere within; 'Toy-boy? Really Sam, what are you suggesting? All consenting adults here, I can assure you of that.' Luke and his silk kimono, swept through the beaded curtain that concealed the hallway from the rest of the house; 'Sam, what are you doing? Put him down. You're so very un-woke. What's come over you?'

'Not you. That's for sure.' I dropped the gagging Buff to the floor where he proceeded to weep in a very un-Dean like fashion.

'Oh dear, another victim of machismo haste,' Luke pouted, reaching past me, to a powder blue jacket, hanging by the door. He produced a twenty-pound note from a pocket and tossed it at the weeping youth. 'There you go now. Never mind the nasty man.'

The buff snatched up the cash, and Luke patted his head fondly, as he eased him towards the front door, 'off you go now, run free. Go on, off with you.'

The lad wiped his eyes, looked at Luke and then at the twenty, and decided to make the best of it, and bolted.

'That's it, run away, run away. Go and get some sweeties, or crack, or whatever...' Luke sighed, as he shut the door. 'Sam, you really must stop manhandling my friends. He's a very talented chap, you wouldn't believe what he can do with an ice-lolly.'

'Luke, this is important.'

'So is he darling, well his father is anyhow. A local bigwig in the Lodge. I was pumping him for information.'

'I bet you were.'

'Sam darling,' he pouted, spreading his arms in a theatrical yawn, 'I've been on my feet all night, and was looking forward to spending the morning on my knees. And you've spoilt my fun.' He was probably telling the truth on all counts. Luke works nights at the Post Office; I try not to think about his daytime activities.

'I'm here about the Major.'

'How is the old bugger?'

'Well, let me think. He was tortured last night. I found him this morning and he's in hospital.'

Luke's face turned to granite; 'Is that so, you better come into the kitchen.'

I watched Luke disappear through another beaded veil. I paused before following, trying to steady my nerves; I'd once had a bad experience in Luke's kitchen; that I've not yet fully come to terms with, but more of that later. I stepped beyond the veil, and into Luke's version of a French country kitchen, A rainbow garden of multicoloured garlic strings, suspicious looking herbs and questionable mushrooms.

'Who's behind this Luke? I'd like to know because they did a job on my place last night too.'

'If I told you, it was the Fellowship of the Upright Gentlemen, would you believe me.'

'The Lodge, of course I would.'

'I warned Monty this would happen. Poor Monty, is he alright?'

'No, like I said, he's in the hospital. They want the Major's curiosity. They left their demand on my bedroom wall. I've agreed to hand it over at midnight.'

'Why on earth did you do that?'

'So I can wring their necks of course.'

'Fair enough, but where is the darling thing? You obviously didn't bring it with you?'

I did a double-take just like in the movies, 'I don't have it. Don't you have it?'

'No, why would I?'

'The Major said you did.' I thought about what the Major had actually said, 'I've just visited him at the hospital… he said your name.'

'I see, so a bashed-up old man, said my name, and you immediately jumped to the conclusion that I had the very thing, that I had sent you to take charge of…'

'Sent, I don't remember being sent…'

'For crying out loud Sam. Why else would I give him your name? Do I have to do all your thinking for you?' On the outside, Luke was a flamboyant queen, a Quentin Crisp on speed, but beyond the face-paint and demi-wave was a shark with a razor-sharp mind, and more cold guts than an abattoir. And now the shark was baring its teeth, 'good god Sam, what is the matter with you?'

'Don't have a go at me, I thought you…'

'You thought! You thought! You bloody well didn't darling. And then you come charging in here, ruining a perfectly delightful morning, shame on you Sam, shame.'

'Alright, pull your neck in Luke, that's enough.' I don't mind the shark sinking its teeth in every now and then, but I'm not sitting through a chewing, when there's a bigger game in play. 'What's going on Luke? What have those tossers at the Lodge got to do with this?'

'I've half a mind not to tell you. Perhaps you'd like a diagram? What about a colouring-in edition with speech-bubbles, would that help? You're a sodding useless oaf Sam.' Luke threw himself down into a chair and pulled his kimono tight around his chest. 'Be quiet, I need to think... did you know wode has antiseptic properties? So when the ancient Brits...' Luke then went off on a completely obtuse angle. He calls it Anti-Zen. His own form of deep meditation. A separation of mind and mouth. I've spent hours listening to him talk about hair conditioners, slow-cooking and the farming of snails, only to hear him reveal the intricacies of a sordid, and previously unfathomable plot at the end of his rambling. It's a neat trick but a bit disconcerting at first; and after a while it just gets bloody irritating, so you'll forgive me if I don't recall every dithering word Luke spouted; I have enough problems mastering blinking.

At this juncture a little background information about the Fellowship of Upstanding Gentlemen, or the Lodge as we call them, seems in order. Broston isn't just a rundown, mind crushingly dull market town, typically found in the East of England. It's actually a rundown, mind crushingly dull, estuary island in the East of England. You can't get into the town without crossing an expanse of water. For hundreds of years the locals capitalised on this peculiar geographical anomaly, by not mixing with the rest of England. They had a fishing fleet and a port, so what else did they need? But then the estuary, called The Wash, began to silt up. As access to larger, wealthier boats began to dwindle, so did the town's revenue. In 1840 the jig was up. Broston was no longer a viable shipping port, and the big boats and profits went elsewhere. It was then that a cabal of the town's landowning elite; the Fellowship of Upstanding Gentleman, stepped in and offered themselves up as the town's saviours. They had a plan to overcome time and tide, which they were prepared to back; as long as they could have a substantial share of the land, and certain shipping rights. All of which was conceded to, quicker than spit dries on a hotplate. In 1848 their plan was completed. The Cut, as it was named, had been dug, and a new offshore port, big enough to handle the largest of cargo vessels had been built. All was merry and bright in the old town of Broston, until the town realised, they'd been had. The port's new train track would take the goods and wealth away from Broston, and the only people getting rich were the members of the Lodge. So everyone in Broston knew about the Lodge; and knew them to be a right bunch of wankers.

'…which is why I never eat cheesecake anymore.' Luke came back to the world of the troubled, with a flick of his hair, 'so the Lodge is willing to pay you say?'

'If it was them that scrawled tomato sauce over my wall, yes. Five hundred quid. But I want to know why they're willing to pay. Why do they want it?'

'Oh do keep up Sam. The Lodge has been after that funny looking thing for years. I was hoping you'd be able to give me some clues when you saw it. I wanted you to take charge of it, take it apart, find us some clues. This is much more your area than mine. Is it valuable?'

'It's not worth a man's life. Not even the Major's.'

Luke raised the teacup to his lips, 'someone doesn't agree with you Sam. And I must say, I find that rather intriguing. I'm intrigued, and a little aroused.'

'Too much information. What are we going to do?'

'We?' Luke's eyebrows would have hit the ceiling if they hadn't been painted on his forehead. 'This is all down to you Sam. This is your mess, don't drag me into it.'

'You dragged me into this Luke. I didn't ask for any of this. Have you any idea how difficult it is to get ketchup off wallpaper?'

Luke wafted his kimono sleeve around in a lazy circle. 'I don't think so Sam,' and then winked mischievously, 'okay sweetie, so where do you think the Major's beastie is?' The demur grin was back, but once again, let me remind you, don't buy into the cliché. It's a big bouffant camouflage act; Luke's a shark hiding in plain sight…in a kimono. It takes all sorts.

'It must be back at the Grove.'

'I'm blinded by your brilliance, really I am. I mean with such insights; we'll have this case cracked before tea-time.' Luke was sharp, but he could also be a really sarcastic bastard, 'obviously it's somewhere in the Grove…but do you know where?'

After some thought I answered, 'in its box, somewhere in the Grove.'

'Right, fine, of course. I'd better go have a look see myself then… no crumpets for Luke, you really are the limit Sam.' Luke pulled a mobile phone from the folds of his kimono and jabbed at the screen, 'Billy? It's Luke, I need a car round here sharpish. To the Grove; you know that place that's always for sale.' He smiled as he concealed the phone, 'guess I'd better get changed then…and I haven't got a thing to wear.'

Billy the Prawn picked us up ten minutes later. Some people think Billy got his name because his family owned one of the town's last prawn fishing boats. It's not so. He just looks like a prawn. It's hard to describe but his complexion has a lot to do with it. It's a shame really because he's a nice, if slightly twisted lad. Luke and I helped him out of a jam once. He'd been caught making sexual advances towards a field of pumpkins; life can't be easy when you're the colour of a prawn.

'You seeing this?' Billy said as the car slowed in front of the Grove.

A police car and a white transit van were parked inside the gate.

'Don't stop Billy. But go nice and slow. I need a gander,' said Luke, dipping down in his seat.

I was sitting in the back and saw the scene well enough; a group of men in white overalls, coming in and out of the house; 'Looks like they've sent it the crime scene guys?' I pointed out.

'I don't like the look of this,' Luke growled. 'Drive to the next junction Billy and drop us off, give us ten minutes and make your way back down, we'll meet you.'

'Right you are Mr Luke ma'am,' Billy whispered as he peered above the curve of the steering wheel.

'Sit up Billy! You'll cause an accident,' Luke commanded.

'Yes Mr Luke ma'am,' Billy obeyed.

Luke and I walked back towards the house, keeping to the grass verge and out of sight of the copper at the gate. We pushed ourselves as far into the hedge as we dared, peering into the gravel driveway. Luke tapped his nose and pointed to a pile of wood, dumped on the far side of the drive. As we watched a figure in white overalls carried another load from the house and added it to the pile.

'It's the oak panelling,' I whispered. 'Why are they ripping it out?'

'You idiot, they're searching the place? And we both know what they're searching for.'

'The box? But why would the police be looking for it? Why would they…? What's going on Luke?'

'Come on, I've seen enough.' Luke freed himself from the hedge, and set-off back along the verge to meet Billy. I stayed for a few seconds longer, and saw another white clown immerge from behind the house, but this one I recognised. It was the unmistakable hulk of Detective Bull. I watched him toss a huge load of wood-panelling onto the gravel, and stretch his double breasted back with relief. I'm not sure which I found more shocking, him being there or him doing manual labour.

Billy dropped us off in Broston, at the top of West Street, outside 'The Lotus Flower;' Luke's favourite Chinese restaurant. China Pete, a dapper little fellow who wouldn't look out of place in an Agatha Christie novel, opened the door; a shining meat cleaver in his hand.

'What do you want, we're closed! Oh Lukey baby!' he squeaked, 'and Sammy baby! Come in, come in, tea yes?'

Luke couldn't resist the opportunity to put on a show. 'You're a life saver, a bloody life saver China Pete, you lovely little sweet and sour cocksucker you.' Pete seemed to appreciate the totally inappropriate compliment; so who was I to judge.

'The cops being there, really buggers up my plan,' I moaned, as we sat at the table.

'A plan,' Luke snorted. 'You didn't have a plan Sam. You had a brazenly obvious, macho wet-dream of violence and revenge, that's not a plan.'

'I had a plan,' I insisted.

'What was it? No let me guess, get the thing, copy the thing, give the thing to the boys from the Lodge and keep the money. A mastermind at work.'

'Fuck you.'

'You should be so lucky. I've told you before, you'd have to wash using real soap and fix me a meal, something other than random roadkill you'd peeled off the A17. But was I wrong Sam, was I?'

'Give over will you,' Luke knew me too well, but for once I knew something he didn't, 'there's something you should know, after you left, I saw Bull back there.'

Luke's painted eyebrows quivered, 'Did you indeed? Now that is interesting.'

'Is Bull in the Lodge?'

'I'm sure he'd like to be. Maybe he's trying to get into their good books.' Luke leant back as China Pete, replete in white-cotton gloves, appeared from the kitchen and set before us a tray of miniature pancake rolls and a pot of tea, 'there you go boys, dig in.'

'Please join us Pete,' Luke requested, placing a manicured hand on Pete's arm. Pete pulled up a chair, removed his gloves, and sat down. Luke moved his hand to Pete's shoulder, and gripped it firmly. 'I'm sorry to have to tell you this, but they did over the Major last night.'

'Again!' Pete squealed, 'those mummy fucking bastards. What did they take this time?'

'No Pete, they got hold of him. He's in the hospital. I'm sorry.'

Pete's shoulders shook convulsively, as huge tears poured down his face. I was shocked, the Major and China Pete! That Major, what a hypocrite!

'He's alright Petey,' Luke went on, 'Sam's already been to see him. Don't worry I'll make sure someone keeps an eye on him. He's perfectly safe.' Luke rubbed a tear from Pete's face with the back of his hand, 'I need to ask you something, do you know where the Major keeps his beast?'

'The thing in the box? No he never told me, never let me see. Are you going to fix these bastards Luke?"

'Of course, all in good time, but,' Luke chuckled, 'tell me is Detective Bull in with the Lodge?'

'No never,' Pete stated emphatically, 'they'd never take him. He's not local. He's from Norfolk. Might as well be from fucking China.'

'Good point Pete, good point well made,' Luke nodded, as he picked a pancake roll from the tray.

'But none of this explains why they want the thing so badly. It's really not worth that much,' I insisted, because I was right.

Luke bit into his roll and stared thoughtfully at its filling, 'perhaps we've got this wrong.' He waved the decapitated fried snack in my face, 'what do you think? Ummm? Look closely…look deep into the roll Sam, look deep into the roll.'

I saw shredded cabbage, beansprouts, possibly pork, possibly cat. A domino fell in the dark space I call my mind, and I remembered. 'It was heavy. It didn't need to be heavy. You think there's something inside it they want don't you.'

'Very likely,' Luke smiled, 'you see the difference a little expertise makes, I would never have known that.'

'What do you think it could be?' thoughts of treasure were filling my head.

'I have no idea. But we need to find out.'

'And by we, you mean…'

I cycled past the Grove around eight o'clock that night. The police had left, but a length of their yellow and black tape was still wrapped around the cast iron gates. I cycled up to the Bull House pub, where I ordered half a pint of Dark Mild. I took my time with my drink, and didn't head back until the sky was as dark as the Mild. I then cycled past the house once more, to make sure there were no lights on inside – there weren't – so I whipped back around the roundabout and sped into the hedge. I stood on the bike's saddle and then with a push, rolled over the green barricade. I landed face down on the gravel drive with a crunch; not very Ninja.

The kitchen door had been replaced by a sheet of plywood, and an official looking, 'DO NOT ENTER' sticker - official but ineffective. Once inside, I stood with torch in one hand and Monkey Scarf in the other, listening to see if my forced entry had stirred up any guards. All was quiet, so I got busy.

If the wrecking team had found what they were looking for then I was wasting my time. If they hadn't then I did have one thing working in my favour; I didn't need to waste time looking where they'd already been. Back at the Lotus, we'd all discussed our individual visits to the Grove. Pete's account had been somewhat freer, more colourful, and wide ranging, but we'd all waited in the empty backroom, whilst the Major went to fetch his hoard. We agreed we'd been in there for no more than a couple of minutes, before the major reappeared, and the same time had been taken replacing the beast. He didn't go upstairs or open any heavy clunking doors. He was an old, stooped man and although fairly quick on his feet, he couldn't have gone far between the backroom and the kitchen to get his show-and-tell. So it couldn't be hidden up the flight of stairs or far from the dark corridor. The nearest room was the kitchen; if it had been in there it certainly must have been found; as the men in white suits had stripped the room back to the aging plaster. But if it hadn't been found, it had to be hidden in the bottom of the staircase or the corridor. Logic got me that far, but I doubted it would get me further. The stairs had been ripped out from top to bottom. If the Major ever came home, he'd need climbing gear to get to his bedroom. The corridor's panelling had all been torn out, exposing a blackened wooden frame and even more ancient wattle and daub plasterwork; some of which had been knocked about; traces of horsehair shone spectral white in my torch beam. I pulled a lump free but saw no point in digging further, as the plaster ran as flush to the ancient brickwork as you'd expect. Several clay floor tiles had been ripped up to expose the sandy bedding underneath, but I couldn't see the Major heaving those out of the way every time he wanted to show his treasure. I would have heard his back snapping, so where was it? I replayed my visit in my head. The Major, being an arse, asks me to wait, walks out of the room with his silly little cane and shuts the door behind him. Minutes later he returns with the box, pushing the door open with his foot, slightly out of breath due to the weight, his hands full of heavy box. I stopped and replayed the image. The Major's hands were full of box. So where was the cane? He hadn't returned with the cane, and he hadn't used it for walking. Why use a cane at all? Why would anybody carry a swagger stick if he didn't need it? He was certainly the product of England's very private public school system, so a bit of rum, sodomy and the lash was probable, but I felt there was a more pragmatic explanation.

I stood in the darkened corridor and tried to imagine the Major poking about in there with his silly little cane. I saw the Major's stoop, and figured it would limit his upper reach; so maybe he needed the stick to reach something high up, but try as I might it was too dark to see anything. And then that domino in my head began to totter again. I checked the wall for a switch, there was none, and yet directly above me was a bare arsed bulb. I reached up with Monkey Scarf and pushed on the light fittings yellowed casing. I heard a click behind me and turned to see a section of the ceiling lowering on two rope pulleys. Sitting within it was the dark wooden box. I removed the box and pushed the dropped panel back into place, it must have been part of a counter lever, because it rode back up into place without sound or protest. The light fitting clicked back, and all was as it had been. As an incredible sense of 'Fuck You' washed over me, I heard the front door open. The sound of beery laughter followed. I legged it out of the kitchen and into the garden without looking back. I heard raised voices and snapped commands behind me, as I plunged headfirst through the hedge and nearly knocked myself senseless on the crossbar of Dad's bike. Torch beams swung above my head as kicked up gravel scattered around me. A face pushed its way through the void I'd made in the hedge, followed by a torch beam and the hand that held it. As it dipped towards me, I rose up to meet it, swinging hard and fast. The face collapsed back into the greenery. I righted the bike and was off down the road, with the sound of Anglo-Saxon curses ringing in my ears.

I arrived back at my workshop in ten minutes flat. Fast Luke and a handy looking Buff Guy – can't remember his name let's call him 33 – were waiting inside.

'Any trouble?' Luke asked, 'you look like you've been dragged through a hedge backward.'

'Not much, and try jumped,' I replied. I opened the box and set the beast down under the beam of my angle poise lamp. Its amber eyes glowed angrily, and it cast eerie shadows about the workshop. I wouldn't have been surprised to see the wings flap in protest. It really was a great piece of work.

'Creepy,' Buff Guy 33 said, with a visible shiver.

'Only to the uninitiated,' I asserted.

'Initiate us please Sam,' Luke chuckled, 'do your funky thing whiteboy.'

I loaded a new scalpel blade into a stainless-steel handle, and then got to work looking for the closing stitch. I knew where I'd hide it; out of sight in a natural crease. I found it under the left leg, a waxed black silk twine, as tough and taut as the day it was castoff. I cut below the knot and in two minutes, I'd cut through every stitch that concealed the beast's cork sealed anus. I tipped the creature over a stoneware mixing bowl, I usually used for collecting the blood from medium sized mammals, and gently removed the cork bung. Out poured a cascade of glistening white powder.

'Cocaine,' Buff 33 gasped.

Luke's fingers delved into the bowl, 'That's sand,' he intoned, 'and nothing but sand.'

'Sand,' the Buff repeated, 'are you sure?' and shoved his hand into the bowl and up to his mouth, 'it's sand.'

Not wanting to be left out, I pressed in a finger, 'Yep that's sand.'

'We're all in agreement then…sand. I can't help but feel a little deflated,' Luke sighed, 'what's the going rate for sand?'

'Not five hundred quid a pop that's for sure.'

'I'm sure you're right,' Luke gave his lower lip a loud suck, 'so…could it possibly have some sort of sentimental value?'

'Sentimental sand,' I said, like the idiot I am.

'No Sam, the creature,' Luke huffed. Lowering himself down onto my beaten-up sofa, he beckoned for the Buff to join him. 'I need to think this through, come distract me sweetness… let me tell you all about omelettes.' I made a hasty retreat; I didn't need to know what Luke was beating into his omelettes.

I went back up to the flat. I had just over an hour before I was meant to make the handover. Why not just hand the beast over? It made no sense to keep it. The Major would be safe, and I'd make five hundred quid. But why were they willing to beat the old man senseless, for a sand filled taxidermy exhibit? It made no sense. Luke was the brains of our little operation, and if he didn't know what was going on, I was never going to figure it out. I'd not been blessed with the smarts. I've worked hard to try and get my share, but it's been an uphill struggle. My old headmaster, Mr Trout once proclaimed to my whole class;

'You are, without doubt, the densest boy this school has ever had the misfortune to teach. By rights you should disappear into a blackhole of your own making.'

I left school that week, and no one seemed to mind. I was fourteen, and no one came looking for me, I simply disappeared into a blackhole of their making.

I was contemplating these things, when I opened the stove to peruse my book collection. My eyes instantly fell on the spine of Major M. Turney's, 'Broston: An Island in the Stream.' I pulled it out, wiped off the black mold and skimmed to the black and white photos at the centre of the book. There were two images of the entrance to the Temple, an Egyptian style folly, everybody in Broston knows well. Two tapered stone columns either side of a metal studded wooden door. The righthand picture displayed a close-up of one pillar, on which was carved, a plump snake, encircling a squatting creature, that was the very likeness of the Major's curiosity. My feet didn't touch the stairs. I barged into the workshop, book held aloft; only to discover Luke rubbing his hands together excitedly, whilst my angle poise lamp cast the creature's shadow across the far wall.

'Sam! I know where I've seen this, it's so obvious. It's from the columns in front of The Lodge Temple.'

'You bastard,' I shoved the open book into his face.

'Yes, that's it,' he exclaimed, 'was it in the old sods book all the time? Blow me.'

'Done,' Buff 33 smirked.

'Luke, I bloody hate you,' I said with more venom than I'd intended.

'Don't be such a brat Sam.' Luke snatched the book from me, 'look at that, there it is for the whole world to see.' Luke read the accompanying information out loud; 'This edifice was built in 1923, and is an exact copy of the Ishtar Gate, which is now held in the British Museum.' Exact copy my arse, that's not hieroglyphics is it, that's our little friend here.'

'I still think it looks creepy.' Buff guy exclaimed, peering into the book.

'Says the guy giving a blow job to the postman in the taxidermists workshop,' I snapped, 'what do you think it means smarty pants?'

'Perhaps it's a mascot or a fetish object.'

'Kinky,' Buff chirped in.

Luke's hand clipped the back of the Buff's head, 'I'll do the innuendoes thank you. Fetish, as in religious object, not everything's sex. Whatever it signifies it's clearly something very special to them, perhaps even sacred. Afterall, you usually find saints and gods on temples don't you.'

'People do crazy things for their gods,' as soon as the words left my mouth, a chill ran down my spine,

'It's true, I had a very nasty run in with some Baptists when they caught me skinny dipping in their indoor swimming pool,' the Buff declared, turning pale at the memory, 'it was like they were possessed.'

'Swimming pool? In the Baptist church; Christ, what do they teach kids these days?' Luke slapped the Buff's thigh. 'The question is, what are we going to do with their little god? Sam, they're expecting you to hand it over,' Luke checked his diamante rimmed wristwatch, 'in just over an hour. Are you going to hand it over? Or do you want to screw with the Lodge?'

'It's not mine to handover or had you forgotten that?'

Luke's face beamed, 'I was just making sure you hadn't. Screw with the Lodge it is, what do you need Sam?'

'Hand me that tube of Superglue,' I spat, 'and get everything out of that fridge and set it on the bench. I'm going to have to work quickly.'

The Black Sluice Bridge is an imposing concrete and steel structure, that protects the good people of Broston, and the numerous waterways that encircle the town, from flooding by the sea. Before it was built flooding was commonplace; which might explain why webbed feet are so common in the locals, and why so many of the town's houses and shops; including my own, had cellars. The only way to protect your house from flooding back then, was to flood the lower levels and move up a floor. Once the Black Sluice was operational in 1946, many of the town's musty cellars were sealed up, or became storerooms - or more recently were rented out to migrant workers for exorbitant prices; chest infections and damp rot thrown in for free. Another thing you should know about the Black Sluice, is that it isn't the warmest place to stand at midnight, in fact it's a mite nippy. What with the constantly bitter Easterly blowing in across The Wash, and a thousand tons of cold water churning beneath your feet, a man's thoughts drift to the need to pee. In normal circumstances, whipping your dick out on that street during the hours of darkness, would be inviting the kind of trouble Luke would enjoy, and I try to avoid, but seeing as the street was deserted, I decided to risk it. No sooner had I got my dick in my hands and through the railings, than a voice behind me whispered.
'Have you got it with you?'
'Hold on a minute pal, I've got my hands full.'
'Not from where I'm standing,' the voice mocked.

51

'Now there's no need for that,' I said, giving the old lad a hurried shake, 'you got the money?'

'Five hundred as agreed.'

I zipped up and turned to face the voice; I saw nothing more than a black swathed outline against a black background. I undid my jacket and pulled out my cargo, wrapped in a black bin liner, 'you don't mind if I keep the box do you?'

At that moment a torch beam cut across both of us and out of the shadows stepped the bulk of Detective Bull, 'what's going on here then?'

'Nothing officer,' my dark companion sang. He couldn't have jumped higher if he'd been plugged into the mains. Bloody amateur.

'Nothing?' Bull sneered, 'nothing doesn't happen on a darkened corner in the middle of the night between two men; that's not nothing, that's definitely something. Hello Sam, fancy seeing you here. What's in the bag?'

'I think you know what it is Bull.'

'Do I? Perhaps you're right. But I wonder, do you?' Bull took a step towards the whining shadow and growled, 'so do you want to be had for receiving stolen goods? Or do you want to fuck off?'

'I'll fuck off if it's okay with you,' the outline whined and off he fucked.

Then it was my turn to receive Bull's full attention, 'hand it over Sam.'

'What's it to you Bull? Why are you getting involved?'

I couldn't see the sickening grin but I'm sure it was there, 'stolen property Sam, that's my business. Hand it over now.'

I handed him the bag and as a reward he placed his right hand into my stomach, twice, at speed; followed with a downward cut to the left ear. Being hit in the ear hurts, it turns your knees to water, pulls the stars from the sky, and makes you feel mighty foolish for letting yourself get punched in the ear.

'I owed you that one twat,' Bull said with conviction.

By the time the stars had returned to their rightful orbits, the Bull was long gone; taking my plastic wrapped package with him. I was hurting but I still managed to smile...it might even have been a smirk. I was sorry I wouldn't be there to see him open his prize.

The next morning, I had breakfast at 'The Church Street Café' – cash only no cards – and one of the few places in Western Europe, where you can still get a kipper and pint of beer for breakfast. I was scraping the plate with a heavily buttered slice when Luke entered the shop. I didn't see him, I was upstairs looking out over the river, but I heard him make his entrance.

'Good morning all! Has anybody here seen an Oliver Reed lookalike in need of a wash? Sammy! Are you here darling?' The sound of old ladies passing-out and aldermen choking on their toasted teacakes, floated up from the ground floor.

'I'm up here Luke,' I cringed.

Luke broke into a rendition of 'The Lincolnshire Poacher,' as he skipped up the flight of stairs; it's a ridiculous song in anybody's hands, but coming from Luke's mouth twisted it entirely:

'When I was bound apprentice in famous Lincolnshire

Full well I served my master for nigh on seven years

Till I took up to poaching as you shall quickly hear

Oh, 'tis my delight on a shiny night to take it up the rear!'

'Good grief, don't you ever just walk into a room?' I blushed.

'I did once. And I didn't like it. So how did it go?' he said, slumping into the opposite chair.

'Not exactly to plan. Bull was there, he took the package.'

'Now that's interesting, the game as they say is afoot. Have you been eating fish?'

'Kippers. I like kippers.'

'But it's fish dear heart. I don't do fish.'

'Not even in your experimental youth?'

'Perish the thought.' A young waitress appeared with her notepad. 'Not for me dear, I'm just collecting my charge here, day release you understand. Do you like fish dear?' Luke leered.

'Oh yes, can't beat a bit of fish. Halibut, I like halibut with chips,' she replied innocently, before retreating into the safety of the double-entendre free kitchen.

'I bet she does, dirty cow,' Luke giggled, 'oysters I can understand. Any man that can swallow an oyster is fair game as far as I'm concerned, but fish, I'll leave that to the labia obsessed,' Luke shuddered at the thought.

'Tell me something Luke, did you expect Bull to show up?'

He winked his reply, 'is that why your ear looks like a baboon's arse?'

'No, that's a fashion thing; you'll all be doing it soon.'

'Baboon Arse by the House of Bull, yes I've heard of that, very now. Come on, let's get over to the hospital. We need to get to the bottom of this.'

'You've said that before,' I sniggered.

'Touché, Sam, touché.'

'Stop right there! Please state your business on this ward?' the elephantine nurse, had obviously made a mistake in her career choice, and would have been much happier as an immigration control officer.

'We're here to see the Major,' I stated, 'Major Turney, I visited him yesterday.'

'Good god the size of her Sam, is she wearing a tent?' Luke was beginning to boil behind me, 'do you think she knows?'

'I'm sorry, he's very upset, he doesn't mean it. Look we're like family to the Major, we just want to know if he's okay.'

'He's not here,' the tent asserted with folded arms.

'What do you mean he's not here, where is he?'

'I'm afraid that information is confidential.'

'Somebody should tell her she looks like a tent, has she no friends?' Luke grumbled, none too quietly.

'I visited him yesterday. I called the ambulance that brought him in. I'm really concerned for his safety, surely there's something you can tell me…'

'Perhaps she's eaten him. I wouldn't put it passed her.'

'Luke shut up! Please, can you tell me where he's gone?'

'Due to confidentiality and the Data Protection Act I'm unable to give you that information,' the nurse intoned as though she'd said it a thousand times already that day.

'Throw her a bun Sam, she'll tell us everything we want to know for a bun.'

'Don't talk to me like that, we have a zero-tolerance policy here. I'd like you to leave please, or I'll call security.'

'Call them,' Luke challenged, raising his voice by two decibels, 'call them, I'll tell them you've eaten my friend! They'll believe me, you know they will! It's not the first time is it. Headline; Nurse eats aging Major to save on beds.'

The nurse's heaving bosom was stretching her uniform to breaking point. I knew I had to calm things down, if one of those buttons went, it would have someone's back teeth out. I grabbed Luke by the arm and dragged him to the lift lobby, pursued by the foaming nurse.

'I'm so sorry, really he's just very stressed. They were very close. It's all got a bit too much for him. Is there any chance you could tell us where…?' I gabbled as I punched the lift buttons with my Luke free hand.

'Due to confidentiality and the Data Protection…'

'You lard arsed troglodyte!' Luke bellowed, 'I loved that man! I've had my arm so far up his arse I've stroked his tonsils.' - I'll let you picture Luke's hand gestures for yourself – 'if he's dead let me have his body so I can start working on our ventriloquist act! It's what he would have wanted!'

Thankfully the lift doors finally closed on us; and Luke fell into a corner convulsing with laughter.

'Nice one Luke. That was awful, you're an utter dick.'

'Me? What about these people! Why does every inadequate in a uniform turn into a Nazi?'

'She was just doing her job Luke! What are we going to do now?'

'Don't strain your strap; we're not done yet.' The lift juddered and dinged; the doors opened, to reveal the huge looming mass of Detective Bull.

'Bugger,' seemed an appropriate observation.

'You, I want a word with you,' Bull grunted. Ignoring Luke, he pinioned me to the back of the lift with the weight of his gut, and roared into my face; 'Where is it? Tell me now, tell me now, or I'll arrest you for interference and hampering my investigation.'

'I'd like to see you try copper.' Luke sneered; completely disregarding my personal safety. 'I'd really like to see you write that report; I confiscated the stuffed body of a male polecat slash badger slash pigeon, from its rightful owner during the hour of darkness. Where would you take it from there Bull?'

'Keep out of this you queer bastard.'

'Sam! He called me names, oh the bully, I'll cry, I shall, I'll cry.'

Bull dislodged me from his gut and turned to face Luke; 'Keep out of this you freak,' his face was molten with rage, 'you and I will be having words soon enough.'

'Words? Will they be words of more than one syllable? Wouldn't it be easier if I brought crayons,' Luke grinned.

'You better watch your back,' Bull snarled.

'Is that a promise or a threat darling?' Luke chirped, as he took my arm and guided me out of the lift. 'Wave bye-bye Sammy, wave bye-bye. The Major's on the eighth floor now Bull, but don't worry I've pressed all the buttons for you.' We saw Bull acknowledged the flashing lights on the lifts control panel as its doors closed, and felt his roar rumble through the hospital's foundations as the lift proceeded on its way. 'Lovely fellow, his mother must be so proud,' Luke chortled as he pranced from the lobby, with the eyes of Broston's ill and ailing watching his every skip.

Luke had enlisted the ever-reliable Prawn to ensure a speedy escape, and so we shifted our endangered selves back to my place at an entirely respectable speed. Three near naked Buff's had been set to guard the workshop, although I'm not sure how much use they would have been against the raging Bull, they had been busy, making the workshop more presentable. An incredibly thin lad with the face of a strung-out Bob Dylan served us sausages, that he'd cooked on a camp stove – it would be though wouldn't it. The whole scene reminded me of Fagin's lair, although with much more explicit sexual overtones. Luke got busy on his mobile, and soon tracked down a beholding contact that worked at the hospital; the information didn't please him.

'This is getting out of hand. The Major was transferred to The Autumn Evening Nursing Home last night.'

'That's not so bad. At least we know he's alive,' I observed, biting into a custard cream – I don't do sausages; never eat anything you haven't stuffed yourself.

'No Sam, that's not good. Who owns The Autumn Evening Nursing Home, boys?'

The Buffs, who were now busying themselves, in a forlorn attempt to make-over my workshop into a boho boutique, turned and answered in harmony: 'Everybody knows that, it's the Lodge.'

'Bugger, that's not good.'

'No, it's really not…we need to get our hands on a uniform and get you down there pronto…' Luke's eyes gave me a full body scan, 'no that's not going to work is it. There isn't enough hair remover on the planet to sort you out. Oh well, you know what they say, if you want a job done right, better get a woman to do it.'

Seeing Luke out of high heels was a shock to begin with, seeing him in flats, a dowdy nurse's uniform and a sensible semi-perm was just disturbing. Watching him shimmying up to the gates of the nursing home, call in via the intercom and still be granted entry was just fantastic –

and I mean that in the old sense of the word fantastic which is, less 'WOW!' and more like, 'UNBELIEVABLE.' The plan was simple enough. Luke was entering the nursing home when the staff swapped shifts. Those places have so many part-time staff, a new face wasn't going to look out of place. Once inside he'd find the Major and judge how he could be extracted later that evening. I insisted on hanging around the perimeter fence, in case Luke needed rescuing. Prawn and his car would be nearby, ready for a reasonably paced getaway. It was a simple plan – so I was expecting the worst.

Two minutes after Luke made his entrance, a red VW Golf, pulled up to the gate, and the driver barked into the intercom. Although I was hiding twenty feet away behind an ailing horse chestnut tree, I knew that voice; Bull was hot on our trail. The gates swung open and Bull drove inside.

I ran across the road, pressed myself against the gate's brick pillar, and watched as Bull extricated himself from the car. Two men in dark suits emerged from the building and blocked his path to the door.

I recognised them both, Robert Morris and Martin Monk; both known heavies in the pay of the Lodge. Monk had a black-eye and Morris' nose carried a flesh-tone Band-Aid; I hoped I'd been the cause of all their woes. Both seemed intent on expressing their dissatisfaction with Bull's presence. It was mostly expletives and posturing, but Bull was looking confident, his swagger said it all, he shrugged them off like flies and retrieved something from the car's passenger's seat. The next moment he was shaking a stuffed polecat slash badger slash pigeon in their faces. Monk and Morris fell silent, as Bull drop-kicked my creation across the carpark. All three of them walked into the nursing home, laughing like chimps on ecstasy. I wasn't sure what game Bull was playing, but our meddling seemed to have formed an alliance between our enemies. We were in deep shit for sure, and Luke was with the Major, in deep shit creek. The mobile phone Luke had forced me to take, chimed out Gloria Gayner's 'I will Survive.'

'Luke?'

'That's Staff Nurse Luke to you?! Right side of the building now Sam, now…'

'Wait Luke…' the bastard rang-off before I could tell him about the approaching shit-storm; so I did as I was told.

Luke's whistling head was poking up above the nursing home's high wooden fence, beneath a limp looking willow.

I couldn't resist a quick dig, 'I thought you had to wear flats on duty Nurse Luke.'

'Shut up you arse, and kick this fence in.'

'I just saw Bull go in, with three of the Lodge goons.'

'So kick the fucking fence in!'

And in, it was kicked. Through the newly created gap, I could see that Luke was standing on a wheelchair, containing the slumped form of the Major.

'The old dears out cold,' Luke stated, trying to force himself under the Major's limp right arm, 'help me Sam, take his other arm.'

I climbed through the fence and pushed Luke to one side, 'leave this to me.' You don't deal with roadkill the size of Roe Deer without learning how to lift a dead weight. Luke followed us through the fence and then we were off in search of the Prawn.

As soon as we got into the car Luke attached himself to his mobile phone, and was garbling away at a speed I was too agitated to take in.

'Were in for it now Luke,' I insisted.

Luke used to accuse me of always looking at the dark side of the street, but I couldn't help thinking we were in for trouble. Sure, we had the Major and we had the real creature, but the Lodge still wanted it, but now they and Bull, knew we had them both. We'd shown our hand. We'd jumped from pan to fire, and ended up in the deep end of shit creek without a snowballs chance or finding a gift horse; and to hell with mixing metaphors.

Luke broke off from his mobile and sang out, 'take us to Pump Square Billy.'

'Right you are Mr Luke ma'am,' Billy trilled.

'Pump Square? But that's right next to the Lodge Temple.'

'It is! I never knew that; imagine, and me a postman,' Luke shot me a mocking glare, 'all these years and I never realised that the Lodge is right next to Pump Square, amazing.'

'Alright, cut it out,' I snapped, 'are you going to take him through to Dolphin Lane?' That's a grimy little side alley that exits out onto Pump Lane - but more of that later.

'Don't be daft darling. He wouldn't last five minutes down there. The old codger needs rest not a blowjob. My god the shock would probably kill him. We're going to put him up at Lucy Biggerdyke's pad. He'll be safe there.'

My heart did something not dissimilar to a twisting, cannonball, double belly flop; 'Are you kidding me, Lucy Biggerdyke's ...I can't go to Lucy's.'

'Sam it's about time you two met. You've been jerking off to her films for long enough.'

'Does she know?' I heard myself squeak.

Luke held up his phone, 'hold still. I just want to add this to my collection.' His phone flashed in my face, 'so that's what a complete twat looks like.'

'Don't fuck around. Does she know about me, have you told her?'

Luke squawked and rubbed his hair furiously, 'Told her! That you watch her films religiously… and by that I mean on your knees. Are you completely mad? She didn't make those films to accompany tea and scones Sam! They're wank films.'

'Very good wank films,' I insisted.

'They've got stories and everything, Mr Luke ma'am,' Prawn added.

'Shut up Billy,' I snapped, 'Luke, have you told her about me?'

'Oh please. She doesn't even know you exist.'

'That's not true. She said hello to me once.'

Luke's mad hair nodded at me, whilst his head shook in disbelief, 'Yes Sam I know I was there. I introduced you, do you remember? You were hiding behind a Yew tree and refused to come out. That's not a meeting, that's… pathetic.'

'We were staking out the park!' I protested.

'Everybody down…not you Prawn!' Luke commanded.

I ducked down; we were passing the Lodge Temple. Looking up I could see the tapered top of the sandstone columns, which displayed the weird hieroglyphs, which we now knew included, the creature that the now stupefied Major had shown me a few days before.

'Maybe we should just get the Major out of town,' I whispered.

'Why are you whispering Sam? We're in a car. Maybe you should leave the thinking to me.' Luke's tone didn't help my nerves at all; his next words totally shredded them as he trilled into his phone; 'Lucy sweetie we're here!'

Prawn pulled the car into Pump Square and stopped at the foot of a set of pink stone steps, as he did so the pink door at the head of the steps opened.

Enter Lucy Biggerdyke; which incidentally was the title of her first film. She stood in the doorway of her Edwardian townhouse looking like a well-oiled goddess, in purple and silver Lycra. The incredible Lucy Biggerdyke, shoulder length red hair, a body Satan would repent to get his hands on, and eyes that would drive Mother Mary to rug munching.

Lucy was Broston's first professional hard-core porn actress. By the time our tale began she'd retired and made good; and opening her 'women only' gym, made her a respected member of the community. She was still as hot as the tip of a soldering iron. I couldn't look at her. I'd already seen too much of her in slow motion action; I was blushing and ready to melt.

'Thanks for this Lucy,' Luke said as they shared showbiz kisses, 'bring him in Sam.'

I threw the Major back over my shoulder and followed Lucy's well-shaped calves through the door. I'd seen those legs from every possible position but only ever via a screen. I was shaking from an exhilarating cocktail of horny guilt and voyeuristic shame. Luke had told me it was called a De Sade Complex, I asked him if there was a cure, he said he'd have to beat it out of me. I declined the offer. I decided I'd just have to suffer in silence.

Once inside the house, those lovely legs took us down a flight of stairs, into the flood cellar, that had been converted into a rumpus room, complete with boxing bags, step machines and a home cinema system that must have been worth more than my shop. The giant TV screen made me very nervous. I couldn't help thinking; Did Lucy watch reruns of her old movies? Did they have weird boxing, porn movie parties that re-enacted the on-screen action – and did they sell tickets?

'Sam! Sam! Snap out of it Sam,' Luke was shouting at me, 'put the Major down before you drop him.'

I did as I was told and then stood in a corner; being that close to Lucy Biggerdyke was too much for this mortal man to take.

You may be thinking that I've saddled Lucy with the name Biggerdyke, just to be perverse, or bigoted but you'd be wrong; it's a very local name. You have to remember this is the Fenlands. We have lots of dykes around here.

We have Wide Dyke, Swan Dyke, Deep Dyke, Heavy Dyke and many others; so a lot of families took on their local dyke names with pride. It just so happens that Lucy Biggerdyke, is six-foot-two and yes, although she worked with dick, she prefers quim. She 'came-out' after she retired from the movies. The Lodge tried to create some static with the local council, when Lucy wanted to open her gym, but most of the locals never blinked. They couldn't see what all the fuss was about; an estuary town values its dykes. In fact the more dykes the better as far as Broston was concerned, you ask anybody, having a well maintained dyke helps you sleep better at night – 'Support Your Dyke' may not be much as town mottos go, but at least it's sincere.

'Sam!' Luke was yelling at me again, 'wake up man! Help me here.'

Luke had the Major propped up and was trying to get something into his mouth.

'What is that?' I asked.

'Speed, a bit of whizz to get the old guy going. Come on Major, a little bit of speedy weedy whizz...come on Major take your gear like a good boy,' Luke growled in frustration, the old guy didn't want to play along.

'You can't give him that,' Lucy protested, 'it could kill him!'

'Lucy I'm out of options, and ideas and I don't know what the fuck is going on, and only this old fart knows for sure, we need to wake him up.'

'Wait...' I dug down into my coat pocket and pulled out a crow feather. I always have a feather or two on me, it's what happens when you collect roadkill, 'have you got a light?'

Luke handed me a lighter and I sparked up, setting fire to the feather. I waited until it caught good and proper, and then blew it out, and held the smoking tip under the Major's nose. He instantly sat bolt upright, coughing and swinging his arms madly at us. You would too, burning feathers stink something foul - I really resisted a fowl joke there.

'Major!' Luke shouted into his face, 'hold him Sam, Major! You're safe, its Luke. Relax, you're safe, we've got you.'

The old man's eyes focused on Luke's face, 'Luke…Luke you bugger, good to see you.'

Luke grinned, 'good to see you too Major. You're safe now.'

Tears rose in the Major's eyes, and he began to slump forward, the effort had clearly been too much for him.

'No you don't. Not yet Major, listen. We have the thing, your monster, we have it,' Luke gave the Major a less than gentle shake, 'but the Lodge know and they're looking for you. I need to know more to keep you safe. I need to fight back but I don't know enough. Why do they want it? Why all this trouble, for a bloody stuffed monkey?'

'It's not a monkey…' I quibbled.

'Shut up Sam,' Luke snapped, 'come on old boy, we need to know,'

The Major raised a hand as if to wave Luke away, and then whispered, 'the box…read the box,' and then crumpled into himself.

'Read the box? What the hell is that supposed to mean?' Luke exclaimed, but the Major didn't answer. The chemical cosh the Lodge had forced down his veins, was stronger than my burning feathers.

'Is he going to be okay?' Lucy asked in a hushed voice.

'He'll be fine. Can we leave him here Lucy? Just for tonight. Sam and I have got to get back to his workshop.'

The gorgeous Lucy agreed, and I was so jealous of the unconscious Major it hurt. I thought about stabbing myself in the foot so that I could stay. All I wanted to do was sit in the shadows whilst Lucy Biggerdyke, ate bananas and dripped chocolate sauce down her ample chest while watching re-runs on that huge screen.

'Sam! Wake up,' Luke shouted - and we were gone.

I'd hidden the Major's boxed curiosity; in the one place I figured the Lodge donkeys would never think to look; my shop window. It was set-up behind my old terrier Fluffy, under a badger that's holding a jar of honey in both paws. It's not a Honey Badger, it's just a regular badger with honey, but I made it to celebrate the works of A.A Milne; it was the best I could do seeing as we don't have many bears in Broston. I brought the Major's boxed critter back into the workshop and placed it under the workbench's lamp.

'Can you see anything written on it?' Luke asked, peering as closely as I was.

'Nothing.' It was just a dark wooden box. 'It's just a dirty black box.'

'Could there be something between the wood, you know like two bits stuck together.'

'No, it's solid timber,' I answered a little testily.

'Laminated that's the word. Is it laminated?'

'It's solid Luke,' I snapped back. 'I know my wood.'

Luke leered at me, 'of that I have no doubt, but what about this box?' Luke cradled his chin in one hand and pointed at the box, 'this was made by a craftsman Sam, someone like you. So tell me, what do you see? Tell me about the box.' His voice hardened as he reduced it to an insistent whisper, 'look at it, and tell me what you see.'

'It's a box, just a simple box,' I cast my eye back over the box and caught myself re-evaluating the joints, 'actually it's not simple at all. It's actually a very complicated little wood box. It's over engineered…there are too many joints, and too many types of joint. It didn't need to be this complicated.'

'Which means?'

I shrugged, and as soon as I did, my dull brain registered something I'd overlooked the first moment I saw the box, 'it's screwed together. But with those joints… it doesn't need screws.'

'Go on Sam, why use screws?'

'Yeah why? Because their needed, which means the joints must be fake. Which means…' I took a flat nosed screwdriver from the wall and in ten minutes I'd dismantled the entire box, 'there's not a lick of glue, the wood plugs aren't real either,' I said as I admired the workmanship.

'What do you see now Sam?' I could feel the warmth of Luke's breath on my neck, as he whispered into my ear.

'Six wooden panels.'

'What kind of wood is it?'

'I don't know the staining's too dark.' I could feel that thought-domino vibrating in my head, 'no it's not. It's a fucking resin, its shellac!'

'Isn't that what you put on pianos?'

'That's exactly right, but…' I grabbed a bottle of acetone from a shelf and took a rag from a draw, 'this is real shellac, bug juice, which means I can strip it back.'

Luke handed me a panel, 'this one first, try there on the inside.'

Five minutes of laying acetone on, and rubbing it off followed, – rub on, rub off, rub on, rub off – and then I spotted it, a slight change within the colour of the wood. The inside of the lid had been inlaid with a paler wood, and then the shellac had been overlaid thick and heavy, until the inlay had been completely obscured. Ten more minutes work revealed words, tiny almost paper-thin, inlaid words, covering the panel's entire face. Two hours later, and I'd revealed the story the box had been hiding for over two hundred years. I almost wished we hadn't bothered.

'Oh bugger.'

'What did you say the head of the creature was Sam?' Luke said with a balking wince.

'It looked like a monkey.'

'But it's not a monkey is it Sam…its Algernon Massingbred.'

I'd be lying if I told you, at that moment, I remembered the entire story, but I recalled the gist of it. Everyone in Broston knows the story of Algernon Massingbred. There's a painting of him in the local museum. He's called the Honourable Scoundrel of Broston; a local antihero. The story gets told on every school trip to the local museum. As I said the Massingbred's belonged to the Lodge, the original cabal, that duped the town. Once the ill-gotten gains had been turned to gold, Algernon stole the lot. Legend has it, he fled to South America and lived like a king, until he was slain by a jaguar two years later, or so the story goes. The box revealed the true story. It seems Algernon got as far as Brazil, but was waylaid by thugs, in the pay of the Lodge. And then, just outside San Paulo, 'the righteous judgement of the Fellowship was carried out.' The text stated his punishment was 'rightfully appointed and justly measured,' but calling it murder would be more accurate. They set a Wandering Spider on him - a vicious little brute with a deadly and peculiar poison, you suffocate to death, in great pain with an everlasting erection; poor old Algernon. But The Lodge weren't done with him yet. They had his head removed from his body, shrunk and shipped back to Broston, where it was set into a 'horrible display' as a warning to others.

'I need a proper cup of tea after that,' Luke declared.

I agreed, a teabag in mug affair wasn't going to do the job; it had to be a pot. I searched for custard creams, whilst Luke mused about Algernon's fate; 'If what the Major told you is true, that he found the creature in the Grove's loft, there are two possibilities. The Lodge presented it to the family, which is horrid. Or the family stole the creature from the Lodge, to give him some dignity. Then the Major finds it and starts digging around in the local archives…'

'The Lodge gets wind of it.'

'And start trying to cover their tracks.'

'But why bother?'

'Reputation Sam, murder is not good P.R. The Massingbred family may not be around anymore, but think about the scandal…or perhaps…' Luke's eyes shone as they narrowed, 'or perhaps the Lodge believe the whole retribution and human sacrifice thing, gives them some sort of power…perhaps they want their Mojo back?'

I have to say, as creepy, macabre and downright ridiculous as that sounded; something about it rang true. I picked up my screwdriver, and hurriedly reassembled the box, 'should we tell somebody… go to the press?'

'If that was a viable option, I think the Major would have done it. Perhaps we should give them what they want,' Luke sighed, 'what's to be gained. What's in it for us, but more trouble?'

'We can't just give up, not after what they've done.' I couldn't stand the idea of the bastards getting one over on us. I pondered defeat and then a dim bulb sparked in the darkness I call my mind, 'I'll tell you what's in it for us. Doing the right thing…putting something right, and getting one over on Bull. Look over there in that draw. You'll find an old coconut; Luke when was the last time you had a haircut?'

'You've got to be joking, get away from me Sam! Billy, you need a haircut!'

Nine o'clock the next morning, I was standing beside Luke, beating on the studded oak door of the Temple. Luke was dressed in a red leather catsuit, and sparkling ruby red high heels, whilst I carried the immaculately polished wooden box under my arm, and Monkey Scarf around my neck.

The mottled face of Robert Morris, one of the Lodge's heavies, opened the door. His eyes fixed on the box, 'seen sense have we, I'll take that.'

'Not a chance sweetie,' Luke cooed, 'is the organ grinder in? Or shall we come back later.' The door opened wide. Luke gave me a wink, and strode in, maxing his camp up to 11; 'Darling I just love what you've done with the place. It's fabulous darling, absolutely fabulous.'

He wasn't wrong. White Ancaster stone covered the floor and walls, trimmed with turquoise blue tiles, that rose into an arched eggshell blue ceiling, littered with tiny gold blue stars. At the far end of the hall, a good ten metres away from us, a lush wall of cherrywood panelling glowed as if it held fire within its grain. At its centre, high above the stone floor perched a golden balcony, that any Pharaoh would have been happy to call his own. A lanky, tall man, dressed in a turquoise velvet jacket, that was a little too short in the arms, walked out onto the balcony. He had the kind of face a vulture would be pleased to own, and he used it to leer down on us. The bastard looked pleased with himself, 'what do you want here?' - it wasn't a question, it was definitely a challenge.

'Dr Hooms I presume,' Luke bowed slightly, 'love the jacket.'

'Hooms? Who's Hooms?' I whispered through gritted teeth.

'That lanky fucker up there, that's Hooms, that's who,' Luke replied.

Hooms gripped the balcony's balustrade, 'Enough with the clowning, what do you want? State your business.'

'We come baring gifts,' Luke intoned solemnly, 'gifts of friendship and reconciliation.' Luke nodded at me, and I placed the box on the floor.

Morris stepped forward and opened the box, 'it's all here your Honour.'

'I take it you want it back, if not just say so, I'm sure I can find it a good home,' Luke grinned gleefully, 'we had thought the Antiques Roadshow, they'd love it, wouldn't they Sam. Fascinating history, very interesting reading, now that it's cleaned up.'

Hooms stifled a yawn and pulled a fob-watch from his jacket, 'come on then, what do you want?' his voice was colder than the stone floor.

'It ends here, that's all. You keep your mascot and your nasty little secret, and we keep our mouths shut.'

'Get on with it, I'm sure there's some clause attached,' Hooms sneered impatiently.

'If anything happens to the Major or us. We tell the story. Simple as that.'

'I see. Check the box again Robert,' Hooms commanded, without raising his voice.

Morris did as he was told, 'looks good Sir.'

'Fair enough, your deal is acceptable, good day to you,' Hooms turned his back on us and stepped out of view.

'One more thing!' Luke shouted.

The vulture face reappeared, arms crossed, glaring down at us like a rabid headmaster.

'Photos and photocopies of photos. All in a bank, for friends with the whole story. So don't fuck around okay.'

'Or what…you'll run and tell? How very predictable.'

'That's right big boy, and your little den here will be discredited, you'll lose your membership, and this little playhouse will be turned into a public toilet.'

Hooms' face tore into a scar of a grin, 'I understand. How very like your kind to link shame with a public convenience. As I said, we have a deal. Robert, show these… gentlemen out please. And then have the floor washed.'

The door opened behind us, and we were out before I'd taken another breath. I turned to congratulate Luke, but his face was livid with rage. 'What's up? We did it. I can't believe we got away with it but we did it.'

'I didn't appreciate the toilet gag. Very homophobic… I'm so annoyed,' and with that, Luke stormed off into town, ruby red shoes clattering on the cobbles as he went.

The Major wasn't too pleased with the outcome either. He wanted a front-page exposé that he could build into a bestseller. But when Luke explained how close he'd come to being an obituary entry, he begrudgingly agreed that his finely honed writing skills, and biting satirical wit, were best spent on other pressing local issues. I'm looking forward to the first of what promises to be a three-volume work, on the history of the Lincolnshire sausage.

I wandered down to the park that sits at the centre of the town. There's a small aviary there, just inside the gates, I like to check it out from time to time; I've had a lot a business from that aviary, but all looked well and healthy. Opposite the aviary, on the other side of the gates, there's a small concessions kiosk, that bears a small metal plaque, 'For Simple Shirley, who loved playing in this park.' I like to pay my respects whenever I'm passing. I crossed to get myself a cup of tea, but my way was blocked by a seething, narrow eyed Detective Bull. There were only two things that had ever been narrow about the Bull, his mind and those angry, angry eyes.

'I want that fucking thing and I want it now.'

I gave him my best Artful Dodger grin, and declared, 'I haven't got it on me governor.'

Bull responded by putting his size 12's on my tatty boots and pressing down hard; 'Talk.'

'okay, okay, I do know where it is…' Sims shifted his considerable weight to my little toe. 'And I'll tell you, I'll tell…but there's something you should know…'

'What's that Sam,' he sneered as he attempted to grind his heel into my toe.

'These boots are fitted with steel totectors, so fuck off,' I put my hand to his chest and pushed his stink away from me.

'You've done it now Sammy. Striking a police officer is a serious offence.'

'Do you want to know where it is or not? Yes or no? I'm sick of your nonsense, and your schoolyard bully-boy tactics,' I was warming up nicely, 'I don't give a shit Bull. You don't scare me, and you never have.'

'Where is it?' he roared.

'I gave it back to the Lodge ten minutes ago.'

'You didn't...' his eyes jumped from slits to saucers, 'oh you fucking didn't...oh you fucking did didn't you,' he grabbed hold of the bars of the aviary and started shaking them like a spoilt two year old brat. The birds didn't like it one little bit. I wouldn't be surprised if several aging budgies died of fright. Then, just as I thought he was going to shake the thing to pieces; he just deflated. His shoulders slumped, his jaw dropped, and his knees nearly buckled under him. He trudged over to a bench by the kiosk and folded up, utterly spent.

Now you can think what you like of me, but I hope nobody would ever think me a cold-hearted bastard; yes Bull was a nasty piece of work, and yes he stank like a mangled badger, but he was almost human too, and I'm used to dead badgers. So, I bought the guy a cup of tea.

'There you go. There's sugar in it.' He took it with a nod. I sat at the far end of the bench, but given his size we were still pretty close, 'are you really that desperate to get into the Lodge, that you'll betray your policeman's oath just to do it?'

He turned to me and sighed and looked back to his size 12's, 'piss off. Have you any idea how much damage you did to my career last year?'

'You mean us solving a murder case you completely overlooked.'

'One dead little fuckwit. One fuckwit down. As if this town hasn't got enough of them,' he'd clearly thought deeply on the matter.

'Not hot on the whole 'protect and serve' bit of policing are you Bull?'

'If you hadn't interfered, I would have been out of this town in a flash, you'd never have seen me again; but now I'm on you Sam…I'll have you for this.' His voice trailed off into a sigh, 'tell me, was it solid?'

'Do what?'

'Was it solid gold?'

'Gold?'

'The gold Algernon Massingbred stole from the Lodge. You know the story. The monkey thing was cast in the gold, that's how they sneaked it back into the country. That bloody silly monkey was solid gold.'

'Wow…I never thought of that,' I really didn't have the heart to put him right, 'but you should know, its not actually a monkey…'

'Piss off Sam. You gave it back to them,' he gave me a look of sheer disbelief, 'all that gold, why couldn't you just mind your own business.'

'What about you Bull? You smashed up the Major's house. You let the Lodge get away with beating him up and robbing him blind. Are you going to do anything about that?'

'Why should I?' his eyes returned to threatening arrow slits, 'and you better keep your mouth shut too, if you know what's good for you.'

'You know what Bull,' I said standing up, 'I'm going to take your advice. I'm going to keep my mouth shut…and you'll never know what you let the Lodge get away with, but just so you know, it was the case of a lifetime, the case of a sodding lifetime. And you blew it Bull, utterly blew it.'

I walked away to a chorus of abuse and the sound of budgies being budgies; the Ying and Yang of existence, in perfect unison.

Luke had an intimate contact at the local parish church; no surprise there; and he arranged for a small and secret service to be held a few days later.

The Major read from the bible, as Luke, Billy and the Vicar, watched me lower the tiny balsawood coffin - my handywork - into the Massingbred family crypt. I'd also made Algernon's head a proportionate balsawood body, and a real mole-skin suit. It was a lot of fuss, but seeing as there were no Massingbreds left to care, I felt somebody should make sure he went off in style. I'm sure that rascal Algernon would appreciate the gesture. The Vicar intoned a few words, and then that was that. We pulled the stone back over and went our separate ways.

As escapades went, it wasn't the most rewarding I'd had in Luke's company, but given the circumstances, I thought we'd done the best we could. And we got away with only minor injuries, all mine of course, but that's just how it goes. I had no idea we'd already peaked, that the zenith of our collaboration had been reached. If only I'd known, I might have lingered, and enjoyed the view for a little longer; but time doesn't work like that; how was I to know, the road ahead was steep, downhill and a dead end.

Chapter 2

HOUND OF THE
BISCUIT BARREL

I was reviewing my Biggerdyke DVD collection, when the phone rang. I let it ring six times before breaking my rhythm.

'Sam&SonTaxidermists, what do you want?'

'Nice phone manner Sam,' a rattled voice answered, 'it's Robin, are you busy?'

I avoided the 'hands full' gag, as I've tried it once, and it's still a lie, 'what's up Rob??' – I heard what I said but knew what I meant.

'Can you come out to Willow Kennel? You know the place, near Far End.'

'Yeah I know it. You want me to…come…right now?'

'Can you come? Are you okay? You sound out of puff?'

'Fine, fine…I just need to finish up here and I'll…come …right over.'

Robin was one of the local vets who occasionally put worthwhile work my way, so I knew what to expect, I was about to benefit from someone else's misery. I closed the shop, not that anybody would notice, jumped on Dad's old bike and set out West. The route took me across the river and along West Dyke, which runs parallel to the Seven Mile Straight; that's a straight piece of road that goes on for seven miles. We're not very adventurous with our names around Broston. Willow Kennel is at the far end of the Seven Mile Straight, just after the Far End Roundabout; which means nothing to you, I might as well say it's by the big pink elephant that sits in Main Street; but it isn't, that's at the centre of the town.

As I dismounted the bike, Robin appeared in the doorway of the white walled cottage, He's usually a well-turned out fellow; sharp haircut, well-pressed Chinos and pale shirts, but he looked uncharacteristically crumpled and worn at the edges that morning.

'You alright Rob, looking a mite haggard there, long night?' I asked.

'It's been a long morning. Thanks for coming,' he said shaking my hand, 'you just missed the police. Come on through.'

My face must have registered some level of surprise, because Robin held a finger to his lips, and retreated inside the cottage. I followed him through the cramped, fusty aired lobby. A mixture of damp coats, well-worn Wellington boots and mouldering super-sized bags of dog food, led into a beige coloured sitting-room. The air was thick with dog hair and cigarette smoke. A middle-aged couple with matching fag-ash hair, were sitting on a sofa balling their eyes out. At their feet sat a younger, red-eyed woman, with a horsy face, holding a smouldering ashtray, from which the older woman, dressed in a beige, too tight onesie, plucked alternating smoking butts.

'Sam's here,' Robin announced, which was rather obvious, seeing as I was standing there right in front of them. 'Sam this is Jack and Cissy Willow and their help Doreen.'

'Morning all,' I nodded not knowing what else to say.

'My babies, my babies, my poor babies,' Cissy wailed, spreading tears and snot all over her face, as she rocked backwards and forwards.

Still not knowing what to say, I went with the safe bet, 'sorry for your loss.'

Robin signalled for me to follow, and as my lungs were eager to escape the locked in smog cloud, I hurried along. We went through a kitchen that was in complete disarray; everything was smashed, the floor covered with spoiled food and broken crockery. Robin and I picked our way through the wreckage, and then moved out of the cottage, heading towards a large wooden shack, festooned with crime scene tape. Above the door hung a tin sign, 'Chihuahuas Do It Standing Up,' Robin looked at me with anxious eyes, 'prepare yourself Sam, it's not pretty,' he swallowed hard, and opened the door.

Robin was nothing if not honest. The floor was covered with a mass of twisted metal mesh, shit, piss and mangled bloody matter; it took me a moment to recognise the deformed metalwork as dog cages. Twenty or so bent and buckled dog cages, crushed into violent and distorted shapes; which was also the fate of their former diminutive occupants.

'Jesus, look at that, mushed Chihuahuas.'

'Twenty-four of them. Most of them died before I got here. I had to put five down. There's another one missing, I hope it got away.'

'What happened? Did the old bird go psycho?'

'No Sam. Four lads broke into the house last night, tied up the Willows and then set about the dogs. The bastards left about three in the morning, but Jack and Cissy weren't discovered until Doreen turned up at seven. She called the coppers, and they called me.'

'Bloody hell,' seemed an apt description of the scene, 'breaking and entering, false imprisonment and dog slaughter, that's some night out.'

Robin raised his hands in frustration, 'this is the fourth dog related incident in a week. On Sunday a Jack Russell was thrown into a wood-chipper. On Tuesday, a Golden Retriever was kicked to death in the park. And yesterday, Mrs Dunlop, one of my regulars had her Fou-Fou, beaten to death in front of her with a spare-tyre. The old girl had a heart-attack.'

'A spare-tyre on her Fou-Fou, that can't be easy. Was it the same lads?'

'No, that's the thing. They've arrested somebody every time; in two of the cases the bastards didn't even run away, but it keeps happening. It doesn't make sense.' Robin sighed, picked up a mangled cage, inspected it, and then threw it across the room. 'Look at this carnage, how do people do this? How can they live with themselves?' Blowing hard through his teeth, Robin shook his head; the poor bastard looked done in, 'let's go back into the house. I've already thrown up twice this morning.'

'You go ahead, I'll just throw some of these into a bag, the sooner I can get them into a fridge the better. Mounting rotten dogs isn't as much fun as it sounds.'

Robin's face turned a nasty shade of green, 'I didn't ask you here for that. I'm not pimping for you Sam. I need your other skills. I want you to look into this mess, it needs sorting, understand?'

I read the rage behind Robin's eyes, I knew exactly what he meant, 'You want me to give them a taste of Monkey Scarf,' I grinned.

'What? What are you talking about? I want you to find out why this keeps happening.'

I had no idea how I was supposed to do that, but it did sound like a job of work. And work pays, 'are the Willow's picking up the tab, or are you?'

'No Sam, I'm not paying you. No bodies paying you. You're going to do it because it's the right thing to do. Let's call it your civic duty.' He wasn't joking, he meant it.

'I've already got a job Robin. I don't do freebies.'

'Sam, if you want me to put any more work your way, you'll do this,' he really wasn't kidding, 'understand?'

I understood, 'no problem Robin. I'll put it on your tab.'

Back in the kitchen, Doreen was sweeping up the wreckage, whilst Cissy, looking like a miserable oversized toddler, busied herself preparing a pot of tea. 'Would you like a cup?' she asked through her snot bubbles.

'Not for me cheers duck,' I replied, the risk of added snot was too high for my tastes, 'Robin tells me there were four of these guys? Can you give me a description?'

A teaspoon flew across the room, hitting Doreen in the back of the head. Cissy's eyes flooded as her fag fell to the floor, 'Sorry, so sorry,' she blubbered, 'you're the taxidermist, aren't you? I've seen you at the county fair. Could you do something with my babies...snort...with the ones...snort...that you can...snort...Will you Sam? Snooooort.'

'It would be an honour,' I smiled, as gently as I could, 'I'll do you a two for three deal how's that?' Robin's eyes shot me a severe look of disapproval. 'In fact, I'll do you a two for four deal; as long as they're not completely mushed, I can do something with them.'

'Thank you, thank you,' Cissy snorted, 'make them look nice. Snort...make something sweet...something to remember them by...they hurt my babies...my poor...snort...babies'

'I know they did,' I replied, giving Cissy my best glum look, 'but don't worry, I promise I won't hurt them. They're already dead. They won't feel a thing.'

Cissy's sobs ripped through the walls. Some people get very involved with their pets. I'm not sure that's an altogether healthy outlook. It's like getting attached to underwear, you know they're going to be rags one day so why risk it? Anyway, that's mc. Robin's eyes flared at me as Doreen guided Cissy out of the room; 'I don't believe you.'

'She asked me Robin. It's what I do. I've got to eat. You want me to turn business down? I've had people bring live pets into the shop to get an estimate; now that's sick.'

Doreen hurried back into the room and set about sorting out the tea; 'They're both in a terrible state. Jack hasn't said a word since the police left. This could be the end of Willow Kennels.'

'You were with Cissy and Jack when they talked to the police. Is there anything you can tell us that might help us find these bastards?' Robin asked.

'Are you going after them? I heard what you did for Simple Shirley. It would be good to know they get what's coming to them,' Doreen grimaced, 'I'd string 'um up by their balls. It's all drugs you know. Cissy said the louts were sniffing a green powder called Scrape.'

'Scrape? Never heard of it, sounds foul. What is it, some kind of speed? Cracker Cane, Angel Must, Crystal Myth?'

Robin's face told me he wasn't impressed by my urban youth speak; 'Perhaps you should talk to somebody who knows something about exotic drugs… a mutual acquaintance perhaps.'

He obviously meant Fast Luke, and I could follow his line of reasoning; sleezy or shady, fringe or frightful, Luke was bound to be in on it somewhere along the line. But I couldn't believe Luke would get himself embroiled in anything so brutal. Luke may be lurid, but dog squishing just didn't have the necessary panache to tweak his decadent nipples.

'I don't see it Rob. I can't see Luke dealing in anything so…grimy.'

'And how much of Luke's deals do you know about?' Rob snapped.

'Luke's dodgy deals are his business, and none of mine. Live and let lust that's my motto.' I had a sudden craving for custard cream biscuits; I needed sugary reassurance. I spotted a biscuit tin on the shelf and decided to help myself. 'I'm sure Luke wouldn't get involved with anything criminal…well not that criminal,' I insisted. I opened the biscuit tin, only to find, it contained some very un-custardy creamy badness, 'Cissy, I think I've found one of your dogs.'

Cissy ran back into the room, looking like a giant toddler, filled with the joy of retrieving its favourite toy. I handed her the biscuit tin. It contained a tawny coloured Chihuahua; eyes protruding, mouth stuffed with Bourbon biscuits and bloody foam. Cissy fainted, hitting the floor with a thwack, that I felt in the back of my teeth.

'Sam! What were you thinking?' Robin blustered, dropping to his knees at the exact same moment as Doreen dived to Cissy's rescue – their heads collided with a crunch I felt in my toes.

'I'm going to go now. I'll drop by Luke's. Don't get up. I'll let myself out.'

I arrived at Fast Luke's, just as the police were climbing back into their vans. There were some very red faces amongst the retreating troops. Their discomfort may have had something to do with Luke standing beside his inflatable white rabbit, shouting the odds in nothing but a pink leather posing pouch.

'Police brutality! Gross invasion of privacy! No to cavity searches without K.Y! Big Brother is Fisting You!'

'Having fun Luke?' I asked as the police vans sped away.

'Tip sodding top,' he replied, correcting the hang of his posing pouch, 'would you like to come in for a spot of rum, sodomy and the lash, my good fellow?'

'I'll pass on the sodomy and the lash if it's all the same with you Luke.'

'Yes, perhaps you're right. Let's stick to drink…I need a stiff one!'

Luke seethed and muttered as I followed him through to his inner sanctum, the Moroccan Lounge; whatever you're imagining right now, it isn't enough. I accepted a silvered glass tumbler, loaded to the brim with vodka; he didn't have any rum as it turned out. I told him why the local constabulary were showing a sudden interest in his lifestyle choices. There was no indignation, no protestations of innocence, no outrage or outcry; perhaps he was all outraged out, or maybe he wasn't as blameless as I'd hoped.

'Are you selling this Scrape stuff Luke?'

'The very idea! Do you think I'd sell anything called Scrape? It sounds disgusting, like something from pensioner's feet. No of course not.'

'Why would pensioners foot scrapings turn folks into dog killers?'

Luke's eyes narrowed into two kohl lined slits, 'Your mind is a cloud Sam, a dense, dark cloud. I've heard about this Scrape, and I'm a little embarrassed to say, I didn't really believe it existed. I thought it was a rumour. Apparently, it's organic, and locally harvested from the river.'

I was shocked; the idea of Luke being embarrassed by anything was difficult to process.

'Sam, close your mouth, before your fillings bring a satellite down on us. I suppose we'll have to get involved now; we can't leave it to those idiot coppers to sort this out.'

'Do you know who's dealing this stuff?'

'Not exactly, but they shouldn't be too hard to find; if the rumours of the source are true. We need to get this stuff off the streets before anymore pooches get pounded.'

'What do you want me to do?'

Luke grabbed his crotch and leered.

'Never going to happen.'

Luke told me to watch the tidal inlet that cuts the town in two. I positioned myself between Town Bridge and the Church Street footbridge, giving me a clear view of both sides of the seawall for about four hundred metres. Being the muscle behind Luke's brain had its disadvantages. Crouching in litter strewn stinky bushes, at two o'clock in the morning was just one of them; still being there at four-thirty was another. My working conditions induced thoughts of division of labour and revolt, that were entirely new to me. My Dad was right when he said, everyman should be his own boss. Being Luke's lacky was less fun than spraying enflamed haemorrhoids with bleach – your own haemorrhoids that is, not someone else's haemorrhoids; I know what I'm talking about, I am the yelp of experience. I was about to give up all hope of moving my legs again, when I heard the cough of a dying engine coming from the West Gate carpark, down by the Church Street bridge.

I watched as four hunched figures dragged a yellow dinghy, and several large coils of rope out of a rusty old transit van, and onto the seawall. A torch flashed up and down both sides of the wall, and then aimed down into the mud. As it was low tide there was nothing but green silt and rotting ship hulls six metres below them. One of the guys; a small chap with badger-hunched shoulders, placed a dirty white bucket over his head, and then laid himself out flat in the dinghy, pushing himself into the sides, like a snail retreating into its shell. The dinghy was then lowered down the seawall into the stinking slop. As soon as it hit the silt, two of his pals ran over the bridge, heading in my direction. The one left behind, a really big bugger with no neck; stood on the wall and swung a rope in an ever-increasing circle over his head. As soon as his partners were four metres down from me, Mr No Neck launched the rope across to them. It nearly knocked them off their feet; it was some throw.

Working in what seemed to be a well-practised routine, the two teams manoeuvred the dinghy into the centre of the river, and then began hauling it forward across the mud. As they did so, the two guys on my side, got nearer and nearer. I wasn't fazed. I was well-hidden and safe enough. They were thin and wiry, perhaps in their early twenties, maybe less, but I knew I could take them, with or without Monkey Scarf; I never leave home without it; but as it happens, they were so intent on watching the dinghy, that they walked right by me without so much as a blink. Just out of spitting range, they stopped and began working the ropes, hauling the dinghy back into the West Gate side of the wall. Given my position, I couldn't see what was happening at mud level, and as I hadn't been sitting on a numb arse for six hours just to miss the main show, I carefully bum-shuffled forward, until I could see the badger-lad working the dinghy. He held a torch in his mouth, a wallpaper scraper in his hands, and was having a good go at some pale green slime, that had accumulated on the side of a half-submerged boat. I eased forward and leaned over the wall to get a better look. I was totally transfixed, watching the little guy working hard for his fix. When he'd amassed a good quantity of goo onto his scraper, he wiped it off into the bucket and started again.

What happened next and all that followed was my fault; I was so bemused by what I saw that I just forgot about being hidden. Without giving my numb legs advance warning of my actions, I stood up. The next thing I knew I was falling arse-over-tit, and barely missed going headfirst over the seawall. I landed on the path with a very audible crunch. There was a moment of uneasy silence, and then I heard the lad in the dinghy yell, 'The rozzers! Get me out of here!'

The haulers on my side bolted. One cleared me with a jump any Springbok would have been proud of, but the second stopped long enough to put the boot in. That was a mistake. I pulled his right foot into my gut, locking it in with both arms. He panicked, raised his foot, no doubt intending to give my ribs a good stomping; his second mistake. All I had to do was roll backwards and let go. I watched him sail over the seawall. His scream ended in a bone jarring splat, followed by a pitiful, terrified howl.

'Help! Help me! I'm sinking!'

In a matter of seconds, I had Monkey Scarf off my neck and was reaching down to help, but my would-be assailant was already waist deep in the stinking filth.

'Get me out! Get me out!' he screamed, 'it's sucking me under!'

'Stop thrashing about and take hold of the scarf!'

His hands gripped the heavy chained end, 'please mate, get me out, don't leave me here.'

'Calm down, just hold on. Oi you give me a hand!' I shouted down the footpath, but his Springbok buddy was long gone. I realised it was all down to me, and that's when I saw the opportunity that was presenting itself, 'so… what's your name?'

'Terry! Terry Wilmott.'

'What were you and your mates doing there? What's with the gunk?'

'Please mate, please get me out!' he squealed, dropping another inch into the ooze, 'it's Scrape, it's like speed in'it! It comes out of that pipe over there.' He pointed to a slime encrusted outlet pipe buried in the West Gate seawall, just above the ship's hull, some two feet below the highwater mark.

'But that's an outlet pipe! It's probably part of the old town's sewer system.'

'Maybe, I don't know? But it's good shit mate. We can cut you in. Just get me out.'

'Don't call me mate. How desperate do you have to be to sniff shit from an outlet pipe? I mean how do you get into something like that?

'I'm sinking!'

'Alright, alright, just hold onto the scarf.' I braced my feet against the wall and pushed back; hauling on the scarf as hard as I could. A moment later I was flailing on my back looking up at the stars. 'I said hold on!' I shouted as I kicked myself up and dropped Monkey Scarf back over the wall.

'I'm sinking! I'm sinking,' he cried, and he wasn't wrong. The mud was already up to his armpits, his fingers barely reached Monkey Scarf's tattered fringe.

I pulled Monkey Scarf back and laid it across my neck, 'sorry Terry, I didn't mean for this to happen.'

'What're you doing? Help me! Help me! I'll tell you everything, get me out! Get me out!'

'Not going to happen Terry. The muds got you. It's the suction you see. I couldn't pull you out with a horse even if I wanted to, and I can't risk damaging Monkey Scarf.'

'Fuck your scarf, help me!'

'It's not just any old scarf Terry. This thing is made out of a gibbon, that's why I call it Monkey Scarf, although by-rights, a gibbon isn't really a monkey, it's an ape; but Ape Scarf just doesn't sound right. The point I'm trying to make is it's rare, one of a kind. I can't risk losing it in that filth.'

'Please!' his eyes were wide and wild with fear; but I couldn't do a lot about that.

'Nothing to be done son, you're going down. Would you like me to sing you a song, would that help? Bit of T-Rex maybe? Do you like T-Rex? Everybody likes T-Rex,' I gave it my best shot, 'Ride a White Swan like the people of the…'

'Fuck you! Fuck you, you fu…,' and off he went, gargling goo and profanity into eternity.

When I looked across to the West Gate side, Mr No Neck was pulling the dinghy, and its occupant into the darkness beyond the seawall, and then they were off and running back to their van. I guess they got what they came for.

'Fuck me sideways,' was Luke's response when I told him about that morning's discovery, 'that's horrible Sam.'

'I know,' I agreed, 'that pipe could come from anywhere; god knows what's in that stuff.'

Luke gave me a look that usually meant I'd said something dumb; but I couldn't think what it could have been; which might be significant but how was I to know?

'I meant the kid,' he sniffed.

'Terry, yeah damn shame. Got any biscuits Luke, I'm starving.'

'You trouble me Sam, you really do. Would you like some scrambled eggs?' I nodded and Luke shouted the order, to whatever Buff Guy must have been lurking in the kitchen. Luke poured coffee from his gilt Moroccan coffeepot, and then slumped back into a pile of cushions so large they were almost a landmass. 'So, what do we know? Chiefly, that the outlet pipe must serve the older part of West Gate; as none of the modern buildings are allowed to discharge their waste directly into the sea. And that means, in all probability, that Scrape originates from somewhere under West Street.'

'Which means there could have all sorts of stuff in it. West Street has more than its fair share of hairdressers.'

Luke's face returned to 'that look', 'what are you talking about?'

'Hairdressers, they use all sorts of chemicals, dyes and bleach and all kinds of stuff. Sniffing that wouldn't do you any good at all. Bit like those hatters in the olden days. Maybe it's like reverse rabies. You know instead of being terrified of water they become terrified of dogs because of these chemicals.'

'Sam, darling,' Luke smiled sweetly as he pointed to the coffee in front of me, 'shut the fuck up and let me think.'

I ate a biscuit while Mr Luke Smartarse, rubbed his plucked eyebrows with his green lacquered fingernails. I do wonder if it was a purposefully hypnotic gesture. I wouldn't put it beyond him to try and lull me to sleep, then again there's not much I would put beyond Luke. Maybe he didn't trust me not to interrupt his train of thought…it's that or I was very tired because I fell asleep before the eggs arrived. Luke let me sleep until he decided to practise chemical warfare upon me. I woke up choking, my throat was burning, and my tongue felt like it had been dipped in toilet cleaner; 'What are you doing?' I cried as another jet of gullet drying perfume hit me in the face.

'You were farting in your sleep. Christ it smells like something crawled up there and died.' Another blast of aerosol saturated the air above me. 'Do something about your diet Sam, before you take the gilt of my coffee pot! Now come on, Prawn's got the car waiting outside.'

Once we were in the car Luke's mouth stepped up a gear; 'Bull's shown his hand. They've put out descriptions of the dog killers. And given the public's propensity for bow-wows I reckon they'll have them by this afternoon. Even Bull will have trouble fucking this one up.'

'That's good isn't it?'

Luke gave me another look of pity mixed with frustration, 'Not really, it's the stuff we need to know about. What it is and where it comes from is much more important than who's selling it on the streets. I fear Bull may cock this whole thing up for us if we don't act fast.'

'People need hairdressers Luke, how would you manage without…' Luke flashed me another look and I shut up.

We were heading out of town, away from the flatlands to the solid ground where the old kings of yore looked out over waterlogged marshland and thought to themselves; 'Now that's a good place to build a town.' Those mad old bastard kings. The thing is leaving Broston always makes me uncomfortable, I've never functioned well in the up-country. The altitude thickens my blood, and hills make me feel bilious, and given Luke's objections to my farts that wasn't a good thing within the enclosed space of a car. So I had to ask; 'why are we leaving town?'

'We need some perspective Sam. I need to get ahead of this thing before the police sweep it under the carpet. Bull won't care about the source once the dealers are out of the way, which means more dealers will take their place, unless we can actually cut off the source.'

'And so it goes,' Prawn reflected in a most thoughtful manner, although he may have been referring to the tractor that had just overtaken us; although an incredibly cautious driver, Billy was surprisingly philosophical for a pumpkin fucker.

'But we know the source,' I added, 'it's the outlet pipe, why don't we just smash the pipe of bung it up?'

'Bung it up?' Luke sneered, 'I think we may need to take a more proactive approach than bunging it up. Now if you don't mind, I need to think…' Luke looked out the window and started listing breakfast cereals and their uses in home baking; I sometimes wonder if Luke's Anti-Zen was just an excuse to ignore us lesser mortals. One thing's for sure, Luke knew more than he was saying, but as that's pretty much a constant, I let it go and looked out the window, searching the curb for roadkill. As Dad used to say, 'When death rests, the taxidermist gets busy;' he said some odd things did Dad.

A mile or so further on, we pulled off down a dirt track that cut across a fallow field. Prawn crawled the car along as the track was more potholes than not; and despite his consummate skill, I still heard the sump scrape stone more than once, and on one particularly nasty dip I heard another sound; a sharp bark of protest from the boot.

'Did you hear that?' I asked.

'Hear what?' Luke responded.

'Have you got a dog in the boot Prawn?'

'No, it's just the way I walk,' he replied.

Luke laughed and turned to face me with his eyes shining, 'Sam, Prawn made a funny.'

'I'm telling you I heard a bark, what's going on here…?' And that's when Luke clamped a damp acrid cloth to my face.

At first all I could taste was chemicals scouring the back of my throat, and then a deep damp smell pushed its way through the fog in my head. It was an old musty dampness, mixed with the scent of an old forest in midwinter. I heard my dad's voice calling out to me. He'd found an owl pellet and wanted to show me how to recover the bones. I opened my eyes and found myself in the middle of a decaying room, tied to a chair with a single candle burning at my feet.

'Easy now Sam,' Luke's voice came from behind me, soft but firm, 'I assure you this is a necessary inconvenience,' his hand rested on my shoulder, 'I promise you, you'll come to no harm.'

I felt sick and dizzy, and my wrists were throbbing in protest, 'good grief, what is this? What are you playing at Luke?'

'Trust me Sam,' Luke insisted.

'Perhaps you should have said that before tying me up.'

Luke pinched my nose and covered my mouth with his other hand, 'count to ten. And breathe out,' his grip on my jaw slackened and I breathed out, 'relax and…breathing in.' He released my nose and I breathed in hard; sucking up the green powder he'd placed under my nose.

'You evil bastard, why'd you do that?'

'I'm sorry sweetie, but I need to see what this stuff does. And to be frank you're the straightest person I know. If it fucks with you, it'll fuck with anybody.' His painted face was stern and very serious; and I wanted to kick it in.

'You could have asked!'

'Sam, face it; if it's not custard cream biscuits or roadkill, you're not interested. How does it feel? Anything strange happening?'

I wanted to rip his eyeballs from his head and shove them up his arse, but apart from that I felt fine. In fact, I remember feeling increasingly fine, sunnier and sharper and exceptionally warm and cosy inside. 'I feel good. I hate your sneaky bastard arse, but I feel...yummy. I love this room. I love this dirty, stinky, rotten room.' The light from the candle seemed to rise from the floor and brighten as it swirled above my head. 'That's amazing, I didn't know they could do that, say, is that a piano over there?'

I wasn't seeing things, it was a rotting, mildewed upright piano, as green as it was black; more mould than firewood, and the most beautiful thing I'd ever seen.

'Sure is Sam. This place used to belong to a music teacher. She became a bit of a recluse after she retired. A regular cat-lady; she lived here with a hundred cats, and a hole in the roof, huddled around a dustbin brazier and her cats for thirty years. Last time I saw her was in November, she was a lovely old girl. The council found her just after Christmas. The cats had eaten half of her. Shame really, but it's what she would have wanted. Would you like me to play the piano? I think I can muster a tune.'

That sounded like the best idea I'd ever heard, 'Please, please that would be great.'

Luke opened the keyboard's lid, formed a claw with one hand and beat out a rhythm on the yellowing keys. It was the theme from Jaws, a somewhat inappropriate tune for the situation, but I didn't care. What my brain knew and what I felt were totally awry, everything was disconnected and discordant; just like that battered and beautiful piano, it was so sweet I wanted to weep; 'That's beautiful Luke just beautiful, play more, play more.'

'Interesting,' Luke mused and then declared sharply, 'Billy, bring it in.'

Prawn appeared in the golden doorway, his face glowing like a peach caught in a glass of sunshine, he'd never looked so angelic; but in his arms, he cradled Shug the Hound of Hell.

Yes, it looked like a Chihuahua but I knew who it was; it was death's own dog. Odin's hound, Ah Pook the Destroyers' pooch; he wasn't fooling me!

The flatland folk know all about the legend of the black dog. To see him is to die. To see him is to know him and to see him is to know death. Unless you can send him back to his master, without knowing your name, your doom is assured.

'But I know your name!' the dog growled, 'I know all your names. You, the arse bandit there, and the idiot-boy Prawn, I know all of you.' We were done for; doomed for eternity unless I took charge, I knew what had to be done. The dog had to die! I lurched forward and then threw myself backwards, the chair's back legs cracked and collapsed. I began tearing at my bindings. screaming at Luke to set me free; 'Shug must die! Shug must die or

he'll take us all to hell! Rip off its head! Rip off its head
Prawn, do it, do it now!'

Luke's knee pressed down on my chest, 'why do you
want to hurt the dog Sam?'

'I don't want to hurt it Luke. I want to kill the
fucker! The beast must die!'

'But why Sam?' he asked, pushing down hard on my
sternum, 'why kill the dog?'

'It's a fiend! Shug the black dog. He'll devour our
souls if he gets the chance! We can't let it happen Luke.
We have to eat him first! Quick, chop him up into little
bits, light a fire and send Prawn out for some beers! It has
to be done Luke, it has to be done…' And then the
chemical cloth reappeared, and the shining world quivered
into darkness.

Round Two began with a far-off hollow bell; I felt
groggy, my back ached, and my tongue was so dry it made
me feel sick. I came to, trussed-up like a chicken on the
cold damp floor. The fluffy headed mutt trotted over and
began sniffing my face. It's hot wet breath, scoured my
nose hairs and turned my stomach. I pushed against my
freshly tightened bonds, and managed to role onto my
back, which amused the dog greatly; 'Luke will you call
your dog off!' I pleaded.

'Since when did I own a dog? I'm much more of a
lizard kind of guy,' Luke giggled from the shadows.

'I mean it Luke.'

'Tell me, what do you think about Roxy?'

'I think she has a stupid name and stinky breath.'
Roxy licked my chin; another whiff of warm doggy breath
assailed my nose. 'Good grief, what have they been

feeding you dog?' Roxy didn't answer which was a great relief.

'Do you remember what happened?' Luke asked.

'Of course I do, it felt great. The world was all butterscotch and roses. Until you brought Roxy in. She was evil, she wanted me dead, and I wanted her dead. I really wanted to kill her... but not as much as I want to kill you now.'

'Sounds reasonable,' Luke nodded and began untying my legs.

'Talk about liberties,' I seethed, 'I'm not some crash-test dummy for you to experiment on Luke.'

'No, calling you a dummy would be unkind. I promise you; it was a necessary evil... and not wholly unamusing.'

'Arsehole, so tell me was it worth it? What did you learn?'

'I learnt we're dealing with an impossible drug. It makes no sense at all. It's ridiculous. Drugs don't do that; bad trips aren't species specific. It's ridiculous. A negative ecstasy snort with an in-built anti-canine twist. It just isn't possible.'

The ropes dropped from my arms and the returning blood flow made everything sting, 'impossible or not, I felt it.'

'Thank you for your participation, it really was invaluable, and I'm sorry,' Luke smiled, offering me his hand. I accepted, and Luke pulled me to my feet, 'so Sam, do you want to take a swing at me?'

'I want to pour caustic soda down your prick and pull out your fingernails. How the hell did you get hold of chloroform?'

'Party favours darling, just party favours,' he held out his chin, 'go on then, get on with it, I owe you a punch at least.'

I was sorely tempted, that sharp chin would have been a fine place to land an uppercut, but I couldn't do it, there was a chance Luke would enjoy it; but retribution was called for; 'I'll tell you what, you owe me a forfeit instead.'

'Very well, what do you want? A massage? A weekend for two at a spa of your choice?'

'No, let's keep it simple. We find a pub and you buy me a pint…' I slipped off my ragtag Bill Sykes overcoat and laid it across his shoulders, 'and you do it, wearing my coat.'

Luke deflated beneath the coat, 'I'd rather have the caustic soda if it's all the same with you.'

The pool players ceased pooling, and the beer soured in the pipes, as Fast Luke; resplendent in high heels, bouffant pink hair, and ratty coat, strode into the Ball House lounge, with the yapping Roxy under one arm. The Queen of Sheba had arrived, and he didn't give a damn who knew it. The Prawn and I quailed in his wake; we were made of straighter but limper stuff. Luke surveyed his stage with a withering glance, defying all to challenge him. You could hear the dentures rattle as the jaws dropped.

'A pint of your best bitter, a Dark Mild, one Campari and soda, and half a lager for the hound,' Luke sang out, with a click of his fingers thrown in for good measure, 'I shall be sitting over there by the window with my bitches. Come on girls, chop, chop.'

I deeply regretted the penance I'd set Luke, he enjoyed it far too much. I should have hit him and been done with it. I could have saved myself the agony of walking across that pub, with all those eyes thinking exactly what Luke wanted them to think. I sat with my back to the glares and groaned into my hands. Luke grinned triumphantly, a sated warrior queen, surveying the scene of her latest victory. I was still moaning when the bald barman arrived with a tray of drinks and a bowl for Roxy arrived at our table.

'No umbrella?' Luke sniffed, looking at his glass with royal distain.

'I'm afraid not...sir,' the barman blushed from his chin to his crown.

'No worries sweetie, never mind. Thank you, keep the change,' Luke cooed as he tossed a twenty quid onto the tray. I swear the barman actually bowed.

'Let's consider our position, as the Vicar said to the Nun; despite our successful experiment, we're really none the wiser,' Luke stated, fingering the condensation on his glass, 'although we now know what Scrape does, we don't know why or where, beneath West Street, it comes from... it's a conundrum for sure.'

'That makes me feel so much better, thanks for that,' I hissed.

Prawn supped loudly on his pint and gave an appreciative sigh, before adding, 'I've been thinking about that...' he paused for another gulp, 'and I think it's rather obvious.'

'Really Prawn, do pray tell, this should be good Sam,' Luke said with a wink.

'We all know about the flood cellars and fissures beneath the town. Some of the cellars in the old town are cut straight into them.'

'Right,' I agreed, without conviction. I was more impressed by Prawn's use of the word fissure; the last time I'd heard that term my dad had been talking about his bowels.

'What if there are secret cellars; what if the government stored chemical weapons, or something like that under West Gate during the war; like they did in those salt mines in Wales. What if they sealed them up and forgot about them, and now the chemicals are seeping out?'

I looked to Luke for guidance, but his face was a silent mask of shock. I suspect he was still processing the idea of Prawn generating a thought; that or the whole fissure issue.

'And after a while these chemicals,' Prawn went on, 'change whatever else is down there. So really the question is; what lives beneath the town, in the pipes and the fissures, that hates dogs so much it wants to kill them?' Luke and I were equally mesmerized. 'It's obvious really, isn't it? It has to be rats, mutant rats. That Scrape stuff must be rat by-product.'

'Rat by-product,' Luke spluttered, 'so sniffing mutant rat shit turned Sam into a dog killer. That's your theory, is it?'

'Stands to reason,' Prawn asserted, 'things happen when you mess with nature; things go wrong. It's like giant pumpkins isn't it, that's not normal, that's messing with nature. They give 'um something to make them extra big and orange and alluring…OW!' Prawn's yelp was caused by my elbow driving into his ribs.

'It doesn't do to dwell Billy,' I cautioned Prawn, giving him an extra jab, to remind him of his solemn oath, to foreswear all future contact with the squash family

'Thank you for that insight Billy my prawn faced friend, I promise to bear that in mind, however in the meantime,' Luke sighed, 'there's only one thing for it. We need to find out where this stuff is coming from,' Luke's painted eyes flared at me from above the rim of his wine glass.

I turned the beermat beneath my pint, and sighed, 'And by we; you mean, me, don't you Luke, me.'

'Everybody's being so insightful today, it must be catching.'

'I must be a real mug,' I groaned.

'Yes, that's true' Luke beamed, 'but it's very endearing.'

Luke had declared his intention to spend the next morning researching in the local library, whilst I was sent to the Town Planning Department to request any subterranean plans that might exist. It seemed a simple enough task. The town council building on West Street looks like every other late Victorian town council building, starchy, pompous and in need of a good wash. The walls are too thin and bow alarmingly in numerous and ever shifting places. Despite being built on solid rock the foundations were so poorly laid, one side of the building was a foot higher than the other, and the drains so poorly dug, you can't pass the place without getting a whiff of something faecal in the air. As the locals say, the council's full of shit.

I was greeted at the front desk by a woman who seemed to be sucking lime flavoured flint. (Perhaps I'm being unkind it's probably the only way to deal with the building's constant stink). Now I'm not very confident around women at the best of times, but official women are something else again, it's not that I'm afraid of them, it's more like they can see me for exactly who I am, and they don't like what they see, and I can't blame them.

'Yessss,' she hissed, summing me up in a glance.

'I'd like to look at any below ground street plans you might have.'

'Below ground? Our street planssss are above ground, not unlike our streetssss,' I half expected to see a forked tongue dart out of her sour face.

'I mean old sewer pipes, the waterways under the town, the old riverbeds and that kind of thing.'

She sniffed, which given the state of the drains had to be a mistake. 'I see, and why do you want to see those?'

An obvious question really, but I hadn't expected it; and I didn't know what to say; 'Does it matter?'

Her mouth narrowed to a papercut slash, 'of course it matterss. You could be a terrorist.'

I was shocked; no one's ever thought me that glamourous before, 'Do I look like a terrorist?'

Her eyebrows dropped, I feared her whole head would be sucked into the sour pit of her face, 'you look like a questionable person to me.'

'Questionable?'

'Decidedly.'

'Thanks very much, what would your question be then?'

'When did you last see a bar of soap?'

I retreated to the library, I found Luke hunched over a large wooden table in the reference room, and although his shirt, cravat and purple kilt deserved their own 'QUIET PLEASE' sign, the helpful library bees were happily buzzing around him; of course, they buzzed off as soon as I entered the room.

'Sam darling!' he exclaimed, 'you frightened them off.'

'It happens.'

'Less scowl, more soap,' he stated with a wag of his finger.

'So I've been told.'

'How did it go at the council?'

I told him exactly what was said, and he laughed, throwing his arms up into the air, 'bugger me,' he exclaimed triumphantly, 'they told us more than their plans ever could.'

'They did?'

'Think about it. Odd thing to say isn't it, terrorists? In this little provincial town? It can mean only one thing…' I'm sure the pause was for effect and not just to give my brain time to catch up; and let's face it there was little chance of that happening, 'it means Prawn might have been right. There is space down there. Space that's not on this bloody map. Room enough down there to store booty or perhaps even chemicals.'

My dull grey cells flickered, 'you mean Billy the Prawn was right?'

'Not about super rats, or at least I hope not,' he clucked, 'I'm looking at one of Major Turney's dire little books. It's not exactly Bruce Chatwin, but we know the Major knows his stuff. And he says there's a tunnel cut underneath the church to protect it from the flood waters.'

'Of course, but the church is on the wrong side of the inlet. West Gate is on the other side, there's not going to be a tunnel under the inlet is there, don't be daft…' I scoffed.

Luke's ice-fire stare looked me up and down; 'Daft? Daft am I? We shall see,' he sniffed, 'you'll never guess who's cellar the tunnel crosses.' Luke gave me a tight-lipped grin and hoisted his kilt into the air, 'never mind the bollocks! Here's the pistol!'

The 'Never Mind The Music Store,' is gobbing distance from the Church Street Café, and directly behind where I'd been lurking the night I caught the lads harvesting Scrape; which I guess means they have a dead body just behind their premises.

The store specialises in punk and hard-core rock music; that's what it says on the window anyway. The owner, Gareth, is totally hard-core. A vinyl devotee and a fan of anything that rocks loud enough to make your ears bleed. He's kept the vinyl faith so long he's considered a Saint in certain circles, and he looks exactly as you'd expect him to look; beard, belly and glasses; the holy trinity of independent record store owners. And for some reason, he hates me.

'Not you again!' he exclaimed as I followed Luke into the store, 'not now, go on, out of it, hop it. I've got nothing for you.'

'What's this?' Luke asked with a gleefully cocked ear.

'Him and his bloody T-Rex records. He does my nut in. Ten years ago, I tracked down a first pressing of Electric Warrior for him, I've never heard the last of it. You got any more Rex in Gareth? Any Rex today Gareth? Any news on the special 45 picture disk Gareth. He's bloody relentless, on and on…'

'It was meant to have Hot Love on the A side and Rip-Off on the B-side, but they mixed the tapes and put a Bowie track on it instead,' I informed Luke. I promise it's a well-known vinyl fact, but Gareth had never bought into it, which I find utterly baffling – 'I'm telling you that record is out there.'

'Bollocks,' Gareth roared back, 'it never happened.'

'That just isn't true. I know it's out there. One day that 45 will be mine.'

'I see,' Luke frowned, adding a mouth click for punctuation, 'moving on now, we've come to see your record collection dear-heart.'

'Peruse at your leisure,' Gareth replied, wafting an arm across the walls of staggered shelves containing the headbanging history of hard-core punk rock.

'I mean the other collection,' Luke insisted sternly.

Gareth steadied himself against the sticker covered counter, 'not now Luke, not in front of him, please Luke, not in front of that…burk.'

'It's too late for that Gareth, I'm sorry, but I need him here. It has to be done.'

'Luke please…' There was true despair in Gareth's voice.

'I'm sorry G, but there's no other way. Trust me.'

Gareth's face flustered beneath his beard, 'that's how it is, is it? Right then…but not a word to anyone else you hear me,' he pointed a trembling finger at me, 'if one word of this sneaks out, I'll do for you.'

'Get it on Gareth,' I grinned.

Gareth led us behind the stock cupboards, through a vinyl veiled curtain and into a low-ceilinged orange lit room. Chrome display shelves lined two of the walls and at the far end sat a silver turntable, attached to the biggest bucket-earphones I'd ever seen, but it was the poster above the turntable that cooled my blood; I couldn't believe what I was seeing.

'ABBA?' I choked, 'Gareth, tell me it isn't so,' but it was so; ABBA to the left of us ABBA to the right of us; it was a veritable shrine to the Swedish four.

'Aha,' Luke smirked.

'Oh duck,' I felt strangely sullied and betrayed and yet a deep well of pity rose for this once proud rocker, 'I didn't realise…I'm so sorry.'

'Shut up,' Gareth snapped and then added meekly, 'if word of this gets out I'm ruined.'

111

'Your secret is safe with us,' Luke assured him, 'but only if…you let us through there,' he pointed to a trapdoor set into the centre of the floor.

'You want to go into the flood cellar?'

'To be exact, Sam does,' Luke nodded at me., 'I'll sit and wait here if it's all the same with you.'

'Be my guest; with any luck he'll fall and break his stupid neck. I'm going back to the shop.'

'Thanks Gareth…' Luke cackled, 'you're a super-trooper.'

Gareth buckled and fled.

'Poor chap. All that thrash and bang he sells to the punkers, and he's the founder member of the East of England ABBA Fan Club. I'm telling you Sam, it's not knowing other people's secrets that matters, it's what people think of their secrets that counts.'

I have no idea if that's right, but Luke knew his business. I got down to work. I hauled open the trapdoor, and nearly vomited. A smell crawled out of the pit that could have bleached your eyeballs and blackened your tongue.

'Oh my good grief. Something died down there,' I hacked.

'Lots of things,' Luke coughed, 'and a very long time ago. Old things wrapped in wet wank socks. Big sweaty camel wank socks,' Luke choked.

'What the fuck is a camel wank sock?'

'I don't know, but I bet they smell like that,' Luke handed me a plastic bag containing a headband flashlight - we'd bought it in a pound shop on the way over – 'now get your arse down there so I can close the door.'

'You're going to close the door!'

'Of course I'm closing the bloody door. You've got a torch! What more do you want?'

'I want the door open Luke. What if I need help? What if I need to breathe?'

'Breathe down there, are you insane?'

'Remind me why I bother with you. I don't have to do this Luke, you do know that don't you? I could go home and stuff a Chihuahua, and be very happy doing it, thank you very much. I want the door open!'

Luke sighed and huffed, opened his scarlet silk jacket, and pulled two twenties from his wallet. These he rolled, folded into two squares, and then stuffed one up each nostril, 'okay, I'll keep the door open. Happy now?'

I slipped the elasticated headband over my ears, 'how do I look?'

'Precious, now fuck off.'

I turned on the light, gave Luke the finger and then dropped down into the darkness. I was showing off; there was a ladder I could have used, but a rapid drop into hell is probably wiser than a slow descent.

'What do you see?' Luke's voice already sounded very thin and far off.

'Lichen, muck and moss.'

'Thank you David Attenborough. Look at the structure of the walls. Tell me what you see.'

I stepped up to the nearest wall and ran my hand across it. It was surprisingly cold, damp and smooth, 'it feels like stone.'

'That's the bedrock. You're looking for a brick arch. Beyond it there should be a channel going off to the right, towards the church.'

'Sounds like balls to me,' I flashed the light around the walls, not expecting to find anything, but there in the furthest corner, low down against the floor, was a three-foot-high brick arch. All but the bottom six inches had been bricked up. 'Bugger me, looks like Major Turney got it right again; but it's bricked up.'

'Are you wearing your ever-so-stylish steel capped boots?'

'You know I am.' Never doubt the usefulness of totector boots. I braced myself against the bedrock, aimed low, and swung my right foot in hard; the bricks crumbled like wet biscuit. 'Okay, I'm through. Looks like it drops down a couple of feet.' Crouching down I peered into the dripping tunnel, 'it disappears off around a bend. I can't tell which way it goes. This torch is crap.'

'You get what you pay for. The seawall is on your left, the church is to your right and Worm Gate is straight ahead. Head for Worm Gate and that's where I think we'll find our passageway across to West Gate.'

'Easy for you to say,' I said through gritted teeth, 'it's not like there are fucking road signs down here.'

'Moan, moan, moan. You've got a crap torch, what more do you want?'

'A gas mask and a sodding helmet,' I mumbled to myself as I eased myself through the arch.

The tunnel beyond it was bricked lined, with a low arching roof, and was so narrow my shoulders scraped both sides, sending clods of moss and wet mortar to my

114

feet. Twelve feet ahead the way was blocked by another pile of rust coloured sludge. The debris was so wet I figured the damage must have been done decades before, and so didn't present any significant risk. I gave it a good shove, which brought another load of bricks down on top of me. Most dissolved-on impact so no harm was done, but the filth was bloody cold, and went straight down the back of my shirt. I'm telling you I cursed the shoddy, long dead brickie who'd cut his mortar to save a few bob; damn his hod.

Eight feet beyond the debris, the tunnel split in two. Both passages were worn smooth, and I could smell the saltwater oozing from the bricks. I took the right-hand tunnel and hoped we weren't due a high tide anytime soon. The tunnel curved back sharply on itself and then ran straight in what I took to be the right direction. Five minutes later, just when I thought my knees were about to explode, the roof lifted, and I could stand up. I stretched my back, thanked the darkness for small mercies, and decided to pick up the pace, and so began jogging along the high but narrow tunnel. I've done some dumb things in my time, but I think that one dunks the biscuit. I didn't see the wall that I ran into, I didn't see the drop in the tunnel that took me under the unseen wall, and I didn't see the pool of stinking water that I fell into until I was under it.

I rose kicking and gasping, trying desperately to find a footing. Thankfully the water only just reached my chin, but in my urgency to get out, I didn't register that the roof above me, was literally just above me. I cracked my head, smashed the lamp, saw stars that had no right to be there, and got a second dunking for my troubles. Shivering from tooth to toe, I pinioned myself between the stone earth and stone sky.

Blinking the water out of my eyes, I tried to focus on the space - or lack of it - that I now found myself in. It took me a good couple of seconds to realise, that I wasn't just seeing concussion induced stars - they were there too - but there actually were twinkling lights swirling above me. The stone roof was a shining shower of snot-coloured stars. I reached up and plucked one from its orbit. It was a glowing mushroom. The iridescent sky was a mass of faintly florescent fungi, broken in places by patches of deep darkness. I bobbed and shuffled forward, positioning myself beneath the nearest black space. The room above my head instantly increased. I was standing beneath a netherworld sphincter, that dripped cold dirty water from the world above; but from where exactly? If I was going to get out of there I needed to figure out where exactly I was escaping from; I shut my eyes and forced my mind into the daylight, to try and plot out my position. In my head I walked from Gareth's 'Never Mind,' past Church Street Café, out of Church Street, towards the Church, which meant I was now standing beneath the graveyard. As my eyes grew accustomed to the light, I could see that an earthy anus or two was still gripping the woody remains of long decayed caskets.

I checked around me for the remains of long dead worthy parishioners, but thankfully there were none. Perhaps the water or Prawn's mutant rats had taken them away. I didn't know and I didn't care. My balls were the size of frozen peas and shrinking fast, I needed to get out, before they became magnetic blackholes that sucked out my lifeforce. My head ached, my teeth were rattling, and my legs were weakening, not a good combination. I knew if I wasn't to take up permanent residency in the graveyard, I had to get moving. I reached up and grabbed at the sodden earth, bringing a barrow's worth of filth down on top of me. Its weight forced me back under the water. I rose, throwing clods of earth about me in mute rage; and then I heard a distinct splash behind me. I turned, and again it sounded. I braced myself against the glowing roof, expecting to see the bared teeth of Prawn's mutant rats appear from the darkness. Again, the splash sounded. But its distance hadn't changed. I figured it might be another, hopefully easier to access grave, and headed towards it. The sound became clearer, changing from a soft splash to a sharp drip with every step I took, until at last I came face to face with a stone wall. It had to be part of the church foundations. I edged along searching for the source of the sound. And then I found it, a carved stone arch, sitting just above my head, no more than two feet wide and a foot high, cut through the middle of a huge stone. The sound of falling water rang out loud and strong beyond it. If the arch led to the church crypt, there would be a way back to the surface, but only if it led to the crypt? That was a big 'IF,' to consider. As I peered into the darkness framed by the arch; my spine quivered; my chances of making it through such a tight space were thinner than the space itself. I really didn't want to do it; but if I didn't try, I knew I was soon going to be unsanctified worm food.

A high-pitched gurgle bubbled behind me. I put my back to the wall, my heart thumping an alarm that rattled me from head to totectors. It was the wrong sound in the wrong place; and its misplaced oddity was terrifying. It came again, a high-pitched slurping gurgle. A wave hit me in the face and slapped against the wall behind me. Something big had dropped into the water. Images of sewer alligators and subterranean greased hippos, flashed through my head. Another wheezing, bubbling hiss, sounded three yards ahead of me – a single thought possessed my mind; 'Mutant fucking rat!'

I tore off my coat and pulled myself up into the arch. Pushing my arms forward, I managed to work myself in as far as my gut. But the cut narrowed sharply, and seconds later my shoulders were wedged around my ears. I couldn't shift another inch. I was stuck, six feet below ground, spitting muddy water beneath an 11th century church; waiting for a giant mutant rat to charge at my arsehole. In that moment I knew two things; blind terror and defeat; and then I heard the water break behind me. Being defeated was no-longer an option. I drove myself forward, ripping my shoulders and back raw. My fingertips found the edge of the stone and I dragged my nose beyond it. I felt something grab my foot and try to yank me backwards. A terrible heat tightened around my shin, and then I felt a sudden cold release, as my boot was wrenched from my right foot. I kicked hard, pulled forward, and tore myself free of the stone. Filling my lungs with jagged air, I fell forward, head over nibbled toes, into a vast bottomless darkness.

I lay on my back, looking upwards, expecting a sharp toothed horror to drop down upon me, but it didn't come. I should have been relieved, but I wasn't. Despite being in one unbroken piece, I was none the less fucked. I'd lost a shoe, my shirt and trousers were gone; as well as layers of skin from my back and chest. I hurt like hell, and there I was, spread-eagled and breathless, at the bottom of a very deep dark hole; exhausted, terrified and utterly fucked.

The shaft was brick lined and about four feet wide. It was either an old well, or a flood drain buried beneath the church. Terror eventually gave way to anger, and anger can be a useful energy. I swore if I ever got hold of Luke, I'd stuff gunpowder down his gullet and shove a fuse up his arse. With this goal in mind, I put my back to the wall, and my feet on the opposite wall and pushed…and quickly discovered that's a totally unworkable form of locomotion. I straddled the pit like a spider, and by means of pressure and the tiniest of grips that made my fingernails scream, I began climbing up the shaft. Now if I'd had to climb up the entire thing in that position, I promise you I'd still be there, but about sixteen feet up my crown collided with the bottom rung of an old iron ladder. My fingers were numb, and my feet wouldn't have felt hot spikes being driven into their soles; but compared to climbing a wall that ladder was a piece of piss. I must have climbed about twenty feet before my poor head hit another obstacle, but this one was flat wooden and looked suspiciously like a cellar door. I gave it a shove and there was some give. Locked it might have been, but I wasn't going to let some stupid cellar door stop me. I put my shoulder to it and shoved until I heard the wood creak, I moved my feet to the next rung, and pushed harder until the wood began to splinter. I was expecting to come up within the church, perhaps at night,

119

perhaps within the crypt or the vestry. Imagine my shock when I broke through the floor of the Merry Fisherman, a public house on the corner of Worm Gate. Not as shocked as those dining in the restaurant, that's for sure. The poor bastards saw a naked, mud and blood splattered mad man come from the bowels of the earth into their midst. If that's not guaranteed to give you indigestion, I'd like to know what is.

'Sammy, what kept you?' Luke beamed; and I have to admit I'd never been so pleased to see the old bugger. I think I very nearly cried.

After Luke had paid off the landlord and bought a round for all present – including a double scotch for me – we retreated to my workshop. Much liniment, antiseptic and more whiskey followed.

'I must say… despite your diet you do have a rather lovely physique,' Luke chimed.

'Shut up and rub harder,' I groaned.

'Oh how I've longed to hear those words from your lips,' he giggled.

'Can we turn the cabaret down a couple of notches please Luke, I'm done in… it was bleedin' 'orrible down there.'

'Very well then, Mr Huffy. There you go, all done,' he said slapping my thigh, 'but don't move, just stay put.'

'I couldn't move if I wanted to. I'm not sure I'll ever move again. I really thought I was done for Luke…and under the church too, that's got to be blasphemy, right?'

'Do stop prattling darling. To be fair, it can't be easy judging distance in the dark…girth yes, distance no. Unfortunately, your little misadventure, doesn't leave us

120

any the wiser,' Luke ruffled my hair and then wiped his hands clean on a scented hand towel he must have brought with him; because I don't own any.

'Sorry I let you down. I'll try harder to die next time.'

'Don't worry about it darling, it's not your fault,' Luke sighed as he stretched himself out on the couch, 'however, we have learnt that there are caverns and passageways under the town, which is important, but it also means that the source of this Scrape stuff…well it could be anywhere.'

'Nothing to do with the mutant rat that ate my shoe then?'

'I seriously doubt it,' Luke placed his hands behind his head and stared at the ceiling, 'things tend to seem bigger in the dark… that's a fact, I wasn't being lewd.'

'Something sucked off my shoe Luke. Can rats suck?'

'Do you really want me to answer that? I believe you saw something but…' Luke pointed at the ceiling, 'you do have a cobweb problem Sam, a serious cobweb problem.'

'Bugger the cobwebs. I'm telling you Prawn was right about those mutant rats!'

'Calm down dear boy, let me focus. If we can't find the source, then we'll just have to catch the supplier before the police do. Perhaps the rest of the crew have a better idea where the stuff comes from… it's a long shot, but the only thing left to do.'

'Hasn't Bull got them yet?'

'No, his incompetence knows no bounds. We'll just have to solve it for him after all.'

'Do we have to? I mean pounded pooches isn't exactly bad for business you know; I could do all right out of this.'

'Sam, where's your community spirit? Think of all those dog owners living in terror and desperation, shame on you.'

'Jesus, you're an arsehole. So how are we going to do it?'

'Greed,' Luke chuckled, 'pure, simple, greed. I'm going to put the word out that I want to get my hands on a large stash of Scrape, and am willing to pay big money. Which means they'll have to get themselves a fresh batch.'

'And we let them deliver it to us right?'

'No, too risky. I'll tell you what, I'll buy you a nice new coat, how's that?'

I spent the night huddled beside the West Gate seawall, hidden beneath Church Street bridge. I was loaded with painkillers, vodka and smothered in Deep Heat, and I still hurt like inexperienced buggery. Using his web of unsavoury associates, Luke had sent out the word, whilst also dropping a false lead to the boys in blue, that would have them searching the other side of town. A move that was sure to rumple Bull's horn. It was a simple plan, but it only made sense if our scumbag dog-killers hadn't stockpiled their merchandise. I had to admit they didn't strike me as the forward-thinking types, so I had some hope, but if they didn't show, we were truly buggered. It was around four in the morning when I heard the rattling rust bucket van, pull up near the bridge. The doors creaked open, and then flashlights double checked both sides of the seawall. They were being extra careful this time. Footsteps followed, and then the sound of a dinghy being dragged along the pavement.

I watched the badger-lad climb into the dinghy, and his two pals lower him down. I heard the mud suck as the dinghy hit the surface. The tallest of the other two figures then sprinted for the bridge. The fleetfooted bastard, was eager to get the job done. This time I was ready for my leaping gazelle. Keeping low and flat, I rolled out from my hiding place, blocking his path. Without missing a beat, he skipped above me, and met the business end of Monkey Scarf at the very centre of his being; that was one Chakra that was shattered for sure.

His big buddy, Mr No Neck, heard him scream as I dropped him over the seawall. The big guy looked to the dinghy, and then at the rope in his hand, and tossed it away. He made for his van, but I put myself between him and his getaway. He had other options, but he chose to charge. Luke wanted him for questioning. But Luke didn't stipulate what condition he wanted him in – I was fine with that – until I saw the knife. It slashed across my line of vision, and then came back round for a second try. I didn't feel obligated to accommodate any second chances. Monkey Scarf smashed his elbow, then it smashed his left knee, then it broke his collar bone.

'Stop! Please stop,' he screamed.

I held Monkey Scarf's business end under his nose, 'do you know the source of this Scrape shit?'

'Yeah,' he looked out to the outlet pipe.

'Beyond the pipe, do you know where it comes from?'

'Only what we've been told.'

'Told by who?'

'No way. Those fuckers scare me more than you do nob-jockey. I'm not telling you nothing.'

'Pal, you're a bad judge of character, and you're forgetting something... you're not my only option. Say hello to Monkey Scarf.' No matter how big they are, they've all got a neck, even if you can't see it.

I pushed the body over the seawall and waited for the splat; but instead heard a thud, a rubbery fart, and finally a pitiful whimper. I shone my flashlight down into the ooze. Dead Mr No Neck was laying across the badger-lad, pinning him to the dinghy.

'So little guy. You know where this Scrape stuff comes from then?'

The shaking shit in the dinghy looked at the outlet pipe.

'Other than the pipe,' I added, 'please, it's been a long night and I've already taken out your two pals, so why don't you just be a smart badger and tell me what you know.'

The little chap couldn't talk fast enough, 'It's the runoff man, it's not even the good stuff. They keep that for themselves. We just sell off the Scrape.'

'Who's they?'

'You know, the guys! The power, the Lodge guys.'

I suddenly felt a lot colder than the night air, 'What the hell have the Lodge got to do with this?'

'They keep the good stuff for themselves. Terry had a job on the council, so he knew about the thing and where they keep it. He knew there had to be a runoff, coz there's

124

so much of the stuff. We tried every pipe for a mile down the river, this is the only one…'

The kid was making no sense what-so-ever; it was all junky speak as far as I was concerned. I had to get him back to Luke, and let him do the translating.

'Can you push No Neck off you?' I asked as kindly as I could, 'I can't haul you both up.'

'Too right, He was a real bastard. He made me do it. Thanks mister, you won't regret it.'

I waited until he'd pushed the body into the mud, and then picked up the dinghy's rope and started to haul him in.

'Thanks man, I didn't really want to get involved,' the little rat-badger rattled on, 'I mean who wants to go out there in the dark and scrape shit off of a boat right…'

'So why do it dickhead?'

'They made me, I was the smallest. They said they couldn't get across the mud without me.'

I had to admit that made sense, 'so what was it with the dogs? That's some twisted shit.'

'Yeah wow, was that freaky or what…them dogs. It was like, you know, just out of control.'

The dinghy hit the seawall. I braced myself and prepared to pull the little guy up.

'You know I'm going to cooperate right. I mean you don't have to hurt me like the others right. I mean I'll talk to the police and everything right…'

I wish he hadn't said that. I hadn't even thought about it. He'd seen me deal with all three of his buddies. And this guy was the talkative type.

'I really wish you hadn't said that.'

'Huh.'

'Sorry, I hadn't thought this through.'

I yanked the dinghy out from under him and let the mud do the rest. Don't think too harshly of me, I felt rotten about it, and I did him the honour of staying put until it was over. I sang him some T-Rex, everybody loves the Rex.

Luke looked disappointed and somewhat frustrated by my news, but I knew he'd get over it.

'That's shocking Sam, I thought they'd put up a fight, but trying to make a run for it…on that mud, what were they thinking?'

'Stoners,' I shrugged, 'Scrapers? What can you do? Good job we got it off the street.'

'Right, I'm sure you did the best you could,' Luke's charcoal eyeliner narrowed to a point. 'The very best you could, given the circumstances.'

'Aha absolutely, that's what I did… the best I could.' I wasn't fooling anybody, and certainly not Luke. 'I did the absolute best I could. Funny thing though, they did say something about the Lodge, you know before they went... off across the mud to where I couldn't hear or reach them. Not even if I tried…. which I did.'

'Obviously, but unfortunately, due to a lack of information… and witnesses, I'm afraid this time the Lodge has outmanoeuvred us. This time they keep their secrets,' slowly and with great purpose, Luke removed a square of paper from the folds of his kimono, 'but someone will have to work it out sooner or later.' Luke slowly unfolded the paper until it obscured him from my view, becoming a huge map of the town's ancient underground system. Although he couldn't see me, I could feel Luke's eye's burning into my head. And then from behind the map came a sharp intake of breath, followed by a tut, tut, tutting; 'Not to worry Sam, sooner or later, the truth will come out. And the sea shall give up its dead… and then you'll be sorry.'

I felt a strange, cold twisting sensation in the pit of my stomach; and to this day I'm not sure, if it was the yearning for a custard cream, some weird waterborne infection or perhaps even guilt.

Chapter 3
THE BLISTER SISTER

I was seeing to one of Cissy's Chihuahuas, when a grey flannel of a man in an ill-fitting brown suit, walked into the workshop.

'Good morning, it is Sam, isn't it?' he offered me his hand, then saw where I had mine, and returned his greeting to his pocket, 'my name is Bernard Teacher, we have a mutual acquaintance, Luke Fassbinder, I'm sorry I gave him my last calling card.'

I nearly split the chihuahua in half. Nobody called Luke by his real name, and who the hell uses calling cards these days? I set the Chihuahua to one side and offered Teacher a chair.

'What can I do for you Mr Teacher? What are you looking for? A table piece, a talking point, a stylish reference to past country glories, or something to scare the local kids at Halloween?'

'No, no, nothing like that; it's my daughter Dotty, Dorothy. She's got herself involved in something, and Mr Fassbender suggested you might be able to help us.'

'Does Dotty know you're here?' He shook his head. 'Does that mean she may not want to be helped?'

'Perhaps… it's difficult to say. Dotty has always been a strongminded girl, but she's a good kid. It's not been easy for her… do you have any children?' Teacher was clearly a shy man, not given to speaking to strangers, and wasn't finding his sales pitch easy. His face was glowing with the effort, and he was fighting to keep the

128

tears rising from his eyes. 'You see my wife June has been ill for a long time, it didn't make it easy for Dotty. There were arguments… I blame myself.'

I don't find talking to people easy myself, but I was in the driver's seat this time, so I decided to make it easy for him, 'what is it you want from me Mr Teacher?'

'I need you to find Dotty and get a message to her. Her mother is dying, she's slipping away fast and…if Dotty doesn't want to be there, I understand but…I don't want her to regret not seeing her mother. Is that wrong of me?'

'I'm no priest Mr Teacher. I take my payment in the here and now.'

'Of course. How much do you charge?'

'Slow down, slow down. You need to tell me some more details, like what she's got herself into, and where do you think she is?'

'I know she's staying somewhere down Dolphin Lane. She was seen there last week. I've tried going door to door but someone like me just isn't welcome down there. They just turned me away.' His voice dried to a whisper, and then all he could do was shrug and crumple into himself.

Looking him up and down, I had to admit the only way a wet-weekend like Teacher would get any attention down Dolphin Lane, was if he was selling children, and not looking for them; 'So what's she got herself into? Drugs, prostitution, selling organs, hamster fudging? Whatever it is, you need to consider that she may not want to come back right now, as difficult as it seems, you might have to accept that she's having too much fun.'

The way Teacher met my gaze – and I hate it when people do that – told me, I'd misjudged the man[the marshmallow clearly had a boiled-sweet centre; and he meant business, he'd do whatever it took to get his daughter back, even if it meant paying someone else to do the dirty work; 'My daughter is not having fun. She is being exploited. She has a condition. Hailey-Hailey disease, it causes her skin to blister. It's a terrible affliction. Holding her hand too tightly can bring on an attack. It's genetic, hereditary. June's condition has become cancerous. My wife never really overcame the social limitations it caused her. She's always been a nervous woman, but Dotty was different. Always out-going, confident. She found a way of making it work for her. She's a Blister Sister.'

He said this as if I should have known the term, and I wasn't going to disillusion him. Business was slow, and a little extra tax-free cash was more than welcome. I nodded in a sagely manner and added, 'that's a pretty extreme scene Mr Teacher.' It had to be right? It sounded bad, and if Fast Luke wasn't willing to get personally involved, it had to be way, way out there.

'I don't expect you to convince her, or steal her away or do anything like that… I just want to get a message to her. Will you help me?'

'You pay me fifty a day, plus expenses, and you'll get my full attention Mr Teacher. Fifty up front, agreed?'

He passed me two twenties and a ten, along with a photo of a dark eyed girl with a high forehead, close cropped hair, and a beautiful smile. The kind of smile that suggests fun, trouble, and the ability to enjoy both.

'That's the newest photo we have, I'm afraid it's about a year old.'

'It'll do fine. Write your number down so I can get hold of you. And tell me something that only you'd know about her, as proof that you sent me.'

He didn't even have to think, 'her favourite food is pancakes with honey.'

'That should do it Mr Teacher, I'll get on it straightaway.'

Teacher nodded, and wiped his face on his sleeve, 'interesting line of work you have.'

'It's just a side-line.'

'I meant the taxidermy.'

'Oh right, well that's a rarefied calling too.'

'What were you working on when I came in? If you don't mind me asking?'

'A Chihuahua. I specialise in small dogs. I'm working on a project for Willow Farm, you might have heard about it.'

His head bobbed glumly, 'yes, a terrible business.'

'True, but on the other hand Chihuahuas do make nifty bookends.'

'That's very…creative. Is there much call for taxidermy these days?' he asked. I could tell he wasn't really interested but was just trying to be polite.

'Not really but it's always been a niche market. Did you know Leonardo Da Vinci was an enthusiastic taxidermist? Amateur of course, but very good by all accounts.'

'No, I didn't know that,' Teacher looked impressed and then confused, 'he was very good in the Great Gatsby.'

'I've never read that one…' Mr Teacher was clearly more tutored than I was, 'well I'd better get on then, it's your money I'm burning.'

My first stop had to be Fast Luke's place. He was sure to have the low down. Luke had shone more torches, in more dark corners of this town – often on his knees – than I could bear to think about. If it was dark, twisted, wrong or repellent, Fast Luke knew of it, did it or had done it; until he'd got bored and needed to find darker kicks to distract himself; the life of a postman is a shrouded thing.

Luke's door was opened by a buff blonde man-boy that I'd never seen before. Fast Luke gets through Buff Guys like other men get through pizzas; one or two a week; more if he's too lazy to cook.

'Hello, can I help you?' There was nothing obviously camp about Buff 52, but he gave me that hungry leer that women save for shoes.

'Is Luke in?'

'Sure, he's in the kitchen, come in.'

'The kitchen? No thanks. Just tell him Taxi Sam is out front and wants a word.'

'Where's your car?' he asked peering over my shoulder.

'Not that kind of taxi. Just say its Sam.'

'You sure you don't want to come in and wait?'

'Not before I get the all-clear.' Once bitten and all that; I think I've mentioned having a problem with Luke's kitchen. It was all down to Buff Guy 1, who was on the scene when I first got to know Luke. I'd called round and Buff 1 invited me in. I wandered into the kitchen to discover myself in the middle of a massed greased-up, fetish freak-out, involving more vegetables than a tossed salad. Not a memory that's easily washed away. The mere sight of a parsnip still triggers frightful indigestion.

Buff 52 shrugged and stepped back inside. I checked-out the graffiti that had appeared on Luke's inflatable six-foot-high white rabbit;

QUEER GO HOME!

A troublesome notion indeed; is there a queer homeland, Queensland perhaps? The front door opened and Buff 52 shouted; 'He says go through to the conservatory, but don't look in the kitchen, not if you value your sight.'

I was more than happy to comply. Ten minutes later a turban towelled Luke flounced into the cactus packed conservatory. It's actually just a rickety lean-too, attached to the back of his pad, but you wouldn't dare say that to Luke's face; 'Morning sweetie, I take it you saw Mr Teacher then?'

'Yeah, I did. A very moving story. Why'd you send him my way?'

'Much more your thing than mine darling, it'll need muscle rather than style.'

'I guess, but an address would be good. Do you know where his daughter is?'

Luke pulled the silk dressing gown tight across his chest, 'Yes, I do know where his horrid little Dotty is.'

'Horrid? How come? What's the problem?'

'Didn't he tell you? She's a Blister Sister.'

I nodded, 'yeah he told me that, I haven't got a clue what it means.'

'Sam, you surprise me. Such a sheltered upbringing. You should get your hands out of those dead dogs once in a while, and get out, really you owe it to yourself.'

'Yeah, yeah, cut the crap Luke, and tell me what you know.'

He winced and tried to look offended but then thought better of it, 'oh alright, you're really no fun these days. The Blister Sisters are nothing special in themselves. Just a bunch of well-organized, disordered personality types, but the scene they're into, 'Blistering,' is something else. Very high-end perversion, attracts a lot of sports stars and celebs. It started back in the late sixties, after the release of the Beatles White Album. You know the track, 'Helter Skelter.' The one that fuckwit Mason got all wound-up about; well he wasn't alone. At the end of the track, Ringo is heard to say, 'I've got Blisters on my fingers' and…'

'Wrong,' I declared, my knowledge of pop culture rarely topped Luke's, so I made the most of it, 'that was Paul not Ringo, and they'd been playing for nearly an hour. It's a really heavy bass line. The birth of heavy metal some say.'

'I'll take your word for it. I can't abide all that Fab Four nonsense. I'm not interested in any boy band, that can't sing and dance at the same time. The thing is, some

134

of the greatly twisted brains of our time, interpreted Paul's wining as a message, and so yet another wrong direction was born.' Luke inspected a cactus that really was too phallic to be true, 'can you guess what I call this one?' he winked.

'Focus Luke. What's the big deal?'

'It's a self-harm gig, not exclusively gender specific, but it's mostly a girly thing. They use hair irons, tongs and whatever to give themselves blisters. I've seen photos you wouldn't believe.'

'Hence Blister Sisters.' Clearly Dotty was a smart girl, and just like her dad had said, she'd found a way to make her condition work for her, by finding folks who appreciated her affliction. 'And guys pay to watch this?'

Luke took the towel off his head, revealing a new peroxide blonde crop, 'they don't just watch. Some people want to abuse you, some people want to be abused. It's a sadomasochistic deal. Girls who want to blister, and guys who want to burn; real up-market stuff. You'll find them in the cellar of number 22. You'll need a twenty to get in … and a clean shirt.'

'Thanks Luke, can you do me a favour?'

'Of course...'

'Next time you think about putting work my way; shove that cactus up your arse.'

At twenty-two hundred hours, I was dressed up to the nines in Dad's old M&S suit; accessorised with Monkey Scarf, and a new pair of totectors. I was hot to trot, and off to Dolphin Lane I trotted. Broston is not blessed with many places of interest or local colour, but ninety percent of all our dark pleasures, dwell in Dolphin Lane - the other ten percent are to be found wherever Fast Luke is at. But unlike Luke, Dolphin Lane's disturbing delights don't appear until well after dark. Dolphin Lane is Broston's sinewy spine, in which all the town's squalor hardened nerves, run hot and jagged. It's only one street, but it hosts enough grim, grime and jizz splattered shabbiness, to keep a fleet of sea-maddened sailors, busy until payday is long forgotten.

I made my way to 22 Dolphin Lane, which incidentally, is two strides down from the Delfino Coffee Bar. They serve a secret recipe hangover cure, that ensures that its many revellers' first place port-of-call after their 'night before.' It tastes like chocolate mixed with Marmite and cat-litter; and can power a tractor in sub-zero conditions; and if that doesn't put you off attending Dolphin Lane, good luck to you. Number 22's front door was fitted with a small, rusted viewing grill. I knocked like I meant it, and half a face instantly appeared; 'Yeah, what you want?'

'I'm here for the Blister Sisters, I'm their uncle.'

'Is that right? You got an invite uncle?'

I held up a twenty and ran it across the grill, 'Yeah here it is.'

The door opened, my invitation was collected, and I stepped into the darkness. As the door closed behind me, a heavy black curtain to my left was pulled to one side. The golden glow of the décor was unexpected and easy on the eyes, but not much else in the room was.

A dozen seedy looking men crowded around two glowing sunbeds, both of which were occupied, by young, well-oiled, naked women. All eyes were on the grilling girls, whilst all hands were busy in pockets. Dispersed around the ogling onanists, were mattresses of different sizes and questionable cleanliness. Stretched out on these, their blistered arms and legs held aloft, were more naked moaning girls. More sweating punters gathered around them like vampires, refracting torch beams and lit cigarettes through the girl's fluid engorged skins. I was glad I hadn't eaten. I made my way around the beds and checked the girls' faces one by one, comparing them to the palmed photo of Dotty, that her father had given me. Dotty was not amongst them. I made my way through the pocket billiard playing perverts and peered into the sunbeds. It was not pretty; these girls were overdone. I could see red raw flesh peeling and puckering into truly vicious taut blisters, but again none of these Blister Sisters were the sister I wanted.

Apart from the blistering sisters, it was a decidedly male scene. It had the feel of a barbeque pit, with all the weekend cooks leering over their overcooked sausages. Whoever the Blister Sisters were, they were not in charge, they were merely assets. I tried talking to one of the baking beauties - a little, oval faced girl with green hair, and a blister the size of my fist on her left breast; 'Do you know Dotty? Is she here?' All I got in reply was a dazed whimper and an unfocused stare. I held my hand in front of her face. She looked right through it. There was no-way I was getting any sense out of those doped-out lamb chops. I was going to have to delve deeper.

On the far side of the room, in the shade of a pillar, I spied a serious heavy, wearing the standard Kray wannabe uniform; dark suit and sunglasses. He was busy looking hard and disinterested, whilst overseeing the pervert's fun and games. My Dad used to say: if you want to know where anything is, ask the help. I put a twenty between his face and mine and whispered; 'so where's the good stuff? I need some real action, not this puppet show.' Ignoring me; he kept watch over my shoulder. I tried again; 'I heard there's something special here. Someone worth seeing. Dotty I think the name was.' That caught his attention. He took the twenty and nodded towards a red door on the opposite wall.

The door opened onto a strip lit corridor, at the far end of which stood a square-shouldered gorilla, guarding yet another red door. I put on my best swagger and put myself in his face; 'I've come to see Dotty.'

'Is that right? And who are you with?' he snorted suspiciously.

'I came with John,' - there's always a John.

'No, which Sports Club.'

My mind went blank, which sport did I look like I might be into? Boxing? Wrestling? I had too much girth for cycling or football, possibly Rugby; I reckoned I could get away with rugby; 'Rugby, I'm with the rugby club.'

'Which club?' the gorilla sneered.

'Which club! Are you kidding me? The club of course! The only club that matters that is! I'm the coach. Do you play? You look like you play. We could always do with a strong man in the... back bit.'

The gorilla's face cracked into a toothy grin, 'Nah, used to do a bit at school like, but got into weights, went a bit off the rails with the steroids, but I'm getting it together now. This is just a filler like, nothing serious.'

'Good for you lad, good for you. Think about it though, we could always use a… silly mid-wicket in the scrum link dance-off.'

'Cheers pal, I appreciate that,' the gorilla was so chuffed he even held the door open for me.

The room was a 1980's Chinese Restaurant throwback. The far wall was covered with stacked aquariums – tastefully lit by alternating coloured bulbs – whilst the other walls were covered in sparkling red and gold flock wallpaper. I suddenly craved a plate of China Pete's pancake rolls, but my appetite was soon ruined. Twelve sporty types were gathered around a long low hotplate, sucking at long metal tubes, protruding from the distended, bloated blisters of a supine naked woman.

One of the supping acolytes; a tall lad with glowing skin, jumped to his feet, ripped through ten star-jumps, and declared; 'Wow that's some weird fix,' and began jogging around the feasting diners. As he reached me, I put my hand to his chest; 'What's got you so happy champ?'

'It's the serum man, high potency electrolyte serum. It's a total rush, give it a go,' he handed me the metal tube and marched out of the room with a whoop and a high-five to the gorilla on the door.

A broad-chested short-arse, in shades and a too-tight black t-shirt, stepped out of my peripheral vision; 'he didn't tell you, it's totally pure and undetectable. The benefits last for anything up to twenty-four hours, but for best results we recommend a six-to-ten-hour window. Private sessions are bookable.'

Knowing I had to play out my part, I took the tube and worked my way around to the girl's shoulder. Her arm lay across her face, shielding her eyes, but I knew it was Dotty. The toned t-shirt was watching me expectantly; I put the tube to my mouth and made to suck.

'Don't be shy,' the t-shirt twat sneered. Stepping forward, he took the end of the tube and stuck it into a blister the size of a tennis ball, extending from the girl's neck. I tried to block the end of the tube with my tongue, but I was too slow; a jet of tepid salty sweet liquid hit the back of my throat. I dug my fingers into my calf and battled the compulsion to vomit.

'Good stuff right?' the twat grinned.

I gave him the thumbs up. He turned his back on me and forgot I even existed. Taking the tube from my mouth, I spat, and put my lips to Dotty's ear.

'Dotty, I've got a message from your dad. Your Mum is very sick, if you want a chance to say goodbye, you need to get in touch. Dotty, can you hear me?'

There was the faintest of acknowledgements, no more than a sigh and the twitch of a finger. But that was all I needed; my job was done, time to go. But fool that I am, I had to ask, 'do you want to leave here Dotty? If you want to leave, I can come back for you.'

Her voice was soft, weak and sounded as if it came from a hundred miles away, 'I… I want to go now.'

'That might be difficult Dotty…'

The far-off breath of a voice replied, 'Please…help me.'

I stood up, stretched my back and beckoned for t-shirt twat to come nearer. He beamed like an honest car dealer and bounded over, 'yes Sir, what can I do for you?'

'Smile,' I said; and he did.

My uppercut put his teeth through his lip, and his head into the ceiling. He was out cold before he hit the floor. 'Time gentlemen please,' I crowed, as I pulled Dotty from the hotplate. Wedging her under my arm, I pointed at a lanky streak-of-piss and told him to; 'Open the fucking door.' My decisive interplay with the t-shirt twat, must have convinced him to play along. Seeing the alarm on the punter's faces, my steroid popping pal stepped into the room. I watched him struggling to do the maths – it was pitiful – so I decided to put him out of his misery. I swung Monkey Scarf hard between his legs; the sound of nuts cracking filled the room; he wheezed, whimpered and doubled over; I put my knee to his chin – nighty night gorilla.

I threw Dotty over my shoulder, took a deep breath, and with Monkey Scarf swinging, charged into the sunbed den. The gathered perverts were no problem, most fled as soon as I appeared; and who can blame them? A screaming maniac, armed with a Monkey Scarf, charging at you, it's enough to give anyone the willies. The room's overseer wasn't so easy. He was primed and looking for trouble. He blocked my path, chin down, fists in the classic guard position. He certainly knew his stuff; but that play's no defence against the Monkey Scarf. I swung the business-end around his guard and hit him with a sonic-crack on the back of the head; that sent him hurtling into a sunbed, that spat sparks across the room as it swallowed

141

him whole. The muscle on the door was next in line. He pulled a night-stick as I came on. I sent Monkey Scarf swinging in, he blocked it with a move straight out of a Kung-Fu movie – which was unfortunate for him, because, as I've mentioned before, Monkey Scarf is articulated. It spun around and around his stick, smashing into his jaw, once, twice, thrice; before he finally hit the floor. His severance cheque would go straight to his dentist. I put my boot to the door, and out into the night we went... naked girl, Monkey Scarf and all.

Obviously, the sensible thing to do, was to take Dotty straight to her parents, or even straight to the A&E department. But I know something about skin, and not just by trade, in my dad's last years his hands started to react to all the chemicals we use, so when it came to treating burns and blisters, I had a fair idea what to do. And to be honest, I saw Dotty's skin as a challenge. Her body looked like a volcanic landscape, marked with old scars of past eruptions and the boiling bubbles of new-born blisters. Even my lightest touch made her wince, living in that skin couldn't have been easy. My trade involves removing unwanted moisture from skin, without letting it become brittle. But Dotty's skin was my trade in reverse. My usual lotions and potions weren't going to cut it, but good old E-45 fixes just about anything, even if it's dead. I buy it by the bucketful. I slapped the stuff on Dotty until she looked like a cone of giant whipped cream. I put her to bed, sat on the floor and watched over her; with half an ear cocked just in case someone decided to try and retrieve their prized performer. I'm going to pass quietly over the withdrawal scene; it was as wretched and pitiful as you'd

142

expect. No one benefits from its retelling; let's leave it at that. Over the next day Dotty rolled in and out of sleep, on the hour every hour, but come that evening she seemed to settle into a slower rhythm, by midnight, her breathing was as slow and steady as a lazy sea, so I kicked off my boots and shut my eyes. When I awoke again it was midday, my head felt as if it were stuffed with rusty razor blades and my craving for custard creams was chronic; I sat up to see a mischievous smile beaming at me from inside a E-45 smeared bedsheet.

'Hello there,' I yawned.

'Hi. Sleep well?'

'You tell me.' I winced.

'Well, if your snoring was anything to go by, I'd say so, but you sure do have some weird dreams about your dad,' she pulled the bedsheet tight around her shoulders. and looked me straight in the eye – and for some reason, I didn't mind - 'I don't know how to thank you.'

'You don't have to, I'm being paid.' As soon as I said it I regretted my words. 'Although I must say…you are very welcome. My friends call me Taxi Sam, as in taxidermist.'

'Taxidermist?' Dotty mused, 'what's that? I know derma means skin. So, your something to do with skin therapy, right? And by the looks of me you know what you're doing, so what's a taxidermist?'

'I mount animals. That is, I remove the skin from dead animals, treat it, preserve it, and display them in interesting poses. It's not as weird as it sounds.'

She giggled and it sounded like sunshine, 'it does sound pretty weird.'

'Really. That's rich coming from a Blister Sister.'

Dotty shrugged; a girls got to live. It was very empowering at first, but it certainly went sour real quick,' her eyes dropped to her scars on her arms and then with a deep sigh lifted to meet me with a solid grin, 'how'd you get into taxidermy then, hospital occupational therapy was it?'

'No, my Dad taught me, it's the family business. Some of the best museums in the world have my dads' work in them…look shouldn't we be talking about you? I mean how are you? Do you want to go to the police?'

Dotty sat back and shut her eyes, 'no, there's no point. The police knew all about it. There's a couple of them in the club most nights.'

'I did not know that,' I answered with a sinking feeling in my stomach, as I tried to recall the faces I'd caved in that night.

'Nobody made me do it,' she smiled with a shrug, '…well not at first, for a while it was a pretty cool scene, just us girls, and then they started giving us this Scrape stuff, you heard of it?'

'Yeah, I heard of it,' I replied, and that revelation made a lot of sense.

'It took away all the pain, and all our control. They just didn't want to let me go, because of my condition, I was a real earner for them. But I'm out now, they'll not bother me again, I know too much for them to give me any trouble.'

'I'm not so sure of that,' as I said this she stood up, and repositioned the sheet, tying it off above her breasts; I didn't look away quick enough, and saw more than I should; I felt myself redden, 'sorry, I... sorry.'

'Sam you've seen everything I've got. This moisturiser didn't slap itself on.'

It felt like my blush was turning into a bruise, 'oh god... Jesus I'm sorry, I didn't think. Nothing happened...I just thought about you as meat.'

Her eyes narrowed, 'meat, gee thanks. That's a pretty male perspective. Nothing new there then.'

'Sausage actually...'

'That's new, Lincolnshire or Cumberland?'

'I shouldn't have done it, but you were in pain. I know how to deal with skin, it just made sense to do something about it. I should have taken you to the hospital. I'm so dumb.'

'I believe you. Thousands wouldn't. Just sausage right. It feels good, what did you use, I recognise the E-45, but I can smell coconut.'

'It's my own basecoat, a mix of glycerine, petroleum jelly and cocoa butter with E-45 for joints and... crevices... oh god. I'm sorry.'

'It's okay Sam. You did a good job,' she grinned, and the sun came out again. I could have looked at that face for hours. But I had a task to complete. I phoned her father, and then made myself scarce. They had a lot to talk about. I went down into the workshop and had a quick chat with Fluffy my old stuffed terrier – he's a great listener, if a little ragged about the seams. When I came back to the flat, I found Dotty still wrapped in my sheet, standing in the kitchen laughing at my cooker.

'What's so funny?'

'It's full of books.'

'Oh yeah. The flat gets damp in the winter...'

'So how do you cook?'

'I don't. Why, do you want something to eat? I've got custard cream biscuits.'

'I'm hungry, really hungry. It feels like I haven't eaten in a week, and I'm not sure that isn't true.'

'Shall I take you over to your parents?'

Dotty shook her head, 'plenty of time for that. I want to eat fish and chips with you.'

'What about your Mum? Your Dad said…'

'Dad said, Dad said. Dad is always saying something, and Mum is always ill. Don't you want to eat with me?'

'Cod or plaice? The guy round the corner delivers. I stuffed his budgie Percy for him. He has him in the shop.'

Half an hour later we were eating fish and chips in the workshop. Having a woman in my workshop, wasn't exactly a new experience, but having a beautiful woman, wrapped in a sheet, and lathered in moisturiser certainly was. I liked it.

'You live here alone Sam? Do you have any family?'

'No, it was just me and dad. He died a couple of years ago. It was just us for years.'

'No Mum?'

'Don't remember her. Nice lady, or so Dad said, she died when I was two.'

'I tried the room at the top of the stairs, it's locked, was that your dad's room?'

I nodded.

'Still miss him huh?'

I shoved a chip in my mouth and tried to make my nodding more varied.

'Mum and me never really saw eye to eye. Something to do with us having the same condition, and all that regular mother and daughter stuff. Too much drama, too much control. I think Mum likes being a victim, and she couldn't stand it when I didn't play along. I moved in with my Gran when I was twelve. She treated me like a person not a disease. When Gran died, I lost it for a while, made some bad choices. Believe it or not the whole Blister Sister scene was the highlight of my life... the things we do to try and escape ourselves.'

'I know what you mean... I really lost it when dad died,' I confessed, 'grief makes people do strange things.'

'That's true. People do strange things, when left alone. I like you Sam. I think I'd like to know you better.'

I was back in nodding mode, 'I'd like that. I'd like that very much.'

Dotty balled the chip paper into her fist, and looked around for somewhere to dump it, 'Thank you, I needed that. Your friend makes great chips. Stuffing budgies obviously has its benefits.'

'Do you want to get back to your folks now?' I asked.

The ball of vinegar paper hit me in the head, 'no Sam, I want you to take me upstairs and cover me with moisturiser while I'm awake... and maybe, if you do a good job, I'll return the favour.'

I choked on my chip.

I'm not going to give you a blow by… no that's wrong; I'm going to be discreet about what happen next. All you need to know is, it was beautiful, the best afternoon, evening and night of my entire life. And not just because of the physical stuff, Dotty talked to me like no one else has ever talked to me, I made her laugh and she made me feel good. It was bliss. I'll never forget it, and every time I think of our time together; it breaks my heart.

The next morning, I delivered Dotty to her parent's trim and tidy apple-white abode on the far side of town. They had pancakes and honey waiting for her. I told her father I'd collect the money later; it gave me another reason to visit the house. I didn't want the money, but I needed that smile in my life.

I went home and crashed-out in the workshop thinking about Dotty, and although I'd seen every inch of her, I dreamt about nothing but her face. I don't think I've ever slept so sweetly, and I know I haven't slept well since. The next day I closed-up early and went across town to visit the Teachers.

They didn't answer the door, so I waited around for two hours, and then tried again, but there was still no answer. It occurred to me that they might have fled the town, and my heart turned to sawdust. I went home; threw a stuffed weasel across the workshop, ate a pack of custard creams, and felt no better. I can't say why, but I was certain Dotty wouldn't have left town without getting a message to me. Something was wrong. As soon as the sky darkened, I went back to their house. The lights were on upstairs, so somebody was in; I knocked until the door shook, but nobody answered; something was most definitely wrong. I ran to the back of the house and climbed over the fence. I tried the backdoor; it was locked. A barge-charge with the shoulder opened it with a sharp crack. I ran up the stairs, fists clenched, ready for trouble. As I reached the landing, I turned towards the light and saw straight into a bedroom. Dotty was lying spread-eagled on the bed. Her head hung over the edge of the mattress, her eyes cold; still and as dull as grey chalk. Six guys in sharp suits, frenzied over her body with long sharp steel tubes. They were sucking her dry. I didn't have time to feel the rage that hit me. I was moving before my head knew what I was doing. I stormed into the room, and then froze, I couldn't believe what I was seeing; Dotty's parents were bent over her pale thighs, supping on her lifeforce through a tube that had been forced into Dotty's body. Standing in the corner of the room, watching over it all, was the tall thin figure of Dr Hooms, replete in his ill-fitting turquoise velvet jacket. I reached for Monkey Scarf, but Monkey Scarf wasn't there. In my panic I'd left home without him. I raised my fists, and then something came down hard on my head.

A forest fire of a headache and the sting of blood in my eyes woke me, in a spinning room. I couldn't stand, my legs wouldn't obey. I crawled over to the bed. Dotty lay there motionless, as pale as milk. I didn't need to check for a pulse. There was no point. I'm more than familiar with the pallor of death.

She'd been severely beaten, probably partly to subdue her and to maximise the swelling of her skin condition; and then the bastards, and her loving parents, had sucked the life out of her. She'd lost so much fluid her system had just collapsed. A heart-attack of sorts; or maybe just a broken heart; how could her parents do such a thing? The carpet was covered in blood, and it was all mine. I heard the police sirens approaching. All the evidence the police would need was there on the carpet; and laying naked on the bed. I'd made a gift of myself. I crawled out the room, fell down the stairs and stumbled out into the garden, crashing through the garden fence; my trail wasn't going to be hard to follow.

I curled up in a stinking alley, with the sound of police sirens whirling around me, as I threw-up my guts and cried my eyes dry. I'd lost what I could never have, and more than I'd ever dared to hope for - and I was likely to be hung drawn and quartered for the slaughter. But what did it matter? The world was dust to me. I walked out into the street, wanting them to find me. Why not get it over with? What was the point of going on?

'Sam! Sam! Get in the sodding car,' Luke was shouting at me from across the street. A blue Volvo drew-up beside me. I looked in the window.

'Taxi for Taxi Sam,' Prawn grinned, 'better get in duck, the wolves are out.'

I did as I was told; a moment later Sam jumped into the car, threw a Kimono over me, and pushed my head into his lap, 'now you behave while you're down there.' I wept. 'It's okay Sam, I know, I know, it's going to be okay.'

'It's never going to be okay again Luke,' I sobbed.

'I know… but somehow Sam, we'll put this right. We'll get the bastards, I promise you that. Come on buddy, I got this, Luke knows what to do,' Luke gripped my shoulders, holding me tight, and then I smelt the chemical cloth close around my mouth, and I've never been so grateful.

Chapter 4

BROSTON BLUES

I was in my workshop elbow deep in Nigel's nether regions; his woodwool had recently been invaded by a family of mice, when Fast Luke barged in. Seeing Luke in daylight hours was an unusual event. Seeing him distressed and in his Post Office uniform was a new and disturbing experience; like catching your dad pleasuring himself with a goldfish – it's just wrong.

'What's that?' Luke shrieked.

'It's Nigel.'

'It's a fucking lion Sam.'

'That's also true, and he has a very strange case of piles.'

'Don't say a word, don't say another fucking word. Get me a drink, I need a drink.'

'Tea?'

'A drink Sam, a sodding drink.'

'I've only got surgical spirit Luke.'

'Fine, fine, fine. Just put plenty of coke in it.'

'I have orange squash.'

'Damn you Sam, you're so provincial. Fine, lots of ice then.'

As I fixed Luke his drink, he fixed his face with a compact; a process which seemed to steady his nerves.

'They've arrested China Pete on public health charges. Christ they might even throw attempted murder at him.'

'China Pete? The Major's China Pete?'

'How many China Pete's do you know? Jesus Sam, yes China Pete. They picked him up this morning…'

'For what?'

'For being four-foot two, you moron. For the poisonings of course, keep up Sam,' Luke snapped.

'I find that hard to believe.'

'Believe it,' he said curtly, 'I've got a man on the inside,' - that wasn't difficult to believe, Luke had many men on the inside – or vice versa.

'I mean I can't believe Pete had anything to do with this shit.'

'I know what you meant Sam. I really didn't want to get involved in anything so… sordid,' – another surprise – 'but if the boys in blue are going to scapegoat my friends, I really don't have a choice.'

It was a month and three days since Dotty's murder, and I was still walking around uncharged and unquestioned. The local news gossip rag had moved onto more lurid things, an outbreak of gastric unpleasantness that had beset the town. There had been thirty-two cases of food poisoning in two weeks. One of which had resulted in the death of a six-year-old boy, with another twelve-year-old in hospital on the critical list. The town's intestinal sorrows had made the national news, and the denizens of the twenty-four-hour media machine were flexing their sphincters like a vegetarian after a bean-feast blowout.

NEW SUPERBUG HITS EAST OF ENGLAND

They'd named the malady, the Broston Blues. The virulent but as yet unidentified bacillus had everyone doing overtime with the alcohol gel and the Sani-wipes. You could get high on the fumes just by walking down the street. Three outdoor smokers had been seriously burnt when a cloud of alcohol vapour ignited during their puffing session – okay not really but you get the point. It was straining times in old Broston town.

'Whose sodding lion is that?' Luke sneered.

'He belongs to the library. Apparently, the kids love him. I had to remove a pound of sucked sweets from his gullet. What have they got on Pete?'

'Got on him!?' Luke's voice rose by several octaves; and somewhere a dog howled for mercy, 'nothing, that's what they've got on him. It's an affront darling. A bloody affront and I don't believe a word of it,' Luke downed his drink and licked his lips, 'interesting, I like that. What was it called?'

'Surgical Orange.'

'I might have to get some of that in, its tangy. So, I can count on you then?'

'To do what?'

'To look into it dummy. Dig around and find out what you can, I'll do the same, and our combined forces shall overcome. That sounded less naughty than I hoped it would, it's all this bug business, it's got me all… cranky.'

'I don't think so Luke, perhaps you should go solo on this one.' I'd been keeping a low profile since the Lodge put me in the frame for Dotty's murder. To be exact I hadn't left the house in three months. If the library hadn't called about Nigel's infestation, I'd probably still be hiding under my workbench. As Dad used to say; there's no therapy like keeping busy.

'Are you still worried about the police? I told you, if they really wanted you, they'd have had you by now. I mean, they've got your blood and all the witnesses from Dolphin Lane, that's more than enough to stich you up, but they haven't.'

'Thanks Luke, that's very reassuring. You ought to take up counselling.'

'Sam, you stumbled in there. They weren't expecting you. They took the opportunity to try and hang it on you, but it didn't work. If you'd been found at the scene, yes you'd be fucked but you weren't…'

'What if they took a photo? They've got to have taken a photo…' I insisted, as I'd insisted at least sixty times before, 'if I get involved in this now, it's like I'm just asking to be blackmailed.'

'You presume too much. The police have a body, and the parents are missing. That makes them the primary suspects. So, for the trillionth time…you have nothing to worry about,' Luke placed his manicured hand on my chest, 'sweetie please, listen. Get off your arse and do something. You need to get out of here, if you don't, they might as well have caught you. Get on with it.' Luke turned his back on me, and then flounced-off, out of the shop to fulfil his raison d'etre – which is being Fast Luke -

156

a rage of primary colours in a world of insipid grey. I shoved my arm deep into Nigel's arse and considered the complexity of life's waterlogged pageant.

I decided to start at the Lotus Flower, Pete's place, which was an idiot move, because it had been closed by the Health Inspector. So I nosed around the other restaurants on West Street; of which there are many. If there was an inside story, I was sure to hear it from his competitors; and I had to start somewhere.

Up and down West Street I trolled, I dipped poppadums in the Indian restaurants. I bought pancake rolls in three different Chinese takeaways. Tapas in the Spanish bar. Blini and smoked salmon in three Eastern Euro bars and a Pukka pie in the chippy. I spent a fucking fortune and discovered nothing but mixing your starters leads to indigestion. It seemed that when it came to China Pete, everyone was equally shocked. It couldn't have been a deliberate act on Pete's part; if there was any truth in the accusations; it was a terrible accident or somebody else was to blame.

Raj, a third-generation nudist, amateur philosopher, and proprietor of the Indian Star encapsulated the mood in his inimitable way; 'When you run a restaurant you take responsibility for everything that goes out the door. If some idiot wipes his arse and doesn't wash his hands, it might as well have been your arse, your shit. I cannot believe Pete knowingly did anything wrong. He's a good man, a nice man, too nice. He employs idiots and now he's paying the price for being nice. You can't run a restaurant and be a nice guy. You have to be a shit. Ask any of my staff, they all think I'm a shit. I'm proud to be a shit, but there's no shit in my kitchen.' I do wonder why Raj doesn't have his own TV series; the BBC are missing a trick there.

Kim Chung, of 'The Oriental Cat,' was at pains to point-out the social impact of such accusations; 'These charges make no sense, no sense at all, but already he's guilty. Everyone thinks he's guilty. His reputation is ruined. Pete will struggle with that, he worked very hard to build up his reputation. It will be very bad for him. Not good for my business either; already tonight I've had three cancellations. Totally fascist thinking: you can hear them saying it; those Chinese restaurants are all the same.'

Vic the Pole, who's actually from Lithuania, and was born with a speech defect that makes him sound like Tweety Bird talking through a tin-can phone, claimed he had the low down. He'd seen the Health Inspectors remove eight large cans of 'Good Flower Cooking Oil,' from the Lotus Flower the previous day; 'It was the same brand that Pete had tried to sell to me, he was getting it wholesale. I told him I didn't want to know. I didn't recognise the brand. Twelve years in the business, I know all the oils. I think Pete bought cheap and now he's paying the price.'

'Vic, that makes no sense. Surely anything nasty in the oil would have been killed off by the cooking process.'

Vic was convinced; 'It only takes a splash, a drop of corrupted oil to sit on a spoon or a worktop; filth grows, it spreads and before you know it,' Vic whistled through his teeth, 'you have the shitting hell.'

It only sounded plausible if you didn't know China Pete. I was sure that dapper little dandy ran a clean house. But I had to admit, it was possible the competition on West Street had pushed him to cut overheads, but that wasn't the Pete I knew, or thought I knew.

I stood at the end of West Street, bloated and bilious, stuffed tighter than a Lincolnshire sausage, and considered my findings; I'd learnt nothing that had taken me beyond my own opinions. I trudged back down the street, past the council offices – where the whiff of sewers continuously lingers – this triggered dark thoughts; how great must the corruption and incompetence be within their building, if they can't fix their own drains? And what chance is there for the rest of the town? What chance for China Pete?

I was down deep in my effluent gloom when a hand gripped my arm. I turned quickly and was confronted and confounded, by the shapely curve of the magnificent breasts of the glorious Lucy Biggerdyke – I nearly fainted.

'Taxi Sam isn't it? Luke's friend.'

I was a little hurt that she didn't recall me from our first – actually second – meeting. 'Yeah, that's me, Sam Taxi, I mean Taxi Sam…' I was also struggling to block out certain video experiences she wasn't aware we'd shared.

'Luke said you'd be here. He wants us back at his place. Where's your car?'

'I don't have a car.'

She looked perplexed; just like she did in that scene from 'Biggerdyke You Like,' when she walks in on the red-headed twins with their oiled cucumbers; 'So why does Luke call you Taxi Sam?' she asked.

'It really doesn't matter. Can you tell me what's going on?'

Lucy was a striking looking woman. She was harder and firmer around the edges than she'd been in her youth, but it suited her. Her physic was due to her gym, 'Fitterdykes' – a very popular, top-class establishment for ladies who sweat together. Her grip on my arm was testament to her personal fitness regime, but her eyes were telling me something - apart from her obvious repulsion to my presence - was seriously wrong.

'What is it? Why does Luke want to see me? What's happened?'

Lucy swallowed - which was distracting - and then pronounced, 'China Pete is dead.'

Half an hour later Lucy and I were back at Chez Luke. We were standing around the heart-shaped kitchen table drinking coffee-laced whiskey. I heard myself say; 'Aren't they meant to watch the guys they put in the cells? Don't they have cameras to stop this kind of thing from happening?'

'There's only so much they can do when a guy goes for his dentures,' Luke sighed.

One of Luke's inside guys had passed the word on; Pete had been found dead in a holding cell. His throat cut with a snapped denture plate.

'I guess he couldn't live with the shame.' I recalled Kim Chung's words concerning Pete's fallen reputation; it seemed he was right; some folks take that kind of thing very seriously.

'Perhaps it was guilt after all,' Luke added without conviction.

'I don't believe that,' Lucy growled, 'this isn't a confession, this proves nothing. I don't believe it.' Lucy choked on her words as tears and snot erupted across her face. Very reminiscent of the closing scene of four of her early films. Lucy was taking it hard, which surprised me, unless I missed my guess, there was more to Lucy's grief than the loss of toothsome pork balls.

161

I decided to keep my info about the dodgy cooking oil to myself. I downed the coffee and made my excuses. It was time for me to get back to the workshop. Being around mammals with pulses is always a stretch for me; I crave the certainty of formaldehyde and bared bone.

Nigel was just about finished, and I really wanted to get started on another pair of the Willow's Chihuahuas. They wanted them defiantly posed, within a glass bowl diorama, complete with sand, cacti and miniature Mexican flag; but I needed to finish Nigel's butt before moving onto such a delicate and artistic project. My motivation was lagging, and I needed inspiration, so I flicked through my record collection – sometimes T-Rex is not appropriate – and decided to play African Sanctus; to make Nigel feel at home. This done, I doublechecked that none of the new woodwool had shifted since that morning's session, which of course, it had. Taxidermy tip #1 always allow stuffing to settle; ramming it home just isn't good enough. A good stuffing takes time and finesse.

It was almost six in the morning before I was done. I was just stitching up Nigel's nether regions when my fingertip brushed a hard cold edge, hidden beneath the skin. I knew what it was, before I pulled it from Nigel's butt. It was a farthing, scarred with a star on one side. It had been placed inside Nigel by the original taxidermist, it was his mark. I'd seen such things many times before, but this mark I knew beyond a doubt; how could I not, none came better than my Dad.

It was an odd feeling working on one of Dad's old projects. It made me feel sad and proud in equal measure; and then that scarred farthing got me thinking about routines and traditions, things that don't change. I remembered eating at the Lotus Flower one night when they were short of staff. Pete worked like a whirlwind, serving and clearing tables, in and out of the kitchen all night, and still working the till, handling the money...but there had been something odd about the way he did it, something I commented on at the time but couldn't be sure about. It gave me an idea, but I had to be certain. I needed to talk to someone who knew Pete better than I did, I needed to have a heart to heart with Lucy Biggerdyke.

Given Broston's conservative nature (capital C, small U), 'Fitterdyke' was a brave name for Lucy to go with, but I guess having made a career out of being a Biggerdyke, she'd earned the right to be as loud and proud as she wanted to be. Being in, and possibly on your face, was not an issue for Lucy Biggerdyke. Twenty-two straight to jerk DVD's, testified to that. Now I've not hung around gyms enough to know if 'Fitterdyke,' is exceptional in its décor or ethos, but I can't imagine there are many male gyms were the smell of sweat is overcome by the scent of lavender oil - and whatever else those ladies were rubbing into each other's hot taut bodies in the seclusion of the steam room; yeah I know that last bit is ridiculous, but what can I say? I'm a man who spends his working day rubbing dead animals with acetone and alum; a man needs to dream.

Perhaps I wasn't hiding my grubby thinking well enough that morning, as my presence at 'Fitterdyke', was certainly making the Lycra wearing early risers nervous; and the girl at the reception desk wasn't being as helpful as she could have been either.

'No, you cannot come in, what don't you understand about 'female only' gym?'

'I understand that; I don't want to join, I need to talk to Lucy? Is she here? Can you call her for me?'

'I don't think so, we've had your sort in here before. Lucy doesn't see fans. She's retired, she doesn't give out autographs or…signed underwear,' this was said with some disgust – and I was shocked to think I was so easily read.

'It's not like that, she knows me.'

The receptionist looked me up and down, and I was found wanton, 'Right, of course she does. So why don't you call her on her phone then?' Not a bad question.

'I don't have a phone. Please, just tell Lucy, Taxi Sam is here.'

'She told me, she is not to be disturbed…and you disturb me.'

That,' Not To Be Disturbed,' set alarm bells ringing in my bonce, and they chimed the warning of a desperate act being undertaken by a grief-stricken desperate woman. The next thing I knew I was sliding over the front desk and pushing my way into the gym, yelling for Lucy. Of course, no one else heard my inner alarm bells; they just saw a deranged male forcing himself into a female gym. The girl on the front desk had her arms around my neck and her teeth in my shoulder before I reached the door. Two ladies of indeterminate age but definite muscle tone, threw themselves into the fray, swinging dumbbells at my head as they dragged me to the floor. I was about to take a beating for all male kind – richly deserved I'm sure – when a school yard whistle blew.

'Hold it right there. What's going on here?' Lucy demanded.

'This pervert was trying to force his way in,' the receptionist panted; despite having her mouth full of my shoulder.

'Sam? Is that you?' I think she did well to recognise me, seeing as my face was hidden by so much breast, elbow and thigh.

'Hi Lucy,' I wheezed.

'What are you doing here Sam?'

'I came to see you, and then I thought…' what was I thinking? 'she said you didn't want to be disturbed…I just…oh never mind. Please get them off me Lucy.'

'Idiot. Girls, it's okay, really, it's just a man being a dick, let him go. He's harmless.' The breasts fell away from my eyes and Lucy's tanned and aerobicized legs loomed above me; ending in a very tight pink, crutch hugging leotard.

'Sorry Lucy, I've been up all night, judgements off. I need to talk to you about Pete.'

The back office was a bizarre mix of porn memorabilia and lost youth ephemera. Pictures of horses and declarations of positive talk, stood alongside posters of Lucy dressed in nothing but a smile and baby oil. I noticed one poster in particular, Lucy holding a stuffed Kangaroo in an opportune position, whilst the legend 'Biggerdyke Down Under' ran across her breasts; it's a great film, a personal favourite.

'Lucy, I need to ask you something? You were pretty upset last night. I know we all were, but you really were struggling there... what was the story between you and Pete?'

Lucy sat on her desk and stared at the ceiling, 'Is that all? You know my background, everybody in this town knows my X-rated story. Look I have a hard time trusting men but is it any wonder? They all want something from me… they want me to be somebody I'm not. But Pete was different.'

I have to admit, looking at her sitting on that desk, in her tight pink leotard; I was amongst that number. The desire of the eyes is a terrible thing. I could feel my face reddening and my pulse quickening; even though I knew Lucy batted for a team I had too many balls to play for – I was embarrassed, ashamed and turned on – it was like being a teenager again; 'You trusted China Pete? Did you know about him and the Major?'

'Of course I did. I'd worked at the Lotus Flower when I left school. Pete was always respectful always nice. When he heard I was starting out in the industry he warned me against it, said I had more to offer than my looks. But I was too young and greedy to listen. Later on...,' Lucy's eyes narrowed, I could tell she was deciding whether or not to trust me; luckily she couldn't see inside my head and decided to risk it, 'I'd got myself in a fix. I was sick of making porn but too keen of the Peruvian marching powder to walk away. Catch 22, I needed powder to do porn and porn made me money, but more porn meant more powder. After five years of sucking cock, I didn't have a penny to show for it. I went to see Pete. He leant me the money to set up the gym. He believed in me when no-one else did, and when those Lodge dicks, tried to block my application, he stood up for me, and he never asked anything of me, not a thing.'

'Not even his money back?'

'Of course. But there was no rush, no pressure. He was a gentleman. And as for Pete and the Major, that was the real thing. It's a shame the Major was so… uptight, but that's not really his fault is it? Different generation and all that, but it's a shame, Pete would have been so happy to be 'out and proud' with the Major.'

'Do you think Pete could have made a mistake, bought some dodgy oil for example, and unintentionally caused the poisoning?'

Lucy shook her head and then shrugged with a sigh, 'I suppose it's possible. But Pete would never have wilfully put others at risk,' she dabbed her eyes, took a swig on an energy drink and then glared me down, 'what do you think Sam?'

I turned my back on her only to come face to face with her bare breasts in the poster, 'fantastic…I mean he was a fantastic fella. Tell me, when you worked at Pete's was he overly fussy? It's just that, I remember him being very particular about certain things, like the way he handled money.'

'You mean those silly white gloves of his. He always wore those when he worked on the till, called it dirty money.'

And that was it, that was what I needed to hear; a man that careful about germs doesn't change his thinking.

'Thanks Lucy that's great. Look, can you answer one question for me, completely unrelated; why keep the posters? If you wanted to turn your back on it all, why the reminders?'

She smiled but her eyes were downcast; 'Remembering where you've been can be useful. Especially if you don't want to go back.'

'Right… I don't suppose you have any spare copies of this one, do you? It's a personal favourite.'

The crushed can hit me just below my right eye.

I left 'Fitterdykes' very quickly, sweatier but wiser. I was convinced of Pete's innocence, a man who fears dirty money, doesn't run a slovenly kitchen, and isn't likely to buy dodgy oil. Somebody had set him up. The question was who, because whoever it was, they were ultimately responsible for China Pete's death.

West Street doesn't come alive until the evening, so I had to think where else to dig around. There was only one place to go, to the man that knew China Pete best. I made my way to the Grove, knocked on the door and waited. The Major's ability to get around had been severely curtailed since his beating, but eventually the old oak door creaked open and there he was, a much-diminished man.

'Sam? What a pleasant surprise, good to see you,' the Major lied. The poor sods' eyes were read raw, 'come on in. Would you like a cup of tea?'

I followed his unsteady steps into the kitchen – which was still pretty much a wreck – and watched, as the Major busied himself with a kettle on a small camping stove.

'I'm sorry for your loss Major. We all liked China Pete, nobody in town's got a bad word to say about him. How you holding up?''

'Thank you Sam, it's been hard… my own fault really, I spent so long insisting Pete and I were discreet, afraid of what people would say. And now, nobody says anything, because nobody knew.'

'Luke and I are looking into it Major; we'll get to the bottom of it, I can promise you that.' I accepted a chipped mug of tea and watched the Major settle himself at the kitchen table. He moved as if everything hurt, which I'm sure was true on many levels, 'I've spoken to Lucy, and she told me that Pete went up against the Lodge for her. I'm just wondering was there more history, bad blood, between Pete and the Lodge?'

'I've been thinking about that too,' the Major said, slumping over the table, 'did I bring this down upon him? Is it my fault? Me and that stupid box. But it's true, Pete did make a point of objecting to every Lodge planning application. And I mean everything, extensions, repairs. But he complained about everybody, he even took the council on once, complained about the plumbing in their own building, said it was a health risk to public health, which seems ironic now. I think it's fair to say, he enjoyed defying authority.'

'Were any of his objections ever upheld?'

'Not that I recall. Although when the Lodge applied to extend their storm cellar, he did force them to bring in an independent structural engineer. He accused the council of being in their pocket; the application still went through but it must have doubled their costs. It was his greatest triumph. I've never seen him so happy.'

I felt a domino drop, but what it signified I wasn't sure, but at least there was something there I could follow-up on, 'that's helpful Major thanks. What are you going to do?'

'Do? I'm seventy-six years old Sam, I don't do. I just wait for the inevitable. But if you could prove Pete's case… I would be very grateful. Truly grateful.'

'I'll do my best Major.'

'Thank you Sam, and if you're right, if they are behind this, would you do me the favour of bringing me their heads on a spike.'

'Can't see a problem with that Major.'

I let the Major drone on for an hour or so, without really listening to a word, and then offered my condolences again, before making my way across town to The Church Café. A place of solace, where they still exchange food for real money rather than plastic, and the tables have clean cotton cloths, and the milk is fresh and not from the far-off land of UHT. I needed brain food, but the kippers were all gone, so I had the vegetarian breakfast, which might surprise you, but being a taxidermist can do that to you; I haven't been able to put fatty tissue anywhere near my mouth for twenty years. I pay a high price for my art.

The serenity of the Café gave me time to think, time to contemplate the situation. The Lodge looked like a sound bet to me, but I couldn't rule-out narked former employees, or his competitors working with or independently of the Lodge. Both were equally possible but given the good vibe all and sundry had about the man, both seemed unlikely and yet the competition angle – meaning good old money, avarice and greed – seemed more probable. I did consider dropping by the local paper to see if their archives had any info on past spats between the West Street purveyors of foreign foods; perhaps someone held a grudge; but at that point I happened to look across the room and saw a blue rinse perm reading the local tomes latest edition.

Local Man's Suicide
After Mass Poisoning Charges

Not the catchiest of headlines. Nor was it open-minded reasoning. They'd clearly made up their minds. Trying to fit actual investigative journalism between coupons, advertisements and deaths can't be easy. I ordered another pot of tea and re-considered the situation. Who would have all the low-down dirty news about what was going on in West Street? I took one sip of tea and then accepted the inevitable. I was back at Fast Luke's in five minutes flat.

A sweaty young black man dressed in nothing but a smile opened the door; 'Can I help you?' He seemed pleased to see me; certain parts of him much more than others.

'You know I could have been the police or a Girl Scout.'

'But you're not, unless you want to be,' he purred.

'Good grief, is Luke in or not?'

Luke appeared in the doorway, put his finger to my lips, grabbed my coat sleave and hurried me inside. Luke led me towards the kitchen, I watched him pass through the beaded curtain, but held my ground – I was in no mood for more surprises.

'Sam what are you doing? Get in here!' Luke snapped; I did as I was told, 'I believe you've met, Dr Rapper.'

'M.D Rapper,' the young man corrected, as he passed through the curtain and stood beside me, butt-naked watching the kettle boil.

'Sorry yes,' Luke sighed, 'that's M.D. Rapper. It's stands for Mighty Di…'

'I don't want to know what it stands for Luke. I've been to see the Major, I think the Lodge could be behind this.'

'Was there ever any doubt? So tell me what you've discovered.'

'Nothing we didn't know, everyone loved Pete but the Lodge. Not a bad word was said. Some say he might have bought dodgy oil, but I doubt it. He was too fastidious for that. Lucy told me she borrowed money from him, and that Pete stood up to the Lodge when she started up the gym. He also objected to them expanding their storm cellar which cost them money.'

Luke coughed and raised an eyebrow, 'that last bit again.'

'It was something the Major said, the Lodge wanted to expand their storm cellar, and Pete made the council bring in independent engineers. It must have cost them a pretty penny.'

Luke slapped his face and opened a cupboard door, to reveal a rainbow assortment of calling cards and Post-it notes stuck to the back of the door. He plucked one and handed to me; 'Look at this…'

BERNARD TEACHER: CIVIL ENGINEER.

I felt my legs give and had to steady myself against the kitchen counter to stop myself swan diving onto the pink tiled floor.

'Lucy's house is in Pump Square, which means it almost backs onto the Temple doesn't it.'

'I guess so,' I was too befuddled to think geography, 'it's certainly close-by.'

'I wonder. I've been thinking real-estate Sam, but maybe it's about access rather than land.'

I tried to follow Luke's line of thinking, but heard nothing but the echo of a dying lightbulb; 'so what's that got to do with China Pete?'

Luke placed his hands behind his head – I had no idea he shaved his armpits, 'Revenge, pure and simple, maybe he'd become too big a thorn for them to ignore. We're not dealing with rational individuals here Sam, look

175

what they did to your Dotty. And you saw Hooms in that velvet jacket, does that look like a rational decision to you?' Luke lifted his teacup and drained it dry, 'listen carefully, the Lodge doesn't take being crossed lightly, even more so when it comes to money; Pete underestimated their bile and their bite. We can't do the same. If we start digging around in their business, they're not going to like it. If we go in, I can't guarantee success, or safe waters once the deed is done. We might be starting something… both of us may come to regret.'

I had seldom seen Luke's painted face so sober or serious. I'm sure neither of us knew where our trail would take us, but looking back, I'm sure my decision was the biggest mistake of my life.

'Screw it, it's what China Pete would have wanted.'

Luke lent forward and kissed my cheek; 'Bless you Sam. Now then,' he exited the room with a flourish, returning moments later, unravelling the underground map of Broston. 'An extension you say? Let's look at this again. You came out from the tunnel at Worm Gate, so we know there's a link between there and Church Street… so what if there's a tunnel, or should we say, the Lodge needs to create a tunnel, for whatever reason, between their flood cellar and Worm Gate?' Luke laid the map on the kitchen table, grabbed a wooden spoon from a draw and began measuring out the distance between the two points. 'It's less than five-hundred yards between the two points. If you're following a natural fissure, you might only have to clear half that distance, maybe less.'

My right foot was starting to tingle, as the memory of a wet sucking heat, pushed its way to the front of my head, 'Luke, why is Worm Gate called Worm Gate?'

'It's an ancient name, it usually indicates an old pagan site; which might be why the church is built where it is.' I must have looked as unsettled as I felt, 'what's the matter Sam? You look positively peaky.'

'Something took my boot. And it wasn't a sodding mutant rat.'

'Alright Sam, we'll keep clear of Worm Gate, forget all about Worm Gate. Let's focus on the other side of the seawall. The point is the Lodge clearly have better information about subterranean Broston than we do; but something's happening beneath West Street and China Pete got wind of it, so they shut him up.'

My mind domino did a double flip, 'Scrape? You think their making Scrape down there.'

'It's got to be hasn't it. The run-off comes from the west side. But there's only one way to prove it. We have to go under West Street.'

I felt my face turn from phlegm green to paper white, 'And by we, you mean me.'

'Yeah, I do. It's up to you Sam. I can't make you do this… but it's this or forget all about China Pete's reputation. And Scrape production goes on unchecked; god knows how much they're making down there… Think about the future Sam, all those dead dogs, too many for even you to stuff. And Dotty's killers keep getting richer and richer… are you going to let that happen Sam? What do you say Sam?'

I'll tell you what I say now; what a manipulative bastard!

It was nearly midnight and West Street was humming with the delights of antisocial sociability. By the look of things, they'd be another busy night in A&E. A very, very busy night if I had anything to do with it. The usual hustle-bustle and brawls were perfect cover as far as I was concerned. Nobody was paying attention to the Bill Sykes look-a-like dipping down a side alley for a piss. Once I was in the shadows, I climbed over the iron gates that barred the way to the council's private carpark, and followed the smell, that led me to the buildings infamously inadequate drains. I pulled the manhole cover aside and unleashed a stink that was ripe, rank and wretched. A sewage outlet pipe ran into the hole less than two feet from the surface – very poor planning – I could just about make out the bottom of the shaft, no more than six feet below. My nose hairs withered in protest. I took off my backpack, dropped it into the stink, and then went in after it.

Once at the sludgy bottom I could see a brick lined tunnel, running off to the right, underneath West Street as Luke predicted. I took a pencil torch from my pocket and put it in my mouth, and began crawling through an inch of fetid sludge, pushing my backpack before me. It was cold hard going and every movement made something unsightly but thankfully unseen squelch and squirt beneath me. It was horrible, and about three metres in things got worse, the stuff started dripping on me, and rolling through my hair and into my ears. It was all I could do not to add my vegetarian lunch to the mire. I must have crawled through that filth for thirty minutes before I reached the end of the tunnel; and saw light.

The space before me was at least twelve feet high, and strung with a web of suspended lamps, fixed to a skeleton of mud blackened wooden props. Plastic pipes of differing colours and sizes crisscrossed the cavern like limp mouldy spaghetti, whilst an older earthenware pipe that lay in the crook of the crossed supports, had been smashed open. A thick grey pus oozed from it; no doubt a mix of mouldy lard and cooking fat provided by West Street's ecologically unscrupulous kitchens. It was like watching boils burst in slow motion. As I watched, a man wearing an official council reflective jacket, filled a bucket with the stinking gloop, and then stepped out of my line of sight. I shifted my position and saw there was a human chain running through the skeleton of struts, passing the slop buckets down the line to a battered cattle trough.

And this is where my tale takes a hard left; and following it becomes an act of faith; I don't have a scientific definition for what I saw, because there isn't one, believe me I've checked my oven and the library, there is no name for what I saw, other than monster.

It was a huge lard coloured worm, pressed tight between floor and ceiling, and was as wide as it was high; of its length I couldn't say, because its end disappeared into the cavern's darkness. I watched as the workers emptied bucket after bucket in front of the beast. The vile mush was then sucked up by the beasts quivering, tremulous lips with a tremendous slurp that sounded so familiar it made my toes curl. It was a sound that a frightened person in a tight pinch could mistake for a thousand scampering rats; and those lips certainly had enough suction to pull your favourite totector boots from your feet. I think it's safe to say I'd found the worm of Worm Gate. A noise came from the back of the cavern, a wild desperate whine, followed by a maddened bark. It was a small mongrel, something out of a Jack Russell via a Corgi. It was dragged across the floor by the Lodges' bullyboys, Morris and Monk. As they grew nearer the lard monster began to vibrate, and a grey green goo oozed from its skin. The attending workers rushed forward and scraped the goo from its mass, collecting it in fresh unsullied buckets. As I watched Morris picked up the pissing pooch and tossed it in front of the creature. The dog snarled in terror and curled itself into a ball. The worm's lard lips reached out for it. The dog snapped and bit and bit again, but the lips kept coming, enveloping its

180

head, body and hindquarters; with a final slurp the tail disappeared inside the pulsating gelatinous maul. I crawled backwards down the tunnel and vomited until I could feel my toenails scratching my throat. Which of course meant I had to crawl through my own puke to get a second look – at least it was warm. I slid out of the tunnel and ducked behind a wooden prop that was as broad as my shoulders. From my new vantage point, I could see a table had been set out to one side of the lard worm. I could see there were men sitting at the table, but I couldn't see what they were doing. I had to get closer. I spotted a pile of broken bricks on the other side of the cavern. It was a good spot, but I'd have to cross a well-lit area to get there.

I bit my lip and slid across the divide, through light and shadow and light and then thankfully, I arrived unnoticed, behind the crumbling bricks. Crouching low, I watched as workers with ditching spades dug into the side of the feeding beast. They pulled squirming red and blue lumps from its flesh, which were then taken across the cavern and tossed into what looked like an old cider-press, Once the press was filled, two workers lowered a wooden lid down a thick metal screw and began turning a hefty looking metal bar down its thread, lowering the press. A silver green fluid oozed from its base. The reflective jackets collected this in more virginal buckets, and these were presented to the men at the table, who hurriedly tested the goo with pipets and an assortment of bottled chemicals. This done, the stuff was then ladled through funnels into very expensive looking champagne bottles. These were corked, wrapped in foil, and stacked in crates.

181

There must have been fifty bottles or more filled by the time they'd finished.

As the show seemed to be coming to a close, I decided to back out the way I'd come. But somehow, I missed judged the angle, and ended up behind a different mud-covered prop. And there they were; three discarded, commercially sized, cans of 'Good Flower Cooking Oil,' - if shouting 'EUREKA,' wouldn't have got me killed I would have done it. Contaminating China Pete's restaurant with the filth from this horror show, would have been a piece of piss. Maybe he'd unwittingly bought it from them, maybe they'd smuggled it in via a connecting tunnel; I couldn't say, but one thing was for sure, Pete would never have bought it if he knew where it had come from … who would?

I reached into my sodden backpack, and removed a small digital camera, and tried to remember the rushed lesson Luke had talked me through; turn on, point, press – I did it all, and the flash lit me up like a flare. The cavern fell silent. But not for long; 'Who's there? Who is it? Show yourself,' it was that bastard's Morris' voice, I'd know that swine anywhere.

As the torch beams focused on my hiding place, I reached into the bag and pulled out Monkey Scarf – I'll never leave home without it again.

I charged in, screaming, swinging Monkey Scarf high and wild. Some jackets fled; some fell but a few had the guts to hold their ground; bloody idiots. Three went down with one swipe. I stomped another with both feet. Drove the camera into the next one's jaw and lashed another two with the business end of Scarf before they knew what hit them. And then came the second wave, buckets and spades raised, ready for action. I went low, swinging Monkey Scarf with both hands. I shattered three knees and then the spades came down. The first blow hit my shoulder and nearly knocked me off my feet, the second swung for my head. I blocked it with Monkey Scarf's linked end and delivered a boot to the guys happy-sacks; down he went. Another wild swing came in from my left, skimming the top of my head. I dropped and lashed-out, taking out the guy's legs, and then I was up and running. But two tossers dived at me from the darkness. One caught my right arm, the other caught my elbow in his teeth. I rolled forward sending my opponent sprawling across the floor. This attracted the attention of the white worm. It lurched forward, crushing struts and pipes in its hurry to get into the action. Its lips flapped and shuddered as it desperately sought to find food. Everybody else in the fight scattered, leaving me and my wrestling buddy alone. Flailing about in the filth, trying desperately to get to his feet. The poor guy didn't see the worm until it was almost upon him. And when he saw it; he didn't have time to scream. The lips closed around his head; there was a deep rumbling slurp; and he was gone.

The falling lights and shattering props were sending sparks and thunderous echoes across the cavern. This must have startled the just fed beast, as it suddenly retracted along its segmented body, and hurled itself backwards into the darkness at an astonishing speed. I took in the scene. It was mayhem; splitting pipes, toppling props and falling rocks; there could be no doubt, the whole lot was coming down. There was no way I was going to make it back to the sewer tunnel. I had no choice. I sprinted after the beast and into the darkness.

The tunnel was round, smooth and covered in slime; I struggled to get any traction, I landed on my face twice, before switching to a tottering skating stride. Ahead of me an ever-diminishing ball of grey light raced on. I dug in my chin and raced after it. I lost sight of the glow for a moment and was immediately pitched into total darkness. I drove on and then the tunnel took a deep dive. My feet slid beneath me; I was going to topple at any second. I folded Monkey Scarf in two, held it against my chest and dived forward, hoping the precious skin would hold. It's as close to tobogganing as I ever want to get. One second I was gaining on the beast's glow, even in danger of embedding myself in its arse end; and then it was gone, vanished; and I was falling through darkness. I dove into a wall of freezing water like a diving gannet. I hit bottom and was enveloped in a cloud of green, black filth that wrapped itself around my legs; I was in the inlet river and the mud had me. If I'd let it settle, it would never have let me go. I twisted backwards and forwards, kicking hard, fighting the suction that was pulling me down; I broke free with my lungs screaming, I swam upwards, fighting the urge to breathe. I saw lights shimmering above me and fought my way towards them. I broke surface and threw myself onto my back, gasping for air. To my right I saw the slime grey face of the sea wall; sighting an embedded iron ladder; I made for it. I caught a rung with my numb hands; and with the last of my strength pulled myself, and the blessed Monkey Scarf, out onto the tidal river wall.

'You alright there duck?' an unseen male voice enquired, 'you shouldn't go messing about in there you know, you could get washed out to sea.'

'I know…' I panted, 'I know. I was night fishing, got pulled in by a fish. A pike I think, long and thin…a real big bastard.'

'A pike in these waters? I don't think so duck, that's sea water that is, that weren't no pike. Maybe a Conger Eel?'

The sky was beginning to swim with colours, as the world caved in about me like a wet cake, 'Maybe, maybe but I'll tell you this much… bang a gong…'

The next day, China Pete's supporters were called to a meeting at the 'Oriental Cat,' Vic the Pole arrived with an iced cake and the local rag's free edition:

Twelve Council Workers Killed in Mystery Blaze.

It was accurate but several thousand miles short of the truth as usual.

Although I'd proved Luke's suspicions about Scrape production beneath West Street, and that there must be a passageway between West Street and Worm Gate for the beast to access both sides of the inlet; Luke was struggling to grasp the greater truth of the matter, namely that a monster lived beneath the town of Broston; 'No darling I don't doubt the existence of a monster, but a worm? A bloody great worm. Are you having a laugh darling? No, it can't be a worm. In old English Worm means snake. It can't be a worm.'

'I know my animals Luke. Snakes don't have segments or slime. I know, I've mounted a couple.'

'But a bloody worm. That's so… uncool. A snake, an eel even, I could accept an eel, but a worm. Typical bloody Broston, so bloody provincial, it can't even get itself a proper monster. It's appalling. It's too much. Too much.'

'Without the camera, we'll never prove any of it,' Lucy sighed, 'and we'll never clear China Pete's name.'

'Don't worry, I'll make sure that all that knew him hear the truth,' Kim Chung nodded wisely, 'and now we can protect each other from attacks from below.'

'We shall warn everybody against using their Good Flower Oil,' Raj insisted with a raised fist, 'and the next time the Lodge want takeaway service, they'll eat my shit.'

Major Turney called for silence with a rap on the table, as he struggled to his feet, 'Sam I thank you. You've done this town a great favour. Once again, we've discovered that the Lodge has been at the bottom of this town's ills. I'm sure with this evil sounding worm driven out to sea, you have cut-off a foul and lucrative venture the Lodge will not soon recover from… we thank you Sam. Next time, next time I'm sure you'll get their heads.'

'No,' Luke said sternly, slapping the table with the sleeve of his kimono, 'no, I'm not having it. A worm? A bloody giant worm. It makes me sick to my stomach, no class, no class at all. Kim, bring me half a pint of Surgical Orange and a straw,'

NB:

Just so you know, Nigel the Lion is back on display in the library and looks great. I will always be grateful to Nigel and his first taxidermist for opening my eyes to one fact; you can only judge a man by his deeds, and any man who values his deeds should be judged fairly.

Chapter 5

THE BIG SHEEP

I'd been sitting in the car at the end of Red Lion Street for three hours, when the inevitable bad luck turned up. It announced itself with a sharp knock on the driver's window. The officer signalled; 'roll the window down,' but I couldn't, they were electric, and I didn't have the car keys. I waved and then gave him the thumbs up. It clearly wasn't enough. I opened the door.

'Evening Sir,' his voice was polite but as taut as his grin, 'is this your car Sir?'

'No, I can't say it is, officer.'

'Whose car is it then Sir?' his voice dropped a tone.

'A friends', I'm keeping an eye on it for him. The door doesn't lock. Not a good idea in this neighbourhood.'

'And what is this friend's name?' if his voice was to get any tighter, he was going to do his larynx a mischief.

'Billy the Prawn, although it might be in Fast Luke's name.'

'Fast Luke, he's a friend of yours is he?'

'Isn't he everybody's friend? I know he'd like to think so.'

'Step out of the car please Sir,' he ordered; clearly Luke was not considered everybody's friend.

'I'd rather not.'

'And why's that Sir?'

'You're really not my type.'

Ten minutes later I was sitting in the cop-shop, as a bullnecked Minotaur in a white shirt and black tie required of me a song, but how could I sing the Lord's song in a strange land? It was impossible, I didn't know the words.

'Do you understand your rights as they've been read to you?'

'Can't say that I do?

'Why not?' Bull spat.

'Can't say I recall them being read.'

Bull glared at the arresting officer, but it was pure pantomime, I didn't believe any of it. I knew I was being played.

'Perhaps your memory's not so good. Shall I remind you of them now?'

'Not much point, I'm afraid my English isn't what it should be? Never finished school you see.'

Bull dropped his pen and levelled a deliberately vicious glare in my direction, 'what are you talking about? There's nothing wrong with your English.'

'But I figure there's got to be something wrong with my England. Since when, has it been okay to haul a guy into a police station, for sitting in a friend's car?'

'I'm reminding you, whatever you say may be used in evidence against you.'

'Go ahead, use it. See what good it does you.'

'Okay, okay,' Bull chuckled, a sound not dissimilar to ducklings being torn apart by a lawnmower, as he lifted his bull sized butt from the relieved chair, 'enough, enough, enough already. Look Sam, can't we just sort this out, without all the usual bollocks?'

'Fine by me. Who needs more bullocks, I mean bollocks.'

Bull slowly lumbered around to my side of the desk, Bull by name, bull by nature. I braced myself for the goring. 'Let's get this sorted now, before things get out of hand. Steve…' he called, 'bring us some tea.'

'Black, no milk or urine for me Jeeves.'

'Sam, please, please… Tell me, what were you up to? Sitting in that car, outside that address… pretty, pretty please.'

Here's the truth, it was a private matter and I meant to keep it that way. Robin, my veterinarian friend, had been called out to a stable on the previous night. He was waylaid by masked ruffians. His wallet was lifted along with his supply of Ketamine. The call had been a hoax to lure him out, the whole thing was a set-up. If folks what to snort horse sedatives that knacker their bladders, well that was their business; I'd rather they did that, than that goddamned awful Scrape; but the beating Robin received was out of order. I wasn't going to sit by and let that go. No one gets away with unnecessary violence against a friend of mine. Especially a professional friend who's supplied me with some very challenging and profitable work. I figured I owed Robin some justice, and his assailants some vengeance. A little taste of Monkey Scarf would've done the trick, but like I said that was my business, and Bull didn't need to know.

'Like I said to your storm-trooper, I was watching a friend's car, as he had an errand to run.'

'I see… sticking to that are we?' Bull's mono-brow was holding back a wave of sweat. I swear I could smell a

190

hint of corned beef in the air, 'so you weren't watching the drug den across the road then?' his face broke into a repellent grin.

I felt my rug of righteous indignation being ripped from beneath me, but I decided to bareface it; 'Perhaps...maybe; someone's got to do it, you buggers are doing precious little about it.'

He nodded slowly, a head that big must be difficult to move quickly, 'That's a point of view; just as long as you weren't thinking about taking the law into your own hands, again.'

I tried not to look as caught-out and non-plussed as I felt.

'We know you visited Mr Stainton at the hospital, and you're a bit handy aren't you Sam? Which is why Luke likes to keep you around, you're his go to heavy.'

I decided not to bite; 'Like I said I was looking out for a friend's interests.'

'Checking out the competition more like. Is Fast Luke looking to expand his grimy empire?' Bull's smirk dissolved as his eyes narrowed, 'you were parked right in front of our observation van, you turkey.'

'The blue transit?'

He nodded as two cups of tea arrived, 'so this is what I want you to do Sam, have a sip of your drink, and then bugger-off back to Fast Luke and tell him Detective Bull says hello and butt out.'

It was my turn to nod.

The drug bust made the local TV news that evening. A huge haul was reported, other charges were expected to follow. I can't easily explain why I felt so crestfallen, after

191

all the good guys had won and the bad guys had gone down. The truth is, I'd been found out; shown to be a meddling amateur by a real cop. It all confirmed my suspicion that I was indeed a lousy Private Dick. You could say I'd lost my taste for dick but that sounds wrong, so let's just say the gum on my shoe had finally lost its flavour; either way both metaphors were equally hard to swallow.

I returned to the day job, seeking solace in my craft. Dad always said being busy is the best therapy, and I'm inclined to believe him, but being a professional taxidermist is a famine or feast way to live. If you get work in a museum or restoring a private collection you can have years of work before you; but if you don't, you can spend hours searching for roadkill to make interesting badger displays, that you've then got to sell at backwater country fairs. I didn't have any museum connections. I work mostly on commission, but I also had a freezer full of semi squashed badgers, and my commissions were as cold and flat as they were. Personally, I wasn't fairing any better, there was no doubt about it, I was cheesed off, Stinking Bishop style. I was doing a good job of feeling sorry for myself when the shop front bell chimed, and the Bull steamed into my workroom.

'Twice in one day, people will talk Bull.'

'Taxi Sam, my main man,' – I hate it when cocks quote T-Rex, and it sounded very wrong coming from Bull's blabbering chops. He was dressed in grey sport sweats, the seams of which could barely contain his revolting form. The man had to be a throwback to a mythical time, or a medical experiment gone wrong. If he

192

ever decided to leave the police force, he'd find a lucrative future in wrestling greased hippos.

'Are you lost? The gym's down the road. You should check out 'Fitterdykes,' I know you'd fit right in.'

'This is where the magic happens ah?' he stated in a Lord of the Manor stance.

'No this is where I pretend to work; my castle and dungeon are out back.'

Bull held up his spade sized hands and spat into his palms, 'I need you to come with me. So how's it going to be, hard or easy?'

'You've seen too many cop shows Bull, I'm working here. These Chihuahuas don't skin themselves you know.'

'Come on. It's important. I'm not dicking around. I need your help. I've got some bigwigs waiting to see you. It's about that drug bust, we need your help Sam. What about it, you want to help out the good guys or what?'

I shut up shop.

We both crammed into Bull's tiny red VW Golf and were soon heading out of town at a brisk pace – with the shock absorbers wincing at every dint and bump. Out beyond the river we went, out into the vegetable fields that had turned this county's mud into money for centuries. The flat lands where crows go to be lonely, and potholes are landmarks. At one very much like the next junction we took a sharp left and headed towards a collection of mud coloured farm buildings. Bull punched the car horn, and as it weakly bleated its submission, the front doors of an old onion warehouse opened, and then closed behind us. I heard the car sigh with relief as Bull squeezed from the passenger seat; 'Behave yourself Sam,' he almost whispered as he closed his door. I could only follow.

Three darkly dressed serious looking men were waiting for us. I thought I was in for a medieval style interrogation; hot pokers and flayed skin; followed by a shallow grave. My face must have betrayed my thoughts, because the older of the three men, a broad chested guy with greying temples quickly stepped forward and offered me his hand; 'Don't look so worried Sam, can I call you Sam? I'm D.I Sims, Special Intervention Unit, pleased to meet you. This is D.S Hobbs and Mr Rawlings our tech guy. Thanks for agreeing to meet us.'

'I wasn't aware I had. What is this about?'

'Nothing's been explained?' Sims was a good foot shorter than Bull but he gave the man a look that would have withered a statue, 'well your presence is optional. But I think you'll want to help us. If I may explain the situation, and if you don't want to cooperate, Detective Bull will buy you lunch and give you a ride home with our thanks.'

'Happy to,' Bull confirmed, but there was more saving face than grace in the tone of his reply.

'So…would you have a look at this for us?' Sims pointed to a canvas dust sheet, 'Mr Rawlings if you'd do the honours.' Rawlings, a flat-faced man whose eyes seemed to cross the bridge of his nose; gently laid aside the dust sheet.

'What do you think?' Sims asked.

'It's a sheep.'

'It's a stuffed sheep,' Sims confirmed.

'We don't say stuffed in the trade. And if you want to be pedantic about it, it's actually a ram…a bloody big ram.'

Professional interest got the better of me; I got down on my knees and inspected the brute. By my estimate the work was at least a hundred years old; definitely no later than 1920, and it was top quality work. The taxidermist had really captured the animals formidable bearing and presence, although the two-foot tear in the underbelly had certainly buggered the overall aesthetic.

'Here's the deal Sam. You've heard about the raid on the drug house, well despite what you've heard, the evidence we've got on them is pretty thin, and they've got a good lawyer and some heavy backing. Which means they're going to be out on bail, back on the streets and back to their old tricks by nine o'clock tomorrow morning. But we can make that work for us, they're small fry, and we want to move up the food chain, nab the suppliers, and we think you can help us do that, with this sheep.'

'How's that then?'

'First things first, can you repair it by seven tomorrow morning?'

I couldn't help but laugh. The damage was extensive, but certainly not out of my reach; I'm bloody good at what I do. 'Sure I could, but what's this got to do with the drug bust?'

'We found it during the raid. It's how they smuggle the dope from town to town.'

'In a stuffed sheep?!' I cracked-up again; 'Are you having me on?'

'No Sam, we're not. We found six kilos of cocaine in its belly. And that's too much for the small-time hoods we've got in the cells. We figure there's a major distributor gagging to get his stash back, and when he does, we want to grab him.'

'But in a sheep?' It was the daftest thing I'd ever heard. 'What's wrong with suitcases?'

'But that's the point,' Sims insisted, 'who'd believe a sheep was hauling drugs? And what would you say if you were stopped, I'm taking it to an antiques shop, a county fair, a museum. You know how people are about antiques, who's going to look at this and think drug cartels? This is big time dealing Sam, big time crooks, real nasty bastards.'

'So, what do you want me to do? Just stitch it up?'

Rawlings knelt beside me; he really did have the flattest face I've ever seen, 'I'd like to fit a bugging device under the skin, a tracker and perhaps a camera in one of its eyes if it's possible.' His voice was thin, excitable and rapid. The kind of voice you expect to come out of someone talking about collectable Star Wars figures or ancient episodes of Dr Who. 'I can adjust my camera for a convex lens if I need to, but I wasn't sure if the entire eye was spherical or if the colour tone is likely to be consistent throughout? And I'd need room for an ariel which we could run down one leg, if that's possible, is it possible Sam, what do you think?'

I looked to Sims for guidance, 'how many questions was that?'

'We need it back where we found it by eight o'clock tomorrow morning, well before the scumbags are released, can you do it? Name your price.'

'What about the drugs?'

D.S Hobbs opened a case, revealing six tightly wrapped rectangles; 'It goes back where it came from. They pass it up the chain. We catch them red-handed, job done.'

'Five hundred quid says they'll never know it's been touched,' I touted.

'Done,' Sims grinned, 'get Rawlings' camera in there and I'll double it.'

Somehow, Bull, Rawlings, the sheep and I squeezed into the VW and made it back to my workshop. Bull had enough sense to piss-off and leave us to it, and so, Rawlings and I set to work. This wasn't an entirely comfortable experience for me. I'd grown accustomed to working alone and Rawlings' flat face freaked me out, every time I looked at him, I thought about the roadkill in my freezer.

'I must say this is fascinating work, I didn't know people still did this?' he squeaked.

'Did what Rawlings?'

'Frank, please call me Frank, I didn't know people still stuffed animals.'

I gave flat-faced Frank a cold hard glare, 'I don't stuff animals Frank, that would be wrong and cruel. I preserve dead animals. I preserve their skins, their colour their texture, their form. It's not like stuffing a turkey.'

'No offense, I admire your craft…what's all that sawdust for?'

'That's woodwool, it's for stuffing. So how much space is this camera going to need?'

'Hardly any, it just needs to stay where I put it. That's the important bit.'

'Shouldn't be too much of a problem,' I inserted my arm in the cavity, 'the things actually held in shape by a wooden frame, so there's plenty of space. You could fix the battery and the wiring along the neck, then run the camera up to the eye. It's just a convex lens, held in place with a stud and a leather lace.'

'Good, I can drill a hole through the centre of the pupil, the tip of the camera's black, so I doubt they'll notice.'

I was impressed, 'sounds good. The horns are hollow you could fit a curled cable in those, that any good to you?'

'Great idea,' he beamed like a joyous bulldog, 'this should be fun.'

'Then all I've got to do is stitch and glue. So which eye do you want for the camera?'

'Let's go with the right.'

I tossed him the glass eye which he inspected closely; 'Nice work, looks handmade, can I use your vice?'

'Depends on what you're into Frank.'

'Pardon?'

'Nothing, help yourself Frank.'

Now it was my turn to watch and learn. Frank drilled a cavity into the back of the eye, fitted a metal cylinder that was thinner than a pencil into the hole, which he then attached to a 9-volt battery, the man had skills. 'So Sam, how'd you get into this line of work?' he asked with his arm inside the rams neck.

'It was my dad's business. But it's all I ever wanted to do.'

'Kind of an unusual thing to get into though, what was the first thing you stuffed?'

'Mounted Frank, we don't stuff, we mount…Fluffy our Jack Russell, he died when I was ten.'

'Wow…that seems kind of harsh.'

'Not really, he was dead Frank. He's still in my shop window, a bit faded and loose at the seams, but I love him.'

Once Frank had the eye and its battery pack and ariel in place, we packed the drugs back into the cavity, along with a small black tracer box attached to each one. 'Can't be too careful,' Frank said, and then I set about the final repairs. Despite my flippant posturing to D.I Sims I knew mending the damage was going to take the rest of the night, definitely a two packs of custard creams job. Having Frank there to make the tea helped but his questions were very distracting. I solved that irritation by placing a large tin of Evostick, and a large jar of Huber's cleaning mixture (petrol, alcohol and turpentine) under a comfortable chair, which I encouraged Frank to utilise. A bit of involuntary solvent abuse never did anyone any lasting harm. Frank was soon purring out the Z's. By five fifty-five the custard creams were gone, and the work was done. At six-thirty Bull and Sims returned, and Sims placed a thousand pounds, in fifty quid notes, into my hand. I let Sims wake Frank up, he was very sleepy.

'Nice working with you Sam, real privilege,' Frank groaned as they eased him into the car, 'man my head's killing me.'

'Too many late nights, get yourself some rest, bye now. You god damned glue sniffing flat-faced bastard.'

I decided to open the shop early. There was plenty to keep me busy. The place needed a tidy, but it always did, so I checked over my tools, swapped some scalpel blades and then looked over some Chihuahua sketches. I had their display to finish, making their little basketball costumes was proving to be more time consuming than I'd expected, but it was going to look cracking. I think it could even have won me a couple of prizes with the Guild. It's funny really…there I was thinking such things, and all the time, unbeknownst, I was hurtling towards a cliff edge.

I thought I heard the dull thud of thunder above the town, but the bit of sky I could see through the shop's front window looked cloudless. I put it down to a sonic boom, there's an RAF base twenty miles down the road and those flyboys get a kick out of buzzing the town. The next thing I knew every alarm in the street was singing out. I stepped outside and saw what everyone else on the street was looking at, a funnel of black smoke twisting in the wind above the town. I did the briefest of mid-air geometry calculations; throwing in trajectory and wind speed, in an attempt to prove myself wrong; but there was no doubting the origin of the smoke.

I jumped on Dad's old bike and was peddling through the gridlocked traffic like a speed freak with half a pound of billy-whiz shoved up his arse. Police cars and

ambulances were screaming out their frustrations as they
fought through Broston's congested thoroughfares; all
headed in the same direction. I took to the pavement and
reached Luke's street in less than five minutes. Smoke and
glass filled the street. Every window on the terrace had
been smashed. Fast Luke's residence of ill repute was
nothing more than a smoking roofless shell. My heart fell
to my knees as a policeman grabbed my arm.

'You can't be here Sir.'

'What happened?'

'We don't know yet, could have been a gas leak,
now come on, get out of here.'

And then I saw it, a prostrate smoking shape sinking
into the deflating form of the white rabbit; the
unmistakable remains of the burnt and twisted
hindquarters of a still smouldering sheep.

I sat on the floor of 'Fitterdykes,' sipping something
a lying bastard drinks machine called chicken soup. It
tasted like sage flavoured shit, which is how I felt, but
without the sage. Not even the sight of Lucy Biggerdyke,
the queen of my lust, resplendent in a purple leotard, could
shift my mind from the image of that smoking sheep.

'We shouldn't presume the worst Sam,' said Lucy
gently, her hand on my shoulder.

'The worst being that I helped build a bomb that
killed my friend.'

'Yeah…that worst,' she was radiant in the midst of
her grief, dreadful in her beauty, and I didn't give a damn,
'we don't know Luke's dead, we don't know it was your
sheep that blew up…'

'Yeah. there must be thousands of exploding sheep in the world. Maybe I should go warn the police, oh no I can't, they're in on it.'

Lucy's sucked in her cheeks, and corrected her bra strap, 'we need to find you a place to lay low until we know what's going on.'

'Great idea, let's call Luke and see if there's room in hell.'

'I know…' Lucy's husky voice was steady and calm, 'we'll put you up at the Indian Queen.'

'Down Dolphin Lane? Are you mad? Can't I stay with you?'

'I'm a known associate. They're bound to check on me, but you'll be safe at the Indian Queen, nobody goes there, unless they really have to. You'd have to be mad to stay there, and they don't think you're mad.'

'No, they think I'm daft.'

'So we've got to be smart, it'll work out Sam, we've just got to be smart.'

'I'm doomed.'

Undercover of dark, cloaked in Lucy's ankle length leather coat, I followed Lucy into the deep shadows of Dolphin Lane.

Now I know I've told you about Dolphin Lane, but let me sketch it out for you again. During the day it's just another narrow seventeenth century street, all pubs and pie shops and doors you don't even notice; but at night those doors open; and then it's the unseemly pulse in the unsightly vein of Broston. The sweat in the groin, the urge that you know you ought to deny. All your guilty pleasures live down Dolphin Lane; and a few darker, rarer examples dwell in the Indian Queen. Most people think it's just another rundown spit-and-sawdust public house, but that's what you're supposed to think; and once you get beyond the doors you can stop thinking and let yourself go.

I kept my head down and the coat collar tight, as we made our way through the public bar, then up a flight of stairs and into the back room of a back room.

'We're in luck Sam, its Slime Night. You'll fit right in,' Lucy smiled, words I'd not heard her say since 'Biggerdyke; Girl with the Golden Fist.'

The room was dimly lit, which was a blessing, because the floor and walls were occupied by a mass of opulent glistening figures. Some were naked, some were barely clad in PVC or brightly coloured Latex. Many of these oddities were crawling on their bellies, across a pink tarpaulin, through an inch of thick soapy green slime; making their way towards a kid's paddling pool, loaded to the brim with phosphorescent yellow goo. As soon as one or two players reached the pool they began squirming about in the stuff, smearing it all over themselves and each other. Many of the naked figures had curved opalescent structures strapped to their backs, some of which were fitted with flashing lights; these I twigged were meant to be snail shells, which meant the PVC clad deviants had to be slugs, which made the utterly naked shell less participants worms. Basically, Slime Night was a lube lovers delight.

'Let's find you a dark corner,' Lucy whispered; but doing so was easier said than done, as there was much swapping of fluids going on in the room's darkest corners.

We eventually found a copulation free nook with a table near the fire escape. 'Okay, Sam you'll be safe here. If anybody offers you a cabbage leaf just say no, and if anybody asks you if you want to play, tell them you're a maggot and you'll take things at your own pace.'

'Good grief, don't tell me you've been here before.'

Lucy shrugged as she pulled on her coat, 'have to come out of my shell sometime Sam. Just keep your head down and… oh yeah, better get naked, you're going to stick out like a sore thumb otherwise. It's all sorted, I've had a word, you can bed down behind the bar when the punters clear out. Just give them a hand clearing up, once the fun is over. There's a shovel and mop behind the bar.'

My face couldn't have hidden my mood if it had been stuck in a paper bag, inside a box in a coal sack, in a darkened room. I started to undress – this was not how any of my Biggerdyke fantasies had progressed.

'Don't worry Sam, remember, just say no to cabbage and you're a maggot, understand, if anybody asks, you're a maggot. Get yourself a beer, you'll feel better. But don't get drunk…not if you value your maggothood.'

Oh the things my eyes beheld that night, corpulent worms merging with glistening slugs, writhing snails enacting hermaphrodite dreams; in pairs, in triples, in seething piles of slimy flesh. What I wouldn't have given for a bucket of salt.

The kids pool had been refilled twice, and the participants were off sipping drinks at the bar, when an aged snail, whose skin was so truncated by time that he would have made a more convincing centipede, approached me with a cabbage leaf in his mouth.

'I've got something for you,' it gargled.

'No thanks, I don't do cabbage, I'm a slug.'

'Really? You look like a big fat juicy worm to me,' it winked with a flurry of tongue and spit, 'never mind I love slugs.'

'No, that's not it. I mean a maggot, I'm a maggot. Now fuck off.'

'Don't get all dicky bird on me ducky. Just passing on a message,' he dropped the cabbage leaf on the table and slithered off to join the reconvening mêlée of wannabe invertebrates. I picked up the cabbage leaf and examined both sides, there was no note or message attached but it did seem to be dotted with a number of tiny perforations. An idea came to me, I needed some light. I strode across the lubricated tarp, and immediately came a cropper and landed with a flatulent splat on my face. The pleasure seeking slimers were clearly enlivened to the scent of fresh meat and began slithering towards me at great speed. A snail with a particularly bright and splendid shell was out in front and closing in. I saw an opportunity. As his slimy hands cupped my thighs, I grabbed the strap of his shell and hoisted myself onto his bloated rump. I pressed the cabbage leaf to his shell and began to read. The twisted bastard was jerking and bucking with such delight that I kept losing my place, but just as he achieved his snot shot, I had it. I slid off the blubbering man-snail and made for the door; 'So long slug fuckers. I'm out of here!'

I grabbed my clothes, slid across the floor and out the door, and up another flight of stairs, which led me to the Queen's garden roof – which is just a poorly lit flat roof where smokers gather in pariah huddles under heated garden parasols. I pulled on my togs in full view of the bemused puffers, climbed up onto the wall and jumped into the darkness.

There were shrieks and gasps, but they needn't have bothered. Being such an antiquated street, all the roofs are interconnected, although at different heights and gradients, so all I did was drop down onto the roof of the slime-fest I'd just fled. I then clambered up another tiled incline, jumped up onto another wall and ran upward along its edge. When I got as far as I could go, I was twelve feet higher than the Indian Queen's garden roof. Then it was my turn to gasp and pant. I knew the gap between my side of Dolphin Lane and the opposite row was narrow, less than two yards, but at that height, it looked a lot wider. I was aiming at a narrow block of darkness above an illuminated street sign advertising, 'Hot Girls All Night.' I was pretty sure there was a low roof with a slight slope above it. Of course, if I'd judged it wrong, I was about to jump into a wall with a long drop to follow. I breathed deep and launched myself across the divide. I hit a very solid wall and then gravity did the rest. Luckily the flat roof was there to catch me. My face was scraped raw, and my nose was broken but at least I kept the use of my legs...what am I talking about it bloody hurt!

Bleeding and shaking and calling gravity a twat, I crawled up onto the adjoining roof and made my way towards a small square window from which flickered a pale light.

'Oh, for crying out loud, you scared the shit out of me?' Fast Luke's cabaret claxon of a voice greeted me as I squeezed into the candle lit attic. Once the candle flame settled, I could see, I was mistaken, it was only Buff Guy 32 and 56, doing their best 'Fast Luke Wannabe.'

'Jesus guys, I thought you were…' At that point what little air I had left in me was expelled by a punch to my kidneys. It had been expertly launched from the shadows by Vic the Pole. I landed at Buff Guy 32's feet and sprayed his shoes with blood.

'Oh Jeez!' he squealed, 'that's disgusting!'

'You is a fucking idiot Sam!' Vic's Tweety Bird voice shrieked, 'you killed Luke, you bloody shitting bastard!' Hearing Tweety Bird use such language, might have been a lot more disturbing, if I hadn't been distracted by the excruciating pain that had been inflicted upon me by a wall, gravity and Vic's sucker punch.

'Hold on,' I groaned, 'give me a moment here,' I pleaded, as I yanked my nose bone back into place, 'whatever you think I did, I didn't do it! Or didn't mean to do it…'

'It was a fucking sheep!' Vic squealed, 'you is the stuffer of sheep!'

'Mount! I mount sheep, I don't stuff them.' A kick connected with my ribs. Perhaps it wasn't the right time to discuss the complexities of taxidermy. 'I didn't know it was a bomb. Obviously, I didn't know. Yes, I stuffed the sheep, but I didn't know it was a bomb. I was set-up by Bull and his buddies. They paid me to stuff the sodding thing. They told me it was for a drug raid!'

Buff Guy 56, stepped between Vic and my ribs, 'Detective Bull? What were you doing with that creep? Who else is involved?'

'Bull and some guy called Sims, Hogg, no Hobbs and Frank Rawlings. Flat-faced Frank built the bomb.'

Buff 56 grabbed my collar and pulled me to my feet, 'what do you know about them, think!'

'I think they were from London, they said they were with the Special Intervention Unit or something?'

'Special Intervention Unit my arse. Bull's a crook. Everyone at the station knows he's as bent as they come. There's no way a high-level team like the Intervention Squad would call a crook like Bull in on a job.'

'They said they were police,' I insisted, 'And Bull is a policeman.'

'They weren't police' Vic spat, 'bloody murdering gangsters is what they bloody is, and you is a bloody idiot Sam.'

'No argument here,' I groaned dejectedly.

Buff Guy 56 wiped my mouth with a rag, 'you look awful, does it hurt?'

I was in mid nod when his left hook bent my nose back the other way.

'I loved that man. You stupid, stupid, hairy twat,' he shouted.

It was time to put things straight, 'Guys leave it out! The next person to touch me, gets beaten to death with their own bowels. Enough! He was my friend too. Do you think, for one minute, that I would knowingly have had anything to do with his death? Luke was the only true friend I had. Yes, I know I was dumb and I'm sorry, but I want to do something about it if I can… okay?' Vic and the Buffs nodded and mumbled at their shoes. 'Now I'd like to put my nose back in place if it's okay with you.'

There was less grind the second time, but more snot and a gush of blood that had both the Buff's gagging. 'How did you know where to find me? Lucy wouldn't have told you.'

'We can see half the town from up here,' Buff Guy 32 said, 'we saw Lucy walking a gorilla in a leather coat down Dolphin Lane, it had to be you didn't it.'

'But why are you up here?'

Buff Guy 56 started to tremble, 'I was in the house Sam. I saw the sheep in the lounge, made a comment about it, and then popped out to get some milk…' he cut-off and stared at his shoes.

'We needed to hide him until we knew who we were up against,' Vic sighed.

'Did you see how the sheep got there?'

'It was just there on the doorstep. I told Luke, you must have dropped it off,' Buff Guy, pushed the tears from his eyes, and turned to face the wall, 'last thing I saw was Luke mounting the sheep with Prawn cheering him on.'

'Prawn too! Ah Jesus no, not the Prawn,' I gulped.

'Yes, remember them that way,' Vic sighed, 'he died doing what he loved. Fruit cake?' Vic held out a plate of sliced dark fruit cake.

'You brought cake?'

'Of course, I had no idea how long we'd be up here, it's best to be prepared.'

I declined, as fruit cake and snotty blood don't mix.

'Luke used to say that bastard Bull gave cocksuckers a bad name,' Buff Guy 32 spat, 'he's so bent he could fuck himself on command. But if he's got back-up, we've got problems.'

I wasn't really following their reasoning; I was too busy wondering if stuffing fruit cake up my nose would stem the flow of blood.

'But why would they do it, why so BOOM?' Vic asked, spitting cake into my face.

'They wanted Luke out of the picture,' I replied, 'and they wanted to put me in the frame. They'll call it a crime of passion. An over dramatic, camp crime of passion.'

'But you're straight Sam, horribly straight. Nobody would ever believe you and Luke were an item, talk about sullying his name.'

'BOOM!' Vic added, sending more crumbs into my face; 'Luke knew too much about too many people. Knowledge can be a dangerous thing…which is probably why you're still alive Sam.'

'Thanks Vic, you're all heart.'

Buff 56 turned to me and gripped my ears, pulling my face close to his, 'now listen sweetie, whoever these people are, they're not fucking around. I need to disappear, and you need to do the same. You know too much, and they can't have you telling what you know. Get out of town and don't hang about.'

'What about Lucy? She's out there trying to dig up some dirt.'

'I'll find Lucy,' Vic swallowed, 'I'll take care of that. You have to leave Sam.'

'I can't go. I need to put this right. And I've got the shop, I can't just walk away.'

'Sam you've got to go, these guys mean business. They're not going to leave a witness hanging around to testify against them.'

'No, I'm staying. Luke was my friend. I owe his killers some vengeance.'

This might surprise you but the only time I ever leave Broston is for the British Taxidermists Guild's annual convention, and that's usually held in Norfolk, which is like Broston lite. Despite all my bellyaching, I actually like where I live. The idea of leaving my home for good was a big deal. I couldn't just walk away. I had attachments, things at home that I needed to deal with, private things, that I couldn't let fall into the hands of strangers.

It was one o'clock in the morning when I crept back into my workshop. I'd cased the place for about an hour before I was sure it was safe to go inside. I went in through the back and gently closed the door, breathing in the familiar stink of home. About a millisecond later, a solid something hit the back of my head and knocked me into a star-spangled darkness.

I heard laughter before I saw the light, and when I saw it, it was too bright and too close.

'Back with us Sam, good lad,' a blurred shape beyond the light chuckled.

'I don't know why you're bothering with the light, I'd know your voice anywhere Bull.'

'Is that right?' I only had a moment to register the voice behind me before a phonebook crashed against the side of my head, 'so who am I?'

'Sims…' the phone book hit the other side of my head, 'you murdering bastards…' it crashed in again, sending flakes of tinsel falling before my eyes, 'why did you do it?'

Sims' face glowered into mine, 'because your friend was scum, and scum needs to be scrubbed out. Harsh measures are needed with resistant stains.'

'You've made it awful easy for us Sam, awful easy,' Bull sneered, he couldn't hold back his glee, 'talk about corroborating evidence. Fuck me, you've done us proud.' His laughter made my skin crawl. 'We really thought we'd have to get creative, spin a bit of a yarn; you know, the rage of spurned bugger boys. But you've laid it all on for us Sam, filled in all the blanks, you sick dumb fucker.'

I let him crow, it gave me time to test the plastic ties around my wrists, they were top quality, no give at all.

Sims gripped my jaw and pushed my head back until my neck crunched; 'And all these chemicals, your prints over everything, your handy work on the sheep and…' His other hand twisted my nose and I screamed. 'Wait, wait quiet now, listen. this is the best bit…and then we found your secret den. The back bedroom, your little shrine, your dirty little secret.'

School yard terror; you know the feeling. The bully has you cornered and there's nothing you can do. Fear and self-loathing. The shame of our own fear, the guilt of defeat. I knew what was coming. The kids point and laugh, and then the school nurse reads your personal diary - in which you declare your undying love for the head-girl - over the intercom system. If you can imagine that, then you might be able to conjure up the razor cold shame and terror that was dry humping my body from head to toe. I knew what they'd found. I knew where they were taking their taunts, and I knew there was no way out.

'A proper Norman Bates aren't you Sam. Look who's here to say hello,' Bull turned the lamp on himself and pulled my father's corpse from the floor. He sat it on his lap and shook it like a doll. 'Say hello Sam, who's been a bad boy then? Gottle of gear Sam, gottle of gear.'

'Leave him alone,' I tried to shout but my voice cracked and withered on my tongue.

'You've got to admire the workmanship,' Sims cackled, 'really you have. You did a much better job than that Norman Bates fella. As I recall his Mum was a real mess, but this is good work. The old man looks a bit peaky but otherwise, it's a real masterpiece, good job Sam.'

I had my reasons, but my reason had deserted me after Dad had died. Later I tried to tell myself it was what he would have wanted, but once the deed was done; what was I supposed to do with his body? What was I supposed to do?

'Don't look so glum chum,' Bull sighed as he wiped away a tear of laughter, 'think of all the work you've saved me. The report writes itself. You're going to be famous Sam. The press love nutters. I wonder what they'll call you?'

'The Taxidermist Killer,' Sims hissed.

'I like it. Can you see the headline?' Bull jeered, 'Local Taxidermist Executes Sordid Lover... with a stuffed sheep and four pounds of Semtex. Daring police raid uncovers his father's stuffed body above his lonely workshop; classic front-page stuff.'

'Hollywood here we come!' Sims roared.

They laughed until they were begging each other to stop. Sims gathered himself, and stood looming above me; 'Now then Sam, this is how it's going to play-out. In an attempt to elude capture and overcome by guilt and shame, or whatever…with the police in hot pursuit, blah, blah, blah, the culprit; heinous bomber and Dad stuffer, jumps into a drain and drowns himself. End of movie. Like it? they'll be writing books about you for years to come. They'll probably put your old man's body on display in Scotland Yard's Black Museum, but you wouldn't want that would you Sam?'

Bull dropped Dad's body at my feet, raised his right leg and placed his heel on Dad's head, 'the psychologists will have a field day with this one,' he laughed and then with a sudden twist, he crushed Dad's skull into the floor.

Until that point they had me beaten, cornered and broken, but all bullies tend to push it too far. Everyone has a breaking point, and they'd found mine and they'd used it against me. Now that the worst was done, they could do no more. I felt the domino in my head begin to spin, and I knew what had to be done; 'It's a cold night to go swimming. I guess I'd better wrap up warm then. Can I have that scarf on the rack behind you?'

Bull stood and searched the coatrack, 'what is this thing?'

'Monkey Scarf. It's half a monkey. I never leave home without it.'

'You're a weird fucker Sam. But it's perfect, the weight of this thing should finish the job nicely,' Bull laughed, 'I'm actually going to miss this guy.'

It was still dark when I was thrown into the boot of Bull's VW. Now their plan was clear enough, but it bears a little explanation. When they talk about drains in Lincolnshire, they don't mean those things you have in your street covered by grates, they mean a field drain which is about twelve metres broad and half as many deep. People die in drains, fisherman fall in, drunks slip in, suicides dive in, and I was next. If the tide is out you fall into shallow water and break your legs, sink into a metre of mud and smother. If the tide is in, then the ice water steals your breath, you sink and drown. The only question is, will your body be washed out onto the salt marshes or be ripped apart by the tide. It was a good plan, but that doesn't mean I liked it.

The car stopped and I was hauled out of the boot. I landed on my poor throbbing face in stinking mud, and was kicked in the side for good measure, before being hauled to my feet by my bound hands; and that really hurts. I could hear the water lapping, so the tide was probably on the turn, but the water was too dark to see, so there was no knowing how deep it was – so there it was, I had one chance or no chance at all.

'It's a bit nippy Sam, you're going to be glad you wore that scarf,' Bull chuckled as he shoved me to the brink of the dark drop.

'So, do you need a push, or are you man enough to jump?'

'Aren't you idiots forgetting something?' I wriggled the fingers of my bound hands, 'that's gonna look odd.'

215

'See that, I said he was a helpful fella,' Bull chuckled as he flashed a penknife past my face, 'don't move. I wouldn't want to hurt you.'

As he stepped in and cut, I bent my knees and pushed backwards making a grab for his nuts. I didn't connect but it spooked him, instinctively he went to push me forward, but I dropped low, and came up fast, grabbing at his groin – and this time I had him – rolling forward I threw him over my shoulder; and down the drain we went.

Hitting cold water, really cold water is like running into a brick wall at speed – and I would know. It hurts everywhere at once and you don't think, you can't think, you just react; you have to get out. I can't say who hit the water first but when I broke surface Bull was beside me, grabbing at my shoulder. He pushed me down and away, and then I was on his back, and down he went, under my feet. He was pulling and punching but he wasn't really fighting me, and I wasn't fighting him. We were both gripped by the same basic drive, to get out of the tearing cold. His hands locked around my ankles and pulled me under, I kicked, I stamped, I thrashed blindly and madly; not trying to hurt him, not thinking anything but; GET OUT. I felt his grip break and drove myself through the water. The water stopped churning, I wasn't going under again and Bull, wasn't ever coming back up.

Which way do you swim in the dark? I had no idea where the bank was or how far away it was, but I heard Sims calling and cursing Bull, and headed towards the abuse. He must have heard my gasps but there was no way he could see who it was making the row.

'Bull is that you, Bull sod it, answer me…Bull!'

I couldn't feel my legs and my arms were going into a flailing seizure, but I forced my hands around the sodden monkey scarf and drove one end into the bank, it sank deep and I hauled myself a foot out of the water. I grabbed the other end of the scarf and using my weight pushed it deep into the mud, and then using what little strength I had left I pulled myself clear of the water and lay there shivering uncontrollably.

'Bull? Damn it Bull answer me…Sam? Is that you Sam? Answer me you bastard,' I heard Sims trudge away through the mud, and then the car door opened and closed, and I heard him laugh.

The beam of the torch hit the water to my left and then swung across the bank; it passed over me twice before Sims finally got a bead on me.

'You lucky git, well it looks like we're out of smart options don't it!' The first bullet skimmed across my back, the second missed my head by inches and plastered my face with mud. I rolled to my left and pulled Monkey Scarf after me. The third bullet nearly parted my hair, but I'd seen the muzzle flash, and launched Monkey Scarf at it, as high and fast as I could. The gun went off again, and then Sims came sliding past me with Monkey Scarf wrapped around his head. He caught my foot as he went into the water. I let him take the shoe, I can always get more totectors – but I was sorry to see Monkey Scarf go.

It took the best part of an hour to climb out of the drain. I thought about ditching the VW in after the bastards, but I couldn't face the walk back to town, not with only one shoe, so I drove to the warehouse where I'd first met the big sheep. Once there my head was as empty of ideas as the warehouse was of sheep.

I tried to think, but it was never my strongpoint, getting warm and dry was more essential. I also had a strong urge to eat custard creams and I really couldn't get past it. My back felt like it was ripped open, my feet were burning with numb cold, my ribs ached, my face was mush, and I hadn't had a custard cream in over twelve hours. The only guy who might be able to work out what was going on, and figure a way out of the mess, was dead, and I'd helped kill him. Soon everyone would know I was a mad bomber that had mounted his own Dad above his shop, which is actually worse than it sounds. They'd have me down as some kind of psycho… and no custard creams. Pain, guilt, cold and no custard creams are not a good combination. And then I knew what I had to do; I had to go see a vet. Robin's veterinary surgery is just outside of town, and would have hot water, medical supplies and possibly custard creams.

The irony of the situation was not wasted on me; there was I contemplating breaking into Robin's surgery and that's how this whole sorry episode had started, with thugs waylaying my friend, irony is a bastard. But when I got there the lights were on inside, so instead of putting in a window, I knocked. Robin answered the door; his face was a road map of bruises, and his right arm was in plaster up to the elbow.

'So, they let you out then,' I observed.

'Sam! What the hell happened to you?'

'Much the same as happened to you. I need custard creams.'

Robin looked me up and down and then checked the street, 'you better come in. What have you been rolling in? You stink.'

'I fell into a drain with some rats.'

'You did what? Have you been bitten? You'll need some shots,' he's always been a very literal guy has Robin, 'let's get you into the wet room. We need to hose you down.'

I threw my clothes into a bin bag and crawled under the shower jets that were designed for washing dogs, but I was dog tired, and as filthy as a foxhound, so it seemed fitting. I sat there mesmerised by the circles of mud and blood that were running down the drain, it seemed a fitting metaphor for my life.

'We really should get you to A&E Sam,' Robin insisted, as I bent over his examination table.

'Come on, you know how to stitch; I'd do it myself if I could reach, just get on with it Rob.'

'This is going to hurt,' Robin assured me, 'this is going to take six stitches...at least.'

'Embroider away my man.'

'I really should give you a tetanus jab first, god knows what filth goes into those drains.'

'You said it, Rob, do what you've got to do.'

He drew up a syringe and then shoved it into my arm, 'Sam...I need to tell you something. I'm a vet, I don't have tetanus shots, but I do have sedatives...' and then the lights went out.

I woke up spread-eagled on a bed, bound hand and foot, and as naked as your favourite porn star – which was odd because Robin and my favourite porn star were standing over me - luckily, I was too beat to show my appreciation of the situation.

'Sorry about this Sam. I had to be sure,' Robin said flatly.

'It's okay Rob. I guess you've heard the worst.'

Lucy was giggling like a loon, 'I told him, you had nothing to do with killing Luke, we were about to untie you…'

'Well…perhaps you better hear the worst before you do.'

So I told them the worst. I told them what Sims and Bull had discovered in my flat, and then I told them what had become of Sims and Bull. As I spoke about what I'd done to my dad, their faces got greener and greener, and then there was silence, a long silence.

'So…' said Lucy, and then fell back into silence.

'That's some story, sounds like you…really…' Rob added, swallowing hard, 'Jesus Sam.'

I decided to make it easy for them, 'I lost it. Went psycho, crossed the line with a box of frogs and a few screws missing.'

They both nodded; Lucy sat on the bed and laid a soft hand on my face, 'we've all done things we regret Sam.'

It was my turn to nod, 'I spoke to Vic and the Buff Guys, they're sure Sims is no copper. Vic called him a gangster.'

'At the very least,' Robin said as he sat on the other side of the bed, 'but seeing as they're both dead it doesn't help us much.'

'Well…I just feel silly now don't I. It was them or me Rob.'

Robin untied my ankles, 'I guess the question is, who's got enough balls and clout to pay off a copper like Bull?'

'The Lodge who else,' I thought it was obvious.

'Why would the Lodge go to such lengths?' Robin asked.

'Money, simple as that. Luke and I hit their pocket pretty hard recently. My guess is we became an itch they just had to scratch-out.'

'If there's one thing I'm sure of,' Lucy considered, 'it's the Lodge's aversion to bad publicity. They've got too much to lose. They tried to remove you from the picture and failed, maybe your safe now, the risk of drawing attention to themselves is too high.'

Lucy was sweet for saying so, but I knew differently, Dotty had said much the same thing, and they still came after her; 'There's going to be a reckoning Lucy; nothing's changed, it's them or me.'

Robin caught hold of Lucy's hand as she went to untie my wrist, 'let's get one thing straight Sam, no more stuffing people okay, it's creepy. And it's just not right.'

'No more stuffing people, absolutely… what about violence, murder and revenge?'

'Can I talk you out of it?' I shook my head. 'Fair enough, I didn't think so. I've got staff coming in soon, and you've had a long night of it. You need to rest up, give those stitches a chance. Just rest up for a day or so, we'll put our heads together, and maybe we can come up with something, okay?'

I agreed, there really wasn't much else to be done. Robin had done a great job of patching me up - the stuff they give animals is way better than the pain killers they sell in Boots. I drifted back to a Thursday morning two years gone.

I was in the kitchen, making a cup of tea for Dad, the third I'd made him that morning, the third he hadn't drunk. I carried the drink through to him and heard myself say; 'What's the matter old man, not thirsty?' But he didn't answer, of course he couldn't answer, he'd been dead for three weeks. His mouth was wired shut and his belly was full of woodwool. The reality of what I'd done, rushed in on me. I don't really have the words to express how I felt at that moment, it was beyond disgust, I simply shattered. I went downstairs to the workshop, made a noose with an extension lead, looped it around the butchers hook we had screwed to the ceiling, and climbed onto the workbench. I had the noose around my neck, and my toes over the edge of the bench; when the shop door chimed. I froze.

'Hello, anybody in? Hello?' it was a musical voice, full of grace notes and warmth, and then came that laugh, high-pitched and as dirty as a truffling pig's snout, 'oh my god, what is that? Is this legal I ask myself? That's outrageous, I love it.'

'We're closed, come back later!' I shouted.

'Where are you sweetie? Can I come through?'

'No stay there?'

'But this is amazing,' the voice came on, 'I've been meaning to look in this darling little shop for years, but I've never got around to it.' And there he was, standing before me, a tall, thin, stick of a man; magnificent in his shining pink bouffant mane, black velvet flares and lime green leather tasselled jacket; 'Well hello there, what are you doing sweetie? Looks ominous.'

'Go away, leave me alone.'

'Is that tea?' he said pointing to the cup I'd brewed for my dad. And there he stayed, sipping cold tea, chattering on like a song thrush; for three hours, until at last, I told him what I'd done.

'Show me,' he said. And I did. 'Right then sweetie, we need to put this right don't we. What's it going to be? Police, Mental Health Act, followed by hospital, medication, institutionalisation, badly fitting pyjamas and sugar in your tea whether you want it or not; or … you could trust me?'

I chose Luke. Luke saved me. I owed him.

I waited until I heard the first customer arrive, and the business of the surgery begin. And then I snuck down the stairs, into the kitchen and out through the surgery's back exit. I wanted it over, I wanted to face the music. I began walking into town, I headed for the police station. Two minutes later, a police patrol car screeched to a halt in front of me; 'Stand still, police officer!' He was out of the car and pointing a Taser at my chest in three seconds' flat. 'Put your hands above your head.'

'You sure, about that?'

'Do it!'

I did it, and the towel Robin had given me to replace my clothes fell to the floor. 'Just so you know, that is not an offensive weapon,' I tried to assure him.

The officer taking my statement had an odd habit of continually placing and removing a non-existent cigarette from his razor thin lips. I told him everything but left out Robin and Lucy as much as I could. When I was done his face was paler than ash, 'thank you Sam. That was very detailed... one question? Why are you telling me all this?'

'It's a crime.'

'To be exact, it's a lot of crimes, a lot of very serious crimes. But why are you telling me, guilt, shame, I don't get it.'

I had to think hard which is never a pleasant experience, but my blank domino mind, suddenly turned over with a double-six, I knew what I was doing, 'if you take me down, I can take the Lodge with me. It's as simple as that.'

'So let's just check... the list. You admit to drowning one D.I Sims.'

'Who probably wasn't a copper at all.'

'Indeed, but you also admit to drowning Detective Bull, who definitely was a police officer.'

'No point in denying it.'

'You also admit to building a bomb. Which led to the death of two of your friends, Luke Fassbender and Billy the Prawn...'

'Not his real name, but it will do.'

'Right, and you're also willing to admit to... well let's just say numerous acts of premeditated violence and destruction, which may have contributed to the deaths of council officials and four or five, as yet unidentified drug dealers.'

'I haven't paid my electric bill yet either.'

I was given an orange paper overall and placed in a cell with a thick blanket, and once there, I did finally catch up on some sleep, sweet dreamless sleep. Seems what they say is true, confession is good for the soul.

It was eight o'clock in the evening, and I was enjoying an egg and cress sandwich with a very good cup of tea, when the cell door opened, and a very serious looking fella in a long coat, flat cap and pale green eyes walked in. He threw a laminated page full of mug shots at me.

'See anyone you recognise?'

I put down my tea and scanned the page, and there they were, 'that's Sims, and that one there's Rawlings.'

'No it's not, that's Raoul Ranid and Simeon Balchochia, and they're both evil bastards; learnt their trades in the Balkan conflicts.'

'There was another guy at the shed … Hogg, no Hobbs, what about him.'

'He's two doors down. We picked him up this morning. He won't be eating anything but soup for a while,' the serious man with the green eyes, offered me his hand. I took it, and if you believe in judging character by the strength of the grip, this guy was a solid gold heavy weight.

'Pleased to meet you Sam. My name's D.I Sims, Antiterrorist Squad; and I'm very pleased to meet you.

That Simeon was always a cheeky git. And just so you know, I like using the past-tense when it comes to that bastard. Good work.' Sims turned and marched out of the cell. I sat there looking at the open door not knowing what to think, and then I heard a bark from the other end of the corridor, 'Sam, shift your arse, you coming or what?'

And out the door I went.

I followed Sims down two flights of stairs and out into the police station's carpark. The backdoor of a white transit van opened as we approached, I followed Sims inside.

It was like walking into a sweaty armpit. The whole of the van was humming and whirring. I could feel the electric pulse through my feet. At the centre of the techno heat machine, sat a thin man with narrow hunched shoulders. His white shirt clung to his bones, as a cloud of steam formed around him.

'Sam this is Bobby, Bobby Sam,' Sims intoned wiping his forehead, 'I'm afraid the air-conditioning is on the blink.'

'It's always been on the blink,' Bobby said bitterly, 'government cutbacks.' He turned and nodded his beatnik beard in my general direction, without making eye contact – which I appreciated - and then turned back to a bank of five small colour monitors. 'Look at this lousy cheap design…I used to weigh twenty stone, none of my clothes fit now.'

'Alright Bobby, get on with it,' Sims said briskly, nudging Bobby with his elbow.

'So, we have some footage of Ranid and Balchochia in the town. But that screen there, sorry Chief…' he pointed to the screen furthest from me, and Sims shifted sideways so I could get a closer look, 'that shows you and Detective Bull leaving town, in a red VW Golf, and this one shows you in the same car, with Bull and Ranid an hour later, travelling back into town.' The screen shifted to an overhead shot, that must have been taken by a helicopter or a camera fitted to a sparrow. It was my workshop, I could see the roof needed looking at, '…and there you are carrying a sheep into your workshop.'

'Impressed?' Sims asked with lifted eyebrows.

'Scared shitless more like.'

Bobby clicked his tongue and nodded, 'Big Brother is in town. This is Bull collecting the sheep and Ranid…And the next picture we have is an overhead shot of the car stopping here.'

I expected to see Fast Luke's soon to be demolished house, but it wasn't; 'That's not Fast Luke's.'

'I believe you call it the Lodge. Funny handshakes and secret signs no doubt,' Sims said loosening his collar.

'Ranid and Bull go in. An hour later the sheep is dropped off here.' Fast Luke's house appeared on the screen. Bobby's fingers spun across the desk, enlarging the frozen picture further, 'delivery made by one Detective Bull.' I saw Bull place the sheep on the doorstep, ring the bell and run away, the coward.

'Delivery by the Righteous Order of Twats,' Sims snarled.

'Nah, he's not a member, he's from Norfolk.'

'Same difference; a bent copper we don't have to bother about, thanks to you Sam,' Sims rubbed his hands together and then wiped the sweat from his face, 'and we

227

all know what happened next; your mate takes the sheep inside and an hour later. Bobby if you please.'

The explosion played out on the centre screen, glass and fire, rubble and smoke competing in a slow-motion dance.

'I'm sorry for your loss. One question?' Sims intoned, 'if I may, why did your mate take a stuffed sheep into his house?'

'I'm the only taxidermist in town. He probably thought it was a gift.'

'Fair enough,' Sims concluded and crossed his arms.

'So we have some night footage of Bull and Balchochia, driving out of town, Bobby went on, 'according to your statement you're in the boot of the VW, which explains why you drove the car back into town the next morning, alone.'

'Good lad,' Sims added.

Bobby linked his hands behind his head and leant away from the screen. Catching a whiff of his overly ripe armpits, he hurriedly re-crossed his arms, swearing silently to himself, 'here's the thing, we've no film of Ranid leaving town, or even leaving the Temple, which is worrying.'

'Why?' I had to ask.

'He's a bomb maker. And bomb makers make bombs,' Sims replied.

My stomach flipped, and despite the weight of all my previously dim and dodgy brainwaves, and catastrophically wrong deductions; this time, I knew I was right; 'If he's in the Temple, he can get under most of the town. I bet my left bollock, he's placed a bomb under Dolphin Lane.'

'Why would he do that?'

'Luke figured it all out,' I answered, 'their making drugs down there,' I decided not to mention the giant worm. 'They've been expanding their operation, using the tunnels beneath the town.'

'And if we expose them, you think they'll blow it,' Sims mused for a moment and then pressed a button on the control panel, 'Team A, Sims here, standby.'

A sharp voice crackled in response, 'Team A standing by and ready to go.'

'Bobby, bring up the street plans again, underground utility maps, anything…'

'That's not going to work. It's a maze of fissures and tunnels down there. The Lodge must have been mining under the town for years. I found a route running beneath West Street that isn't on any map. They could have undermined the whole town.'

Sims leant over Bobby, staring at the street maps that were flashing up on the monitors, 'Major Turney said you were a good man to know Sam, and his recommendations don't come lightly.' I confess I blushed, it seemed I'd misread the blustering old buzzard too. Sims sighed and pressed the intercom button, 'Team A, stand down. We're calling it off.'

'Wait, you can't call it off. We don't know there's a bomb, not for sure. Why don't you gas the bastard, that will do it.'

'We don't do gas.'

'What about badgers? You gas badgers.'

Sims' finger was suddenly in my face, 'the Antiterrorist Squad don't do badgers, and the indiscriminate use of gas in urban areas has been frowned on since 1918. I repeat, stand down Team A, stand down and come back to base.'

Ten minutes later a large box van pulled into the car park, and twelve figures dressed in those black-on-black delights, that just scream out; YOU ARE GOING TO DIE, began filing back into the police station's basement. I joined them for drinks and sandwiches, and not a custard cream in sight; which says more about the British Police than I'd dare to say.

'Your attention ladies and gentlemen, we now have two possible scenarios.' Sims stood beside a whiteboard, red marker pen in hand, 'Ranid is holed up in Temple waiting for Raoul to get him out of town; which thanks to Sam here, isn't going to happen…' Sims pointed a finger in my direction, and there was a slight murmur of appreciation. 'However, whilst he's been there, it's likely, he hasn't been idle. The chances are he's built himself another bomb, probably demolition charges, which he's placed somewhere underneath the town. Where we don't know. We have to presume he intends to set them off at his new paymasters bidding.' Sims paused and shuffled his feet, 'or, knowing this creeps M.O, he'll set them off when confronted with capture.'

He then rattled on about plastic explosives, time delays, second stage blasts, demolition configurations and such like, but I really wasn't paying that much attention. As far as I could see the problem was still the same, how to get the flat-faced fucker before he levelled the town. My head came back into the room when I heard him say; 'we need ideas ladies and gentlemen, plans of ingress.' A projector turned on and the lights went out. There was the street plan of Broston, projected on the whiteboard. And I saw it:

'It's easy, 'I heard myself say, 'we'll knock the back-end out of Biggerdykes,'

'I beg your pardon,' Sims snorted; all eyes were on me.

'Send a team to blow through Lucy Biggerdykes basement, she lives in Pump Square. The Lodge applied for planning permission for an extension under the Temple. I bet it lays flush with Lucy's basement...'

'Bobby?' Sims Barked.

'Getting it now,' Bobby answered, from somewhere in the throng. A second later the extension plans were on the board. The plans showed the extension did indeed lay alongside Lucy's basement.

'You go in there, blast through. They won't see you coming.'

'But they'll bloody hear us,' someone retorted.

'Bye, bye, town,' Sims sighed.

'Not if I go in first,' I heard myself say, 'I'll sneak in and distract them until you can get in there. There has to be a passageway that leads from Worm Gate to Pump Square, Luke sure thought so, it's no more than five hundred yards.'

'Sorry Sam, thanks for your help, but perhaps its best you sit this one out. Maybe you should step-out and let us get on with the briefing; if you don't mind.' Sims words were kind, but his scowl glowed at me through the darkness.

Mind? Why on earth would I mind? 'Sure, sorry, just trying to help. No problem, I'll go find myself some biscuits. I can't believe you lot function without custard creams, not me I need my sugary fix, best of luck then, mind how you go, good luck, good luck, bye, bye,' all eyes were back on me, as I made my way out the door and closed it behind me; 'Arseholes!'

Sod that for a game of soldiers. While the big boys planned and pondered, I got on with it. I made my way to their van and helped myself to one of their nice black-on-black all-in-ones, along with one of their walky-talkies, and a big black rubber torch; that Fast Luke would have loved for all the wrong reasons. All in all, a nice bit of kit, but what I wouldn't have given for Monkey Scarf; I felt naked without it.

Twenty minutes later, I was standing in the church graveyard, beside a moss-covered horizontal stone that read; 'Beloved Sarah Vaughan, Known to the Lord, 1785.' I took a few steps back and jumped, stamping down hard on 'Known to the Lord;' and I kept doing this until I heard a splash echo in the darkness below; I mumbled an apology to Sarah, took a deep breath, and stamped my feet repeatedly into the stone like a raging toddler; 'You will give, you will give, you bastard stone you!' I ranted, and down we went.

The water was just as I remembered it, sodding cold. I went under twice before regaining my balance, and then stood there nipple deep in water, waiting for my eyes to adjust to the dim light of the glowing fungi. I sighted the shelf I'd fallen from on my first visit to the netherworld. It was way above my head, far out of reach. I followed the line of it, and away to my left, I spotted a crescent-shaped void within the illuminated soil; it was narrow but almost within reach; I hoped it was the entrance to a fissure, not just the result of some recent mudslide. I pushed myself beneath the water, leapt up and by the very tips of my fingers, pulled myself out of the water and into the darkness. I reached for the torch; but the lens was smashed, and water flowed from its innards – so much for government issued equipment; you might as well go to the Pound Shop. But what could I do? There was no going back. I tossed the casing into the water and headed off into the darkness.

The air was thicker than Heinz soup with the fumes and farts of a million wriggling worms. But that's no big deal, once you've had rancid badger fat under your fingernails you can withstand most stenches. I worked my way through cracks and water eroded channels, clogged with matted colourless roots, and sludge of every description, but I just kept going, keeping a picture of Sims projected map in my head, and vengeance in my heart. Some passages tapered off into fractures no bigger than my wrist, others ended in weirdly contoured blocks of immovable bedrock; but I just kept telling myself, that every false trail was leading me to the right path – I've read far too many self-help books. But let me tell you, trying to reverse up a tunnel, whilst the world above slops and drips down onto you is about as much fun as it sounds; none at all; and did I mention it was sodding cold. I was face down in a two-foot-high crevice, covered in an

233

inch of mud and eating my twentieth worm, when my luck finally turned. I heard a squeak in the darkness to my left, I turned my head just in time to see a pink blur of a tail pass through a livid white veil of roots. No mutant rats this time, just big fat ones. I pushed my arm into the roots and felt the flow of air against my skin. Somewhere beyond that veil there was a passageway. Getting to it wasn't going to be easy, the way was narrow, no wider than a shoebox but that's the way I had to go. I shimmied around and wriggled towards it. With my chest and back against bedrock, head bent to one side and arms outstretched, I pulled myself forward, and then I felt something snag at my waist. I pulled harder and heard a grinding crunch and then I was free. I breathed a sigh of relief and then realised I'd just lost my walky-talky; 'Bugger.'

Every movement tore at my uniform, and the slightest roll of my shoulders, dug my flesh into the rock, but I wasn't stopping. I was butt deep and going deeper before great clumps of sodden sod began slopping down onto me. I remember thinking, 'I'm burying myself alive.' But I swallowed down my fear, along with a mouth full of grime, and a worm or two for extra energy. As soon as my nose cleared the curtain of roots, my wriggle room gave out; I could go no further. I was stuck. I tried inching backwards and felt the weight against my shoulders shift. A Zen moment of clarity flowed over me. Going back would bring the mud down on my head. It could be a handful or half a ton, but even a buckets worth would be enough to smother me in that crease of the earth. I pushed out every breath, pulled my stomach in, and punched forward with everything I had. Wrestling with my bodies

234

need to breathe, I yanked, kicked and fought the good
earth. My grave closed in around me as my blood turned to
acid, and my lungs turned traitor. My chest tried to expand
as my throat clamped shut. I was suffocating myself for
want of air, but I knew my last gasp would seal me in
forever. The world around me became heat and fire but
there was no light, just an accelerating darkness
swallowing me whole. I felt my body pass from my
control as I began to spasm, and then the earth under my
left elbow shifted and suddenly I was falling. I landed on
my back in a shallow pool of ice water, convulsing,
coughing and gasping for air. I've never felt such relief –
worth a thousand and one wanks for sure.

The water I was laying in was a bitter and gamey
brew. I've had pies with thinner gravy. Once I was able to
stand; the chamber's height offered no restrictions; I
kicked about in the pool, and it was then I realised I could
see the water's surface shimmer. A dim white light was
emanating from a column at the centre of the pool; a good
ten yards from where I stood. The chamber was vast, and
that meant the entrance to the Lodge couldn't be far away.
On the far wall, on the other side of the chamber, I saw
what I thought could be a manmade arch and headed
towards it. My foot caught in something beneath the water
and I fell flat on my face. Something was snagged around
my boot. I pulled hard and raised my leg above the water.
My foot had caught the sleeve of an official Broston
Council reflective jacket. A white arm bone, swung from
its cuff. I shook the jacket free and then dug about in the
water. I felt something smooth under my hand; I knew
what it was before I saw it; a fleshless, human skull. I

235

tossed the thing across the chamber, the echo of its smashing and that of my convulsive retching bounced off the walls, and skimmed back across the water to me. When I caught my breath, I had to laugh – a bloody taxidermist, and one that's stuffed his own dad; scared of a skull; what a wanker.

As the echo of my laugh died away, the column at the centre of the chamber, slowly uncoiled, expanded its segments, and began tasting the water with its foul, gelatinous maw. I could see by the beast's light that the pool was thick with the bones, and not all of them were human. I saw the skulls of sheep and cattle, as well as many canine bones. Such an array and assortment could only mean one thing, the bastards were feeding it, and had been feeding it for a long time. My foot disturbed a shattered horse's scapula, laying below a layer of silt. I made no sound, just a ripple in the water and a puff of mud; but the beast sensed it, and its head flicked towards me, its lips quivering. I held my breath, frozen to the spot. As the silt around me settled I saw a horse's thighbone. The beast turned its head away sending another wave across the pond. I dropped to my knees and felt about in the water – I needed that horse's thigh bone. The silt swirled, the water undulated, and the beast turned back. Head down, lips rippling, as it sped towards me. There was nowhere to go; I watched transfixed as the worm's lips flexed and expanded, trembling with the dreadful suction created by the creature's pumping segments. Nearer and nearer it came, pushing a wave of filth and broken bones before it. My fingers felt a curved edge, it wasn't what I wanted but it would have to do. The tidal wave of the beast's charge broke against my chest as I rose from the ossuary pool; a horse's rib in my hands. As the lips reached for my face, I plunged the bone down through its gelatinous flesh and into the mud. The worm thrashed the waters, its writhing body whipping the chamber into a maelstrom of white water and tossed bones. Believe me, I had no wish to kill the beast. It was not to blame for the folly of the greedy men that had fed its hunger and exploited its uniqueness. I did not want to hurt it any more than I needed to; but I needed to reach the other side of the chamber; its writhing coils barred my way and threatened to bring down the roof with its maddened thrashing. I did not want to do what I did. My hand found the horses thigh bone, I smashed one end against the rock face, creating a jagged point; and then it was my turn to charge. It was not a clean kill, but a slashing, filthy business. As the beast's head fell, I stabbed upwards, as its head swung past me, I slashed. As the body threatened to crush me, I severed chunks of flesh from its flank; and when its head dropped in agony, I ran up its snout, dragging the bone blade after me, tearing a jagged rift in its flesh. As the creatures writhing agony increased, I dropped from its back, and ran towards the head; slashing and cutting as I went. As I neared the head I sighted a vestigial lump, a grey disc that may once have been an eye. I aimed at a point no more than a foot behind it, and charged, full tilt, bone lance forward. It sank into the creature's flesh, and I pushed it in, to the very head of the bone. The beast quivered and dropped; its pale ghostly glow dimming, as its flesh turned to the colour of ash. I sat before the slaughtered beast, and I swear; if I'd had time, I would have felt guilty. But I didn't, I had to get on; I hobbled across the chamber and into the tunnel beyond.

I was as calm and empty headed as I've ever been. There was no fear of getting lost because I was already lost, there was nowhere else to go but forward. I was either going to end up where I bargained or where the tunnel ended, with any luck that would be the same place. When I got there, I'd worry about what I'd find and deal with it as best as I could; as Dad might have said; get your arse moving son.

I'd been mistaken, the tunnel I'd taken was not man made but another water torn fissure, worn smooth by time and trickle. If the beast's lair had been an echo chamber, that tunnel was ear by which it heard. Sound does strange things underground. It bounces off rock, gets swallowed by mud, and skips across water. And then all those elements collide to make their own unsettling sounds, rumbles and slurps that are not easily discounted by the imagination; and there's always, always a syncopated discordant drip, drip, drip. All those sounds collected in that tunnel, each degrading to its own distorted pattern. If hell is full of tormented souls, no one will know who is screaming, so when you get there, don't hold back, let yourself go, have fun, make a noise, nobody will know. In the middle of the din, I heard a dry rattling cough. And for a moment, I wasn't sure it wasn't my own. I stopped and crouched straining to hear, searching through the noise, peering into the darkness, that echoed back more indistinct and lightless noise; and then came another cough. I froze, again the cough sounded. It was a real hack; fruity with real body, somewhere ahead of me, someone spat and groaned. Feeling my way on all fours, I worked my way forward as slowly and silently as my sopping wet clothes would allow. The channel bent sharply to the left, narrowed, and then ended abruptly six feet above a vast well-lit pool, that was as clear and still as a sheet of glass. At the far end of the pool there were six twisted stone pillars, almost a yard thick at their base from which hung strings of construction lights. I heard another cough and stepped back into the shadows, as Flat-faced Frank stepped out into the light. Dressed in chest high waders with green braces, Frank pulled a child's yellow duck shaped dinghy behind him through the water. Lodged between the duck's wings was a reel of thick yellow and black cable. As I watched Frank circled a column in a slow heavy stride, winding the cable around the pillar as he did so. Once he'd completed his circuit, he fixed the cable in place with strips of gaffer tape and moved on to the next. Slowly and methodically, he went about his job like a true craftsman, only moving on when he was sure the cable wouldn't budge. The only thing that seemed to impede his progress was his nasty cough, I hope the bastard had inhaled something nasty from my workshop.

It might not surprise you to know that being a taxidermist doesn't often involve the use of explosives, but seeing that I now knew Frank's trade, I figured it had to be some kind of cable charge he was laying; and thankfully it looked far from complete. I prepared myself to beat the shit out of him.

The sound of an outboard motor echoed around the chamber, as a long thin wooden punt – the type they used to use for hunting waterfowl on the marshes - appeared from the far side of the pool. On board were three men, two of which I recognised, the Lodge's favourite heavies, Morris and Monk. The third figure sat at the front and seemed to be wearing a cloak. Morris stepped out of the boat and threw the cloaked figure over his shoulder. Lucy Biggerdyke's muffled screams bounced around the cavern.

'What's this?' flat faced Frank asked.

'Just an extra, we want to make sure this one goes down with the filth.'

'Very well,' Frank replied as if he'd just been offered a cup of tea, 'hurry up and tie her to a pillar, I'm nearly done here. You can take me back with you, save me the walk. Here…" He threw the roll of gaffer tape to Morris and busied himself fixing one end of the cable to what looked like a junction box screwed into the first of the six pillars.

'Bugger it,' I said to myself, but louder than I'd intended; I held my breath as my words echoed out across the chamber.

'What's wrong?' Monk enquired, his voice echoing across the water.

'Bugger who?' Morris replied.

'Bugger what now?' Monk retorted.

'Bugger both you bastards!' Lucy railed, giving it plenty of decibels.

Lucy fought them all the way and managed to land a kick to Morris' shin, before they finally had her pinned to the pillar. 'Bitch!' Morris yelled, returning the blow with a slap. I had a strong urge to remove his eyeballs via his arsehole. I thought about going all Ninja and taking them by surprise, but the chamber was too bright, and the distance I had to cover, too great. So I had to stay put, bide my time and watch; I didn't enjoy it. Once the two thugs had secured Lucy to the pillar, they covered her mouth, and both copped-a-feel, with obvious grubby delight. I promised myself I'd make them pay for that. The thugs then jumped back into their ride and chugged across to Frank; 'Come on Ranid, you finished yet? Let's get out of here,' Monk urged, 'I don't want to be anywhere near this place when it goes.' Ever the professional, Frank wouldn't be hurried; he ignored the coaxing and ran a slow eye over his handywork. I could see him ticking off a mental checklist, slow and sure. Once he was satisfied with his craftsmanship he climbed onto the punt; and with sadistic waves to poor Lucy, they disappeared into the darkness beyond the pillars, pulling their inflatable duck behind them. I watched as Lucy pulled forlornly at her bindings and then broke down into tears.

'Excuse me miss, is this the route for the number ten?' You should have seen the look in her eyes when she looked up and saw me standing there, it's as near to love as I'll ever get.

'This is going to hurt okay?' I told her, she nodded, and I ripped the tape off her mouth.

'Shit kicker! That hurt,' she shouted, 'how did you find me?'

'Pure luck.'

'That counts too, we need to get out of here, they're going to blow up half the town.'

'Hold on a minute, let me think…'

'We haven't got time for that, we need to go!'

I took hold of Lucy's hand and led her over to the junction box. It was a thing of simple beauty. A linked series of points with one line feeding in. I tore it off the wall, tore it apart and threw it into the mud; 'Well, there you go, that's going to bring them back down here isn't it…are you ready for that?'

'We can take them can't we?' Lucy gasped.

We probably could have, although having Monkey Scarf handy would have made it easier. But I didn't want to put Lucy in harm's way. 'Maybe you should try make it out before they arrive, how did they get you down here?'

'Sam, I'm a big girl. I was a major porn star for four years. I've handled more dicks than I can remember, and more cunts than you've had hot dinners.' - absolutely true - 'Luke was my friend too. I'd really like the chance to settle the score with these scumbags.'

'Fair enough. Any idea how many of them are left up in the Temple?'

'I can't be sure but maybe seven or eight. I think most of them have gone out of town for the day.'

'Now there's a surprise. How did they get you down here?'

'There's a spiral staircase. It was a bloody nightmare getting down it.'

The sound of an outboard motor kicking over echoed across the water.

'They're coming, I wish I had Monkey Scarf. You got anything sharp?'

Lucy shook her head and then an idea flashed across her face. She hiked her top up to her neck and removed her bra. This done her face dropped but nothing else did, as

242

she examined the bra and then spat; 'Bugger I thought they were underwired.'

I just smiled, it was just the encouragement I needed. I clambered up the pillar, grabbed the cable and pulled it down, the lights flickered and went out.

'Great…what do we do now?' Lucy's voice sounded nervous but determined.

'You know that scene in the 'Health Spa Spankers,' when you surprise those two college girls…'

'Sam!' her voice was incredulous, 'you saw that? That was the first European production I was ever in.'

'I've seen all your movies Lucy…often. You remember the scene right, with the hot mud?'

Lucy's eyes shone, 'oh that scene, sure, I get it.'

'That's my plan…apart from the fucking them with a loofa bit.'

The sound of the outboard grew nearer, and the voices of Flat-Faced Frank and Robert Morris became clearer; Morris was not happy, 'The lights have cut out. You must have tripped the fuse.'

'Don't be an idiot the charges aren't wired into the mains. Where's your torch?' The torch beam cut through the darkness; 'hold this thing steady, go to the last pillar. Come on, get on with it. To your left…straight…good. Closer…my god what's happened here? This is sabotage!'

And that was our cue. I couldn't see Frank as I rose out of the water, but I heard his scream. I reached for the shriek, hooked my arms around his waist and launched myself backwards. He landed under me, and I sprang onto his chest, pushing his head down into the water. It was too dark to see him go under, but I heard the flat-faced bastard's screams become spitting gargles, and then frantic bubbling grunts. I also felt his right eye pop beneath my thumb – as revenge goes, it would do.

I looked across to see Lucy squatting in the water. She was holding a torch above her head, its beam trained down beneath her thighs, onto the head of the franticly flailing Robert Morris.

'You okay there Lucy?'

'Give me a moment Sam…' Lucy slowly and deliberately lowered herself into the water. Morris' desperate garbled screams echoed across the cavern. No doubt about it; being sent to hell when you're so near heaven can't be easy. Lucy's eyes stayed firm and clear, as the water reached her waist, and then it was done.

'You okay Lucy?'

Lucy gave me the thumbs up, she looked none the worse for her experience. The first time doesn't have to be the worst, not if you take it at your own pace.

'Nice work Lucy, time to go.'

We jumped into the punt and headed into the darkness. Some twenty feet away, another set of stone pillars flanked a doorway, carved straight into the bedrock. Beyond it I could make out a spiral stone staircase.

'Does this come out at the Temple,' I whispered to Lucy, and she nodded. 'Listen, when get up there find an exit. Get out into the street and start screaming, Sims is watching the place, and they'll come running. Just get out, okay, I'll deal with the rest.'

'Sims? I thought that was the guy you killed?'

'No, but I will if he lets us down.'

Up the stairs we went. Slowly but steadily one stair at a time, around and around we went, listening for footsteps coming down, expecting to be discovered at any moment; and then finally, there it was, right in front of us; a glowing cherrywood door. I edged it open, and saw the Ancaster stone covered floor, of the Lodge's main hall. We were beneath the hall's balcony, whilst directly ahead of us stood the studied wooden door that led to the street and freedom; and it was open. Between us and the door, were six or seven besuited men, emptying boxes of files and papers into the centre of the hall.

'What are they doing?' Lucy whispered.

'Preparing to torch evidence would be my guess,' I answered, as I pulled the door shut.

'Whatever happens Lucy, get out that door, Sims' men are watching this place. As soon as you raise the alarm they'll storm in and fix these bastards. So just get to the door, okay?'

Lucy nodded, her face flushed as she took hold of my hand and placed it on her most scrumptious, firm, warm, right breast, 'Sam… strap it on and oil it up. I want you to be mean and vicious, I want you tear me apart, I want you to give me all you got…make me come or die trying?'

'Biggerdyke Takes Holy Orders, Smut Productions 2008. The final scene with Mother Superior in the winepress, a classic of the genre.'

'And the only decent bit of acting I ever did.'

'It's a personal favourite. I need to see that again.'

'If we get out of this, we'll watch it together.'

I ran into the hall, baying like a hellhound with raging toothache. I barged into three box carrying suits: flooring the first with a combination punch, jab to throat / knee to groin / forehead to nose. The second suit dropped his box, screamed, and let loose a lefty haymaker that ended its arc in the face of the third suit; knocking him out cold. I drove my fist up into lefties chin, snapping his head backwards; lights out.

'Come on then, let's have it,' I challenged the remaining suits. It took them three seconds to make up their minds, and then they were on me.

Lucy barged her way through the fray, sprinting for the door, sending suits skidding on their arses, as she went. From the centre of the melee, I saw her reach the open doorway; just as Monk stepped back through, blocking her path. He took in the scene with a glance, waited for Lucy to come within reach, and then swatted her sideways with the back of his hand. I saw him, look at the suits swinging in on me, grin like a snake, and then go after Lucy. It was time to stop buggering about; yes I had four guys pummelling me, but not one of them could throw a decent punch. I grabbed the nearest one by the head, pulled him to his knees and then put his head on backwards with a snap. It was enough to give the others pause for thought. I pushed them aside and launched myself at Monk, knocking him to the floor. I landed heavily and Monk rolled free. As I scrambled after him, Monk brought his knees to his chest and launched both feet into my face, I rolled sideways but not quick enough, the blow shattered my collarbone and damn near took off my ear. Monk was about to have another try when Lucy sprung from the floor

246

and landed knees first on his chest. I grabbed his legs, and locked my arms around them, shouting at Lucy to; 'Run! Run! Get out of here.'

I felt the shot before I heard it. It flipped me round like a spinning coin. I looked up, saw Hooms standing on the balcony, a smoking shotgun in his hand, and then I knew I'd been shot; and as soon as I knew it, everything hurt all at once. An electric storm of pain ricocheted from bone to bone, joint to joint, gathering charge and heat as it went. I couldn't move, I just lay there watching Hooms take aim. I turned to see Lucy looking at me, frozen in the doorway, our eyes met, the air cracked, and Lucy's head exploded.

In my head, a double deuce domino, span and fell. I had total clarity. I saw my left arm. The bone was exposed above the elbow, the flesh blown away. I was squirting blood like they did in bad Kungfu movies. I had minutes to live. I had a choice; try and stop the blood and die or kill them all and die trying… and those had been Lucy's last words to me, 'die trying.' The decision was made. I saw Monk curled up in a ball, clutching his chest; heard him wheezing, as he tried to catch his breath. I grabbed hold of his leg, pulled him across the blood splattered floor towards me, and pushed my face into his; I tore off his nose. Clamping my hand over his mouth, I watched him drown in his own blood.

I got to my feet, everything was numb but throbbing, I was cold but burnt to my core. I figured I was dying; it wasn't so bad.

'And for what purpose all this pain,' Hooms sneered from his balcony, 'look what you've done, look what you've done. But what have you achieved? Nothing, nothing.'

'I've thrown a spanner in your works that's for sure. You need to go check on your pet worm. See how it's doing, before you finish your loony leader speech.'

Hooms face reddened, 'What have you done?'

'I think…' it felt as if the floor beneath my feet was rocking, and my feet were sinking into its bloody tiles, 'I think, I've ruined your day. And you know what … that's enough for me.'

'You're pathetic. Do you think this will stop us? Do you think you've won? We've been the uncrowned kings of this town for over two hundred years. Do you really think you can impede our progress; a little man like you? We grind your type under our heels. We are the Lodge, we were born to rule…'

'Hooms!' I had to interrupt his rant, who wants to die with that garbage in their ears, 'we have a saying in taxidermy, and it's this… get stuffed.'

The shotgun rose, its muzzle expanding as it reached out to touch me; I thought about cake, I thought about glass blowing, I thought about the wonder of a sunrise, the glory of a good cup of tea and a lovely custard cream; and I knew the truth of Anti-Zen, I was Anti-Zen – and it was all okay with me. A solid ball of heat spun me about and threw me to the floor. I lay on my back looking up at the beautiful vibrating blue and gold of the Temple ceiling; and I remember thinking; 'be with you soon Dad, get the kettle on, set a place for Luke and Lucy, custard creams all round.' And then Hooms was standing above me; locking and loading his shotgun for one more round of fun.

'I'll feed your flesh to the worms in our nursery tanks, and use your bones to build my thrown,' he jeered, as he took aim.

A thunder cloud exploded, enveloping me in a swirling cape of dust and shadows. And there was Luke riding a swan, like the people of the Beltane, his hair grown long and filled with stars, a frog in one hand that declared; 'Man, life's a gas. Life's a gas... get it on, get it on...' And there was Lucy, driving a Rolls Royce because its good for her voice... and then the Jeepster turned up and turned off the lights.

Sims assures me he put three bullets into Hooms; and told me he enjoyed doing it. The other Lodge members, immediately surrendered, and the majority of those that had already fled the town, were rounded up within forty-eight hours.

I was in hospital for ten days, unconscious for four, when I awoke my left arm was gone and my chest looked like a moon crater. Sims visited me on the sixth day and got straight to shouting the odds about my reckless behaviour, but once he'd got that off his chest, he was actually incredibly decent about the whole thing.

'I'm sorry we didn't get in their quick enough to save your friend. She certainly had an interesting past, a real character.'

'I'm sure her future would have been a lot brighter.'

'Indeed... look Bobby's done some maths, made a digital mock-up of the demolition charges across the site. Turns out, the blast may not have brought the street down; but it certainly would have undermined it. Bobby thinks they were trying to link their flood cellar and the whole area beneath Dolphin Lane with a breach in the seawall near Worm Gate. You know anything about that? Any idea why they needed so much space?'

'Greed?' I'd decided not to enlighten him any further, lest they dig around too much and find something they shouldn't. 'Perhaps they were willing to wait for the street to fall in… they could claim innocence and buy up the land cheap.'

'Could be… once we've finished hauling through their paperwork, we'll have a better idea. How's the arm?'

'Gone. Didn't you notice?'

'Sure. Look, I'm going to leave you out of my report, you'll be as clean as a whistle by the end of this, so do me a favour, keep your nose clean, stay off the radar.'

'Thank you I will, I'll do my best.'

Vic and the Buffs visited, they brought fruit cake and filled the room with so many candles they set the fire alarm off; my tent sized nurse gave them a right telling off, bless her, she's a dragon but she's got a good heart – I bet it's in a jar in her locker. The girls from 'Fitterdyke,' visited; and brought me fruit juice and an honorary membership card, they say I'm not allowed to use. They intend to keep the gym going and I hope they do; it's what Lucy would have wanted. I did offer to take Lucy's movie paraphernalia off their hands; they said they'd think about it. I must check in with them about that.

The official story was the thinnest tissue of lies I've ever heard. If you'd tried to wipe your arse with it, you'd be touching base on the first swipe. The local rag sold it, the public bought it…

Deadly Shoot Out Temple Siege!

…and then forgot it.

Luke's cremation was a small affair; there wasn't a lot left to cremate. All the unusual crowd were there; Robin, Raj, Vic and I, alongside Buff Guys 7 to 32. I was expecting a boisterous send-off, full of colour and spice, but I think we all felt the loss too deeply. The Post Office sent a nice wreath; pink flowers in the shape of a fist which seemed right on so many levels. We scattered Luke's ashes along Dolphin Lane and drank a toast to him in the Indian Queen; it's what we think he may have wanted. Although, I'm sure if we'd asked him, he would have thought of something much more entertaining. And there it was done.

So, just like I said, a simple story of boy meets girl; boy gets girl killed, murders drug dealers, terrorists, coppers and his best friend; and gets away with the lot. Gets away with it but doesn't walk away entirely unscathed.

As for me…well Taxi Sam has a shop to run, Chihuahuas to stuff and badgers to pose, these things don't skin themselves you know… but first things first, I've got an arm to build, and I've just had word from Robin, that the local zoo has reported a death within their baboon troop; yummy.

EPILOGUE

Now here's an odd thing, and I'm quoting here; 'the bodies of two holiday makers, Mr and Mrs Teacher, were found murdered in their holiday cottage in Mousehole Cornwall on Thursday morning. Mr Bernard Teacher, a well-respected government civil engineer and his wife June were last seen on Wednesday night at a local restaurant, where they were regular customers. They retired for the evening sometime before midnight and were not seen again until their bodies were found by their cleaner, Mrs Whittle, also of Mousehole, the following morning. Police have yet to release further details, but sources close to the investigation have revealed that both Mr and Mrs Teacher had been severely beaten in a prolonged and savage attack. Police are asking for anyone that may have information on the Teachers' or their attackers to come forward and…' blah, blah, blah…

… bugger, wonder what happened there then???

Neil S. Reddy

Taxi Sam in Pink Noir, was originally published by Weasel Press USA in 2017, it's been significantly edited and rewritten for this publication because it needed it, and it needed it because I didn't get it right the first time, and that's nobody's fault but mine. My thanks to all those that spoke so well of the original version, I hope you'll be pleased with the improvements, and enjoy Taxi Sam and Fast Luke's adventures in and beneath the sleepy town of Broston... wherever that might be.

Tim Youster

Tim Youster was born and raised in the dry middle lands, but now lives on the wet coastal fringes. He'll happily take a stab at designing anything from your book covers to ya pantomime promo, the weirder the better.

When he's left to his own devices, he's been known to make weird photo portraits, odd pictures of Mr Toad and exciting illustrations of GIANT FIGHTY ROBOTS! He's a dog person, but has a cat and some fish. So that didn't go according to plan.

www.etsy.com/uk/shop/TimYouster

Other titles by Neil S. Reddy published by
Dank House Manor.

Jubjub Juice
Byron Beyond the Firmament
Trash Island
Interzone Xpress Boogie.

Weasel Press USA Publications.
Cause for Concern
Not Kafka
Miffed and Peeved in the U.K

Taste and See

Tales in Liquid Time.